One Bite at a Time

Brandon Faircloth

Fountaindale Public Library
Bolingbrook, IL
(630) 759-2102

Published by Brandon Faircloth.

Copyright 2018 Brandon Faircloth

All rights reserved. This book may not be reproduced in whole or in part, in any form or by any means, electronic or mechanical, including photocopying, recording, or by any information storage and retrieval system now known or hereafter invented, without written permission from the author.

This book is licensed for your personal enjoyment only. This book may not be re-sold or given away to other people. If you would like to share this book with another person, please purchase an additional copy for each person you share it with. If you're reading this book and did not purchase it, or it was not purchased for you, then please purchase a copy. Thank you for respecting the hard work of the author.

Please visit Verastahl.com for up-to-date news, links, and contact information for Brandon Faircloth.

Other Works by Brandon Faircloth:
Mystery
Darkness
On the Hill and Other Tales of Horror
Whimsical Leprosy
The Outsiders: Book One
You saw something you shouldn't have

Table of Contents

It's not a window. It's a door. 1

The House Spider 6

The Everlasting Flesh 12

Mr. Jinkies 19

On the Inside 26

My apartment has a roach problem 32

A thing called Candleheart killed my brother. 44

Everyone in my town has vanished except for me and the demon. 55

I helped pull a dead girl's body out of thin air. 68

I convinced my friend that I'm a vampire. Now he's hunting me. 77

I survived a stay at the Apocalypse Hotel. At least so far. 87

Someone replaced Independence Day with a snuff film. 97

Ol' Mr. Horsehair 104

Yesterday morning I found bloody teeth in my pocket. 111

I keep killing my husband and he keeps coming back. 120

Come see what's in the tunnel. 129

On the Rooftop 144

Do not accept a download of the app called "Polterzeitgeist!" 146

See you next October 155

Have you ever heard whistling on a lonely road? 164

Something came back with us from the woods. 168

The Trick 177

I found a serial killer's cell phone. 184

I thought my neighbor was dressing up like a scarecrow. 220

The Ghosthound 234

It's not a window. It's a door.

When my sister gave birth to Emily, it was a big deal in our family. My husband died last year, and I doubt I'll ever bear children of my own, and even seven years ago Emily was the first grandchild in the family. She was a sweet and beautiful baby with wide green eyes and a bright, cheerful disposition. Even as an infant she had personality, and this only grew as she got older.

I live in Alabama, and my sister lives all the way in the outskirts of Waco, so even though we are a close family, I only get to see my sister and niece at major holidays and for a few days every summer when they come stay with me. Which is what made her suggestion that they come visit last month a bit strange.

We talk on the phone every Sunday, and that evening we had just been chatting about nothing in particular, but I could tell she was stressed or preoccupied. She said her husband, Rich, was very busy at work lately, but that should ease off by late April. And she said Emily was doing well in school, though she was a bit too focused on drawing these days. She said it with a laugh, but I know my sister and something was wrong. I almost asked, but thought better of it, figuring she'd tell me when the time was right. Within a few minutes she had brought up them coming to visit. I was surprised but happy, and at first I assumed she meant during Emily's spring break, but she meant just a couple of days later.

At this point I couldn't help myself, and I asked if everything was okay. Had something happened with Rich? Was Emily okay?

She gave a brittle laugh and said everything was okay, but she wanted to see her big sister if it wasn't a bad time. I told her it wasn't, and by Wednesday afternoon they were there.

I had just seen Emily at Christmas when everyone had met up in Ft. Worth for the holidays. At the time, she had been the same bright, joyful girl I'd always known. She would flit from person to person, telling jokes, listening to stories, always ready to talk, but never rude or demanding. I know she's my niece, but she was perfect.

But when they arrived at my house in March…she was just different. Her eyes looked dull, and while she still talked and was polite, very little of her old spark seemed left. After we got her settled in the living room, I took my sister into the kitchen to grill her. What was going on with Emily? Had there been some trauma or signs of abuse? When did this all start?

My sister, to her credit, was patient with my barrage of questions. She said that it had started about two weeks after Christmas, and no, she didn't think it was due to anyone abusing her. That while she was more subdued, Emily still ate okay, made good grades, and didn't get into trouble except for her drawings.

I had given Emily an antique case full of drawing chalks at Christmas, and while she had seemed only mildly interested at the time, sometime in mid-January, she had started using them more and more. My sister said she would draw windows on walls throughout the house and much to her own dismay. She had scolded the girl, explaining how hard it was to get that kind of chalk off the walls, and forbidding her from drawing on walls outside of her own room.

For a time it worked, as the child focused her efforts solely upon her own walls, drawing windows over every open space she could reach before going back to wipe away earlier, more crude works. This continued for weeks, and a clear pattern emerged. She was drawing the same thing over and over again. Not just the same type of thing—a window—but the same one.

My sister said if you compared them side by side, they all looked nearly identical, but she realized over time that details were being added, tweaked, refined. Almost as though she was focusing the lens of a camera to get a clearer picture. What was strange, aside from the obvious, is the window panes were largely blank. She expected a child's drawing of a window would mainly be about what was on the other side, but the panes contained no details other than the cut and imperfections of the glass.

At this point in talking to me, she realized how long we had been in the kitchen and, with a panicked look, she rushed back into living room. I followed, and we found Emily where we had left her, sitting on the sofa with her hands folded, staring off into space. I crouched down and spoke to her for a few moments about the fun we would have while they were visiting, and she responded normally overall, but it was still very muted. I made them dinner, and later on she was tucked into bed with her promise to wait and start any art projects in the morning with us.

A few minutes later, me and my sister were back on the sofa, drinking wine and talking. I told her it was best to let Emily keep at it until she tired of it, as it was almost certainly just a phase, and she was welcome to draw wherever she liked in my house. She seemed unsure, but finally agreed, hoping the child would move past it quicker with all the fun distractions we could provide. We talked about going to the zoo, the amusement park, the movies. Eventually, with the help of the wine, my sister began to relax and I steered the conversation away from Emily.

We talked about work, and then local gossip from our respective towns that meant little to each other, but was still good for a laugh. Then we talked about Rich. I had known Richard for two years before my sister did. We had met in a sophomore Intro to Philosophy class and quickly became inseparable. He was from Tennessee originally, but he had lived all over the world and carried an air of exotic intelligence and wisdom about him. We were best friends and more, and we pushed each other to be more and be better both physically, mentally and spiritually.

When I was a senior, I invited my sister to come visit, as she was starting to look at colleges. I introduced her to Richard, and within a month they were dating. Within a year, they were married. And did I ever have misgivings or sad nights about it? Yes, of course. But I understood it was for the best and was necessary. It was meant to be and I had to accept it.

As we talked, she began to drift off, fighting to focus as she told me about how Richard had grown more distant lately and wasn't as concerned about Emily as she thought he should be. I commiserated in a vague way and her chin drooped to her chest as she finally fell asleep. I considered that sitting like that, bereft of the lively sparkling eyes and wryly curling smile that had always made her so charming, she looked like she was dead. A pale dead toad.

Banishing the thought, I kissed her head and gave her a shake. We stumbled to bed, and the next day our week of fun began.

Zoo, park, movies, go-carts. We did it all. And Emily participated dutifully, but with no real joy. And every afternoon when we returned home, she went to the empty guest room I had designated as her art room and drew on the walls.

The drawings were remarkable. Whatever they had been originally, they had become almost indistinguishable from the real thing now. And Emily worked amazingly fast, but with such a level of detail, it still took hours to complete a version before starting another. My sister wanted to stop her, but I held her back from interceding, and by the fourth day I had run out of fun suggestions and we decided to just let her go until she burned out, so long as she rested and ate.

On the sixth day, Emily woke me in the blue hour of early morning. When I looked at her, she nodded and led me to the room. All had been scrubbed away except for one, last example in the middle of the back wall. I examined it closely and then bent down to smile at Emily and kiss her forehead. I told her we would wait and show her mama that night.

Emily slept most of the day, but she went outside and played in the afternoon, which delighted my sister. That night, after a dinner where Emily ate and talked more than she had all week, we took her mother up to show her the art room. She entered slowly, looking left to the scrubbed wall and center to the impossibly perfect drawing there, and then her gaze continued its trajectory to the right and landed on Rich, who stood there beaming at us. Her eyes widened, and Emily ran forward to hug her daddy.

My sister took a step forward and then caught herself. She asked what he was doing here and was anything wrong. He had taken a deep crimson length of chalk out of his shirt pocket and given it to Emily with a nod. She ran back to the drawing as he stood and smiled at his wife, saying it was really good to see her, to see all his girls. My sister glanced at me, but I barely noticed, as my focus was on Emily as she finished drawing a red knob on the expertly replicated dark gray frame she had labored on the night before.

She had barely finished lifting the chalk from the wall when the knob began to turn. I felt the buzz of excitement that had been building in me for days swell and explode. I turned to my sister, not able to resist stealing a glance and a shared smile with Rich in the process.

"It's not a window."

My sister blinked confusedly, her face paling now. "What?"

I fought down the maniac urge to laugh. "It's not a window. It's a door."

As I spoke, the knob had completed its third slow revolution and the door opened—first, just a crack, and then enough to let something in. The lights dimmed at its entry, which was a momentary kindness for my sister, as I don't think she truly saw what dragged her back in. I saw too late that the door was swinging back closed, and neither Rich nor myself could reach it before it shut with a brittle snap and became chalk on a wall again. I pounded the wall with a curse, but Richard put a comforting hand on my back, telling me to check the lines, that it would be okay.

Stepping back, I pulled out the piece of glass I had received from Greenland six weeks earlier. Part of an original door. Looking at the drawing through the glass, I could see the lines of power fading, seeping away like water at the slight imperfections that existed. I told Rich the same and he smiled. It was okay, he said, because we had a sweet little girl who would keep trying until it was just right. He looked down at Emily, who was now holding his hand, and she returned his smile and nodded.

Feeling overcome with love and pride, I went and hugged them both. We would keep going until a door was perfect and stayed open. And what a glorious day that would be.

The House Spider

Three weeks ago I went to see my best friend Kameko in Japan. I had recently had problems with a guy I dated, Chet, turning stalkery when I broke things off, and I wanted some time away from dealing with that. More importantly, I was excited both because I've never been to the country (or much of anywhere), and I hadn't seen her in person since a few weeks after college graduation, which had been almost five years ago. She had lived in Tokyo for a couple of years when she first moved back, but when her grandmother had died, she inherited the woman's home out in the country about 20km from Osaki. It was a large house that had been in the family for generations, and based on the pictures she had sent me, I was excited to stay in such a neat place too.

She came to pick me up at the airport, and after hugging and talking excitedly for a few minutes, we headed to her car. She seemed just the same as she always had—smart, funny, and full of life—but I know her too well. I could see something was worrying her as we drove through the beautiful countryside, her pointing out this cool thing or that historic site with a fluidity that made me wonder if she was making up some of the facts and names as she went. I laughed inwardly at the idea of her making up tourist facts, but when she took a break from pointing things out, I asked her if everything was okay.

She glanced at me with a nervous smile. "You always do that. Yeah, everything is okay, but I've been debating on when to tell you about the…unique feature of my house."

I had been smiling back, but I felt the expression slipping away at her tone. "What's that?"

"Well, you know this is an old house I have, right? My great-great grandparents built it over a hundred years ago. And I had never even been to it while my grandmother was alive." I could tell she was trying to build up her courage to get it out, and before I could respond, she finally did. "Well, the house is kinda haunted? Kinda not really?"

Her voice went up at the end like she was asking for my confirmation.

I raised an eyebrow. I had been expecting her to say the plumbing was bad or that the wiring was wonky. Not this. And kinda? What did that even...

"What I mean is, it's not a ghost. It's a yokai. Which I can tell you don't know what that is. Ok. It's kind of a general term for a wide variety of creatures and spirits in Japanese folklore. And apparently they're real, at least some of them, because I have one."

I felt disoriented. I'd have thought it was a practical joke, but Kameko hated pranks and I could tell she was serious. I considered if she was on drugs or having a mental issue, but knowing her, that seemed unlikely too. So, I decided to just roll with it.

"Okay. Weird. So what kind of thing do you have? Can you see it?"

She nodded slowly. "Oh yeah. And it sounds way creepier than it is. It's just a really big spider."

Unexpectedly, a burst of laughter pushed its way out of my throat. "Fuck. I thought you were serious."

Kameko was frowning and shaking her head, her eyes going between me and the road. "I am. And it's not really a spider, at least not a normal spider. But it's about the size of...well, like that show Lassie. It's about Lassie-sized. And it's lived there since the house was built, at least according to the letter my grandmother left me when she died. It doesn't hurt or bother anything or anybody, and most of the time it stays out of sight. Occasionally it'll come out to watch t.v. if I have it on. It likes game shows for some reason. But the best thing is it keeps the house immaculate."

I blinked. "Your border collie-sized spider ghost is a maid."

She shot me a look. "Not a ghost, a spirit, or part spirit, or whatever. But yes, it cleans. Never when you're around, and it has to be through magic, but I haven't had to lift a finger since I moved in."

I turned in my seat to face her more directly. "Okay, what's the deal? Is this a joke about me being messy? I don't get it."

She sighed. "I know how it sounds. But I didn't want you being terrified when you saw it, and you know I never would have invited you here if I didn't truly believe it's safe. It was weird for me at first too. Now I kind of look at it like having a fucked-up family dog that doesn't die."

I opened my mouth to say something else, but I had no words. Finally, deciding I'd just have to let this weirdness play out, I said okay and settled back in my seat.

When we arrived at the house, I was awestruck by how beautiful the house was. It was also very large, especially by Japanese house standards. We went through an outer gate and into a meticulously maintained garden. I gestured around and mouthed "spider?", which got me a withering look as Kameko mimicked my gesture and mouthed "gardener". I grinned and shrugged, and then we went on inside.

The interior of the home put the outside to shame. It was spotless, but I wouldn't have expected less from Kameko anyway, and it managed to be extremely clean and orderly without looking sterile or uninviting. I glanced around, simultaneously happy to be there and nervous, and finally I asked where it was.

Shrugging, she led me deeper into the house. "It's hard to say. It keeps to itself mainly, and it won't ever approach you, even though it doesn't run if you approach it. I guess in theory, it would let you touch it, but I've never tried." She gave out a short laugh. "This sounds so weird actually talking about it to another person." She suddenly stopped and turned, giving me a quick hug. "I'm really glad you're here."

It wasn't until that evening, after we had eaten dinner and settled in the living room to watch t.v., that I saw the yokai. I had caught motion out of the corner of my eye and started to turn when the shape I saw froze me in place. If anything, Kameko had underestimated the thing's size. It moved silently into the room and slowly moved up a back wall until it was perched against the high ceiling. I heard Kameko's voice near my ear, telling me to breathe, that it was ok. To go ahead and look at it, it was fine, it didn't mind. With great effort, I turned my head more to see it more fully, taking in its dark form in the flickering of the light from the television. It reminded me somewhat of a tarantula, but with large sets of black eyes, 3 smaller surrounding a larger, on both sides of its face. I could feel it glance down at me for a moment, but then it seemed to go back to watching t.v.

If it had been anyone else, I would have run away then. As it was, I spent the next day trying to convince her it wasn't safe for her to stay, and she spent another two convincing me everything was fine. Ultimately, she won out. I stayed for another five days, had a great time, and by the end I actually waved bye to the spider as it crept across the foyer the day I left to return home. It glanced at me again, gave a slight nod, and went about it's strange business.

By the time I arrived home, the entire trip seemed surreal. I was also exhausted. I put down my suitcase, cleared out a spot on my messy bed, and fell asleep. I woke five hours later, and seeing the piles of clothes, the furry dishes in the sink, and the general messiness that I could only partially blame on preparing for the trip, I found myself wishing I had a ghost spider maid of my own. Shaking away the thought, and after a depressing look in the fridge, I went out for pizza.

When I got back, everything was pristine. I felt a combination of wonder and terror. Had the spider somehow followed me here?

That's when I saw my suitcase. It had been set against a wall and emptied, but I when I got closer I could still see a small bulge in the front pocket at the top. The pocket was partway unzipped, and I used the light on my phone to look inside. There was an egg in there. A strange, leathery black egg the size of a large chicken egg, its surface shiny except for intermittent dull flecks of green. Even at a distance I could see the egg had been opened from the inside and was empty.

I ran outside and called Kameko. She answered sleepily, but woke up fast when I told her what I had found. She said her yokai was still there, but she guessed it had a baby? She said she would try to find out what she could, but to be very careful, as not all yokai are the same, and some are very dangerous.

I debated getting a hotel room, but ended up going back in, promising myself I would run at the first sign of trouble. When I entered, I saw it. It was halfway up the wall of the front hall, looking at me with eight small eyes of dark blue, like sapphires. It was the size of a small kitten, and its legs and body were covered in what looked like white fur. Its head was the strangest part, as aside from its eyes, it looked more like the head of a weasel than a spider. I saw it open its mouth in a toothy yawn before giving me a small warbling greeting.

It was almost cute. Which probably meant it would kill me and fill my body cavity with eggs. I regretted the thought and swallowed.

"Are we cool?" I felt like an idiot talking to a little monster on my wall, but it just blurted out. Then it nodded.

"Going to live here together and get along, not hurt each other?"

Another nod.

"Okay, cool I guess. We'll try it out. Welcome home." The creature gave what I decided was a happy warble and nod before moving away down the hall.

In the days since, everything has gone very well. It's still bizarre, of course, but I've adjusted quickly, and had no real concerns until this morning, when I found the body in the guest room closet.

I had gone upstairs to get a raincoat out of the closet, but I had trouble opening the door. When I did get it open, I saw a man's body, wrapped neatly in silk webbing, sitting in the closet floor. I screamed, but before going into full panic mode I realized the man was wearing a black ski mask. I studied him closer to the extent I could see through the webs. He had dark clothes, and a long skinning knife was clenched in his right fist.

I recognized that knife. Chet used to carry it around in his truck the times we went out. I felt my stomach clench. I managed to slip the knife loose with some effort and used it to free enough webbing to remove the mask. Chet's face was hollowed and drawn, and I could see that his throat had been ripped out.

It's hard for me to say how long he had been there, but I had seen enough to know what had happened. I grabbed my raincoat and went out. When I returned home that night, every trace of him was gone. For the tenth time I considered calling the police, but what could I say? In the end I sat down and turned on the television. It only took a minute to find a game show to watch.

The Everlasting Flesh

"You always give back what you take out."

The single line of black type was the only blemish on the thick, cream-colored card I was handed as I entered the mansion's front foyer. The man handing them out, impeccably dressed in a cream-colored suit the same color as the card, was solemn in his work, but that didn't stop Jonas from giving a laugh and patting the man on the shoulder as he took his card. The man shook from the impact of Jonas' meaty hand, but his expression remained unchanged. Seeming disappointed, Jonas turned to me and rolled his eyes before pulling me into one of the parlors off the main hall where people were talking.

I had met Jonas six weeks earlier when he contacted me after buying one of my paintings from a gallery downtown. He said he was an art collector and had been very impressed with my work. Did I have more he could see and perhaps buy? Yes, of course I did. Would I meet him for lunch one day and bring my portfolio? Yes, of course I would.

In the weeks since that first lunch, we became friends and Jonas became a patron of sorts. He bought five more of my paintings, but he also started talking about me needing an actual studio rather than just painting out of a spare room in my apartment. I was always leery things were going to veer towards strangeness or turn sexual, but it never did. He never really asked anything of me at all until this party, and it never even occurred to me to refuse.

He didn't tell me much going in, other than it was a social club of ultra-wealthy people that was kind of weird. No orgies or anything like that he assured, and it was up to me how much I participated in any activity, but his precautionary preamble was enough to make me intrigued without really being worried.

Once inside and mingling, I began looking for signs of strangeness, but found few. The oddest thing was that it looked like no one was drinking anything other than water. When I asked Jonas about it, he said alcohol was discouraged at these things, as it could dilute or corrupt the experience. What was the experience? Jonas just gave me a melodramatic lift of the eyebrows and a wink.

We talked to a few people, all clearly wealthy, a couple of whom I even recognized from some article or television show. Then an announcement was made to come into the main ballroom. People filtered from our room and several others, coming together into a large room lit by two massive crystal chandeliers and bare of adornment except for a large platform towards the far end of the rectangular room. It was near this platform that the forty or fifty of us gathered, being beckoned up by a small woman who stood atop it at a podium.

She welcomed us all, saying that per custom, seven people had been predesignated for tonight's "journey" and everyone else had been put into the random pool for the remaining three slots. She asked those three to come up first, each holding up a black stone that apparently indicated their right to participate. When she asked for the remaining seven, Jonas chuckled and grabbed my arm, guiding us to the front.

I was starting to get nervous now, and I wanted to ask questions, but there was little time and I didn't want to make Jonas angry or embarrass him in front of his weird friends. So I kept quiet as we were ushered through the heavy double doors behind the podium. We were in a smaller room that was empty except for two lamps and three men that were clearly some kind of guards. The woman gestured to the men and they proceeded to open the only other door in the room.

This door was of metal and was locked by both an electronic lock tied to a keypad and three bar locks that even the large guards had to grunt to slide out of place. When the doors began to crack open, I could feel cool air rush out to greet us, scentless but carrying a strange weight about it. The woman led us in, and that's when I first saw the body.

It had been a middle-aged woman and was dressed in a gauzy white dress. She had brown hair streaked with grey that cascaded down onto the stone dais she was laid out upon. Her skin was pale and clean, and at a glance she could have just been asleep. But at more than a glance, that clearly wasn't right. She was too still, too inanimate. I couldn't help myself at this point. I leaned over to Jonas and asked if that woman was dead. He nodded, continuing to talk as the woman gestured for one of their group to come forward.

Jonas told me in lowered tones that the body was over 500 years old, but had never decayed. It happened sometimes, he said. Such bodies were called incorruptible, and it was sometimes viewed as a sign of sainthood. This woman, he said, had been a miller's wife in eastern Europe, and had apparently just dropped dead one day. They didn't embalm the body, of course, but it still did not rot. Eventually it was claimed by a local church, and a small monastery had been built around it for a time before it changed hands and ultimately wound up here.

But why? I asked. He pointed to the front where the woman had spread open a slit in the dress to expose the flesh of the body's stomach. This process, Jonas said, was called "wet cupping". It was commonly used as a form of alternative medicine on the living, but it had been discovered that if it was used to extract fluids from an incorruptible body, the fluids could be drank to various effects.

I felt myself involuntarily jerk back. I could tell by his expression, which was much different than his normal relaxed and jolly face, that he was serious. What effects? I asked.

Visions, euphoria, intellectual and artistic breakthroughs. It was kind of like acid, but without any risk of brain damage or long-term physical harm. And while some people did have "bad trips", it was pretty rare.

While he was talking, I was watching the procedure unfolding before us. The woman had several tiny glass cups on a table nearby. With practiced precision, she took a small metal tool that almost looked like a toothbrush to ten different spots on the skin. As she did so, a black liquid would begin to well from the spot, and she would apply a cup, which had some mechanism on it to vacuum-seal it to the flesh. By the time she was done, all ten of the small cups were filling with the black liquid. She then went back to the first one, slid a thin piece of metal underneath its edge with amazing speed, and righted the cup. Wiping down its sides with a cloth, she handed the brimming cup of black ichor to the first participant, an older Hispanic woman.

The woman's wrinkled nose told me of the smell a moment before I smelled it myself. The scent was of dead flowers and decay, and I felt my gorge rising. I wanted to tell her not to drink it, but it was too late. After her, the rest followed in turn, including Jonas himself. They all seemed okay, and Jonas said that while it smelled terrible, it didn't taste bad, and it was perfectly safe. The woman handed me my glass and they all waited, staring at me expectantly.

I'd like to say that I told them no. That I handed it back, or threw it to the ground, or told them I wanted to leave. But I didn't. I was scared and weak. I didn't want to lose Jonas' friendship or his patronage, and I could feel that I was on the precipice of something.

So I held my breath and I drank it. Jonas was right, it didn't taste bad. I felt it slide down my throat like some kind of foul milkshake, and then it was gone. I braced myself for some kind of reaction, but none came. When I looked questioningly at Jonas, he was grinning. Clapping me on the back, he told me that I'd done great. That it would probably be a bit before it kicked in.

We all retired to a room filled with sofas and chairs, and while the other guests, the non-participants, were around, they kept a respectful distance. I felt my head getting lighter as I sat on an overstuffed leather sofa in a dim corner of the room. My vision began to dilate, and then the room fell away entirely. I was flying through some dark maelstrom, and I sensed it was the land of the dead, or at least one of them. I felt my body pick up speed as it hurtled downward through black clouds and purple arcs of lightning, and before long I could see the ground below me. As my descent slowed, I found myself shooting out across the landscape, grey ashy lands of bare earth giving way to dark forests, then to massive cities carved of towering red monoliths of crimson rock and dark sinew. I began to scream and cry from joy and terror, and then I was back in the room. I looked at my phone, and only a few minutes had passed.

Jonas dropped me off at home in the early hours of the morning. He had told me he was proud of me, that he had wanted to see how it would affect an artist of my caliber, and not to tell him, but to show him what I had experienced through my work. Over the next few months I began doing just that. I was painting at an incredible pace, filling canvases with depictions of the things I had seen and images I continued to see in my dreams. Jonas bought many of them, but he was not alone. He bought me a new studio that had room for a full gallery, and by the end of the first year I was selling paintings as fast as I could finish them.

In many ways, that time and the months that followed have been the best of my life. I wish I could say I had enjoyed them more, but most of my time has been spent feeding my drive to paint, as though I'm trying to express corruption out of a wound. Still, I have become very successful doing the thing I'm most passionate about, so I wasn't about to complain.

Yesterday morning, three men broke into my studio and kidnapped me. They zip-tied my hands and pulled a black bag over my head before gently leading me outside and into a car. Two hours later, I was back in the room with the body. They had secured me to a metal table that had not been in the room before, thick leather straps over my thighs, torso and, after removing the hood, forehead. I could only turn my head slightly, but it was enough to see the body and to see that the men had left the room, shutting and locking the door behind them.

I called out several times, but got no response. My pleading turned to angry rants, but soon I was tired, my fear overwhelming any sense of indignation. I didn't know what was going on, or what was going to happen, and the uncertainty made it much worse. I found myself glancing periodically over at the body from the corner of my eye, but nothing changed. More time passed, and I thrashed against the straps, but they didn't budge. After holding out as long as I could and harboring some insane hope that this would prompt a response, I wet myself. Still nothing.

Finally, as I felt my urine cooling against me and my heart starting to slow as I accepted I wasn't getting out of this, I began to cry. Softly at first, and then thick streams of tears ran down the sides of my face and into my hair. That's when the lights went out.

It startled me, but it didn't stop me from weeping. Whatever new torture they were going to subject me to, I might as well cry while I could. Eventually I quietened, silent rivulets still coming from my eyes and pooling in my ears. That's when I heard something.

It was a small, stealthy sound. A rustle of fabric, then the light scuffing of flesh across the marble floor. I had not fallen asleep, and I knew no one had entered the room unless it was by some silent, secret entrance, as the main doors made too much noise. And the sounds…they were coming from the direction of the body.

I remained perfectly still, half-frozen from fear now. I listened as I heard the small noises of movement come closer, felt the unmistakable sense of another's presence close to me in the dark. My head immobile, I could tell there was a face floating above me. I heard or felt no breath, but I thought I knew why. I wanted to scream, was opening my mouth to, and that's when I felt the rough, dry tongue on my cheek.

The fleshy appendage raked itself carefully, almost thoughtfully, across my cheeks before following the trails of my tears down into my hair and even into the cups of my ears. I held myself perfectly still, as though I was being tasted by some venomous snake and was trying to avoid the subsequent bite. The tongue did its work meticulously, occasionally revisiting my cheeks and the corners of my eyes. Then it was gone. A moment later I felt a light kiss upon my forehead.

I heard another slight rustle of movement, and moments later the lights turned back on. The body was back on the dais as though it had never moved. Soon the double doors were opened, and I was escorted back outside to a car where Jonas was waiting inside.

He told the driver to take us back to my house, and while I was so shaken I didn't even want to talk, Jonas wasn't deterred. He apologized for how I had been taken, saying that it was always that way the first time to minimize any resistance. Now that I knew what was what, the next time they would just send a car for me.

The next time? I asked. Yes, he said with a sour look. It would take a few times to give back what I had gotten, but by then I'd be ready for another round, he assured. And it would get easier. I asked what the fuck he was talking about.

He frowned, looking genuinely perplexed. "You always give back what you take out. It's part of the deal. And you'll want to do it again, believe me. It's life changing." He gave a laugh. "Just don't scare me like that again. When you took so long without crying…I was getting worried. I've seen other people not cry, and I've seen what happened to them. She has other ways of taking it back, and believe me, it's not nearly as pleasant." His face looked haunted, and he looked as if he wanted to say more, but in the end he just turned and looked out the window.

I was returned home, ten hours after I had been taken, and since then I've been thinking about what I should do. But I'm writing this not as a cry for help, but as a word of warning. Be careful what thresholds you cross and know yourself before you do. Because things have a way of getting paid for, and sometimes you may not like the price.

Mr. Jinkies

When I was little I loved Scooby-Doo—the show itself more than the titular character, who I always found a little disturbing if I'm being honest. But I loved the ghosts and mysteries, and I loved Velma, who was always smart and determined to keep the rest of the Scooby gang on the right path. Apparently I loved the show and Velma so much that when I was about four I would run around the house yelling, "Jinkies! Jinkies!", much to the annoyance of my brothers and long-suffering parents. It was told to me as a cute story when I was older, but I could read between the lines.

I even had a little stuffed rabbit that I named Mr. Jinkies. I remember a friend of the family had brought him to me, a kind-looking older man in a gray overcoat, and I loved Mr. Jinkies from the start. I had nightmares a lot when I was small, and sleeping with Mr. Jinkies seemed to be a magical cure-all for them. It may seem silly, but I slept with that rabbit until I went to college, and ten years later, I still had him in a box of childhood toys and keepsakes in my attic.

I mention all of this because last week I went up into the attic looking for Mr. Jinkies. My best work friend, Melanie, has a little boy that has been having night terrors for months. They've tried sleep studies and child psychologists, but nothing has helped. I was kind of embarrassed, but seeing how worried she was, I felt like I should at least suggest a different option. I told her about how Mr. Jinkies had helped me get over my childhood fears, and that a similar thing might work for her little boy. Her eyes lit up, as much out of desperation as anything I think, and she asked if I still had Mr. Jinkies.

My first thought was actually to lie. I didn't really want to give up my favorite childhood stuffed animal. But pushing down that first selfish impulse, I swallowed and nodded with a smile. I thought so, I said. I'd look and bring it the following day. She gave me a hug, telling me that she'd tell her little boy how it had helped me and that it would do the same for him. I hugged her back and tried to push away the strange anxiety I was feeling.

When I went up into the attic, it didn't take long to find the right box, as it was labeled "Stuffed animals and Mr. Jinkies". I opened it up and pulled him out, studying him in the dusty late afternoon sunlight streaming through the attic window. He looked just as I remembered him. Brown fur except for a white belly and paws, long ears that flopped at the tips and black glass eyes that you could see yourself in. I felt a small surge of excitement run through me holding him again and, squeezing him to me, I felt a strong urge to call Melanie and tell her I didn't have him anymore after all.

But that was silly, of course, and I told myself I could always get him back in a few weeks whether it helped him or not. The idea that I was planning on taking a new toy away from a small child never really occurred to me, and if Melanie looked strange when I told her it was just a loan of Mr. Jinkies, not a gift, I managed to ignore it.

Still, I felt good for helping them out, and the next day she came in glowing. She said the rabbit had worked like a charm, and they had all had the first good night's sleep in months. I told her I was happy for them, and I was, but I admit I had to fight the urge to ask how many nights she thought they'd need him.

Then it was the weekend and I was busy getting ready for a family barbeque. My older brother couldn't make it, but it was the first time I got to spend a day with my parents and my younger brother Bailey in a couple of months. He was just starting graduate school, and so he would sneak off occasionally to study when he thought he had met some sociability threshold for the next hour or so, but I was busy helping our mother in the kitchen while Dad got the grill ready outside.

We were making hamburger patties when I mentioned that I had let Melanie borrow Mr. Jinkies. I jumped when the bowl my mother was holding shattered on the floor.

"What did you say?" I was looking at my mother, her face white as a sheet and her mouth trembling, a mound of raw hamburger meat and ruined porcelain splattered on the floor between her feet. "What name did you say?"

I was confused and scared by how she was acting. "Mr. Jinkies. My stuffed rabbit." As I was speaking, she was coming across to me swiftly, her hand clapping across my mouth as I finished "rabbit". Shaking her head violently, she resisted my efforts to pull away.

"No, no. You don't ever say that name. Not ever. Where did you hear that name?" Her eyes were wild, and for the first time in my entire life, I was actually a little afraid of my mother.

She lowered her hand from my mouth and I pulled back some, but she still had a firm grip on my arm. "You know, my stuffed rabbit I had when I was little? Mr…I mean, that was its name."

Her grasp on my arm tightened. "Who put you up to this? Was it your brother? Bailey is too young to remember, but Alan would know." She gave me a small shake. "Tell me the truth."

I felt my fear turning into anger as I yanked my arm away. "Chill the fuck out, Mom. I haven't even talked to Alan in like a month, and since he didn't show up today it will probably be another two before I see him. What's the big deal about a stuffed rabbit?"

I could see my mother trying to regain her composure and only partially succeeding. She wiped a strand of hair from her face and gestured to the table. "Sit down for a minute." When I pointed at the mess on the floor, she waved it away. "I'll get that up when we're done talking. But I need to talk to you about this now." Her face softened as she motioned for me to sit again. "Please, honey."

Slowly I sat down. I felt disoriented, as though I was having an entirely different conversation than the one my mother was in. How could it be this big of a…

"You never had a stuffed rabbit."

I laughed. So it was some weird joke. "Yeah, sure. You'll have to explain that to the kid I gave him to." I tried to stop there, but I felt compelled to add, "Loaned him to." She was shaking her head again. I pushed on, explaining how I remembered getting him, naming him after my favorite catchphrase from Scooby-Doo, how he helped me with my nightmares…

She interrupted me, a finger stabbing the air in my direction. "Oh, you had nightmares. And you did know a Mr....you know. But it wasn't some stuffed toy."

I felt my stomach beginning to sink. It wasn't a joke. She was really upset. "What was Mr. Jinkies then?"

I saw her wince at the name, but she went on. "We never knew for sure. When you were about three, you started talking to something nobody else could see. You were just learning to talk, and it's not uncommon for small children to babble off and on to themselves. But instead of lessening, as you got older it got worse. By the time you were four you were telling us stories about Mr....Mr. Jinkies. About how he was this funny creature that told you stories and sung you songs. That was about the time the nightmares started."

"At first we thought it was just normal night terrors. Took you to the doctor, saw a child therapist a couple of times, but nothing seemed to help. Then we started seeing the marks on you."

I frowned, my skin starting to prickle. "Marks? What kinds of marks?"

Her lips had started trembling again, and she covered her mouth with her hand as she went on. "Bite marks mainly. Small and not shaped like anything we knew. Some scratches too." She looked up at the ceiling, her eyes wet and glistening. "My God, we were so terrified. We didn't know if someone was abusing you, or if some animal was getting in at night somehow. We went and stayed at a motel for a few nights, but it made no difference. The nightmares and the marks kept happening, and as time went on, you were getting more and more where you wouldn't talk to us. You would only talk to Mr. Jinkies."

She let out a shuddering breath and looked back at me. "Eventually we brought in specialists. A man who was a former priest and an expert in, well, occult-type things. He said something had attached itself to you. Over the next few days, he tried to get rid of it, and it looked like it worked. You stopped being attacked, stopped having dreams. You were young enough that we swore to never tell you about it, never talk about it again." Reaching forward, my mother grabbed my hand in hers. "But now I don't think it ever really left you. These memories you have about this toy...none of that ever happened. I think it just hid inside of you and waited."

Pulling my hand away, I felt a mixture of fear, anger and guilt. "That's not possible. I held that rabbit in my hands this week. It was real."

She shrugged. "I believe you, and I can't explain it. But I can tell you that didn't happen when you were growing up, and whatever you gave to that little boy, him and his family are in danger." She grabbed my hand again. "But don't you take it back. Whatever you do, don't you take it back. Warn them, tell them to burn it. Maybe that will work. But don't you ever see it or touch it again. Promise me." Her grip and gaze were desperate and hot, and I found myself nodding even though I knew it was likely a lie.

After quick excuses and good-byes, I headed out, telling my mother that I was going to call Melanie on the phone, but I wouldn't go by her house. I did call, but my car was already pointed in her direction. After the third call went to voicemail I gave up. Thirty minutes later I was pulling up in her driveway. There were two cars parked there already, but at first I saw no signs of people. Then the front door opened and Melanie came out.

"Hey, what're you doing here?" She was friendly, but she seemed tense as well. She came down to meet me and gave me a hug. "Sorry I didn't answer the phone a few minutes ago. I've been running around like a crazy person this afternoon. I'm about to give Sidney his bath, but if you want to come hang out for a few minutes it won't take long and we can visit."

I wasn't sure how to react. I had half-decided I was going to be walking into some horror show when I arrived, but instead everything seemed pretty normal. Melanie was staring at me, waiting for a response, so finally I just nodded, mumbled something about just dropping by to say hi, and followed her inside.

The interior of the house was messy, but normal "small child in the family" messy. She led me back into Sidney's playroom and I felt a small chill when I saw the little boy on the floor whispering something to Mr. Jinkies. The rabbit stared passively back with its black gaze, but even at that distance I thought I could hear some kind of low, scratchy response to the child's words. Sidney looked up at us as we approached, and I found myself struck by the shadows I could see under his eyes now. He looked sicker now than he had even in pictures I'd seen after his night terrors had started. I almost mentioned it to Melanie, but something held me back.

With some mild protests and reluctance at leaving the rabbit behind, Sidney went to take his bath. I sat down in a large, overstuffed chair that was likely used for reading stories and taking naps on most days. From the angle I was sitting, Mr. Jinkies' back was to me, but I still couldn't keep my eyes away from that small brown form.

Then I saw it was moving. Or rather, something was moving inside of it. At first I thought it was my imagination getting the better of me, but then the movements grew more obvious and I saw the first bone-white legs of the thing that was coming out from around the edge of the rabbit's cocoa fur. I tried to scream or move, but I couldn't. I was frozen in place, and by more than fear. It was holding me somehow.

It slowly pulled its impossible length from inside that small toy, wet strings of yellow ichor trailing back to what I could only assume was a gaping wound in the obscured stomach of the stuffed rabbit. It looked like a centipede more than anything, but its legs were thicker and had too many joints, and its face had so many eyes and mouths. It raised up until it was at eye-level, its body and legs moving side to side languidly as it regarded me. It makes no sense, but that terrible face seemed simultaneously tiny and enormous, its eyes boring into me until they were the whole world.

That's when I remembered everything. I remembered this face of Mr. Jinkies and the true face behind it that was somehow much, much worse. I remembered its low, scratchy voice that had seemed so funny when I first heard it as a child, but had soon become the discordant tune of my terror and pain. I felt myself urinating and I didn't have the presence of mind to care or feel embarrassment. I was too focused on the words emblazoned across my mind.

Leave me here or take me back. It is your choice.

I didn't wait for Sidney to finish his bath before I left. I haven't answered Melanie's calls or texts, and I called work to tell them that I'm not coming back. I'll change my number in the next few days as well. I thought I would feel more guilt or shame, and I do feel some, but not much. I keep thinking about an old joke my Dad told me once.

Two hunters are wading across a river, their boots strung around their necks, when they see a grizzly bear looking at them from the bank. The bear starts towards them and one of the hunters takes off running in the other direction. He's making slow progress barefoot on the riverbed, but when he looks back his friend hasn't started running yet. Instead he's putting back on his boots. He yells for his friend to come on. Freshly booted, his friend starts running, soon catching up and starting to pass his barefooted friend as they make it to the far shore with the bear close behind. As he passes him, he yells back, "I don't have to beat the bear, I just have to beat you," and leaves his friend in the dust.

I wish I was a stronger person. A better person. I thought I was, but I'm not. I can't have that thing near me again, whatever it is. I have to be rid of it, really rid of it, forever this time. I could call this a confession, but I think you have to repent to really confess. And in the dark, quiet hours that I lay awake, worried I'll hear a stealthy rustle across my floor or the thump of a stuffed rabbit flung against my front door, I'm at my most honest.

And if Mr. Jinkies comes back, I've already made a list of other children I can give him to.

On the Inside

I don't like to be away from home. I was diagnosed with severe agoraphobia when I was twenty-five, and for years I tried to overcome it. My father was still alive then, and he would always encourage me to go to therapy and slowly push my boundaries. My primary triggers are open spaces and crowds of people, so if someone sees my house they often joke about how it's in the middle of an open field.

That's by design. My father built this house for me, you see, and it has views to a wide-open world while still having walls to keep me safe. It has a good-sized back yard and garden, but it's all enclosed in a ten-foot wooden fence, so I don't feel so exposed when I'm out in the sunshine. He always said that he wanted me to have a place I could love now, but when I was ready, I could also use it as a jumping off point to a much wider world. All I had to do was step out my front door.

He died two years ago. For the first six months after his death, I actually went out more, driven by the idea of making him proud. But over time, any sense of pride or duty were smothered by my fear and grief. It became easier to just avoid the world and sink into the stillness of my quiet little life.

Not that my life is bad. It isn't, and the point of telling you all of this isn't to make you feel sorry for me. My father left me very comfortable financially, and I am lucky enough to have an online document review job I can do from home. I'm healthy, fairly happy, and I have friends that come and visit me often.

I also have a wonderful two-year old cat named Tibbers. My friend Alicia brought him to me a couple of months after my father passed away, and initially I was resistant to the idea. I like animals, but I've never had a cat before. It wasn't until that first night that I knew I was going to keep him.

I had set up a box for him in the bathroom with high enough walls and enough weight in the bottom that I thought he couldn't jump out or tip it over. He cried for awhile, but I tried to ignore it, figuring it was best to let him tire out and go to sleep. And it seemed to work. The pitiful mewling from the bathroom tapered off and I finally felt myself drifting off to sleep.

I awoke some time later to a warm pressure against my side. I sleep on my stomach usually, and as I reached back I felt the kitten's small furry body draped against me, his front paws and head on my back with his bottom half resting on the bed. As I touched him, I felt a sleepy purr rumble through my fingertips and ribs. That's when I knew I loved him.

Most nights, that's still how Tibbers sleeps at least part of the night. He'll prowl around too, of course, but before the night is over I usually find him propped in that odd half-sitting, half-laying position against me, fast asleep.

That's why two nights ago, I didn't think anything when I felt weight settling against my side. I drifted back off contentedly, and it was some time later when reached down to pet Tibbers. Instead of soft fur, I felt something hard and semi-rigid. I quickly woke up, but in those first couple of seconds of coming out of the fog of sleep, I felt ridges and small, spikey protrusions in spots. I let out a scream and fumbled for the light on the nightstand, screaming again at what was illuminated.

My sheets had a small pool of blood on them, and it was easy to see from the wound on my side where it had come from. Something had been biting me or sucking on my side, and as I jumped up from the bed, I saw it move under the sheets away from me. Tibbers had come running into the room from some night-time exploration at the commotion I'd made, and he saw it too. The shape darted back and forth as though not sure which way to go, and that hesitation gave Tibbers the time he needed to jump on the bed to try and catch it.

I felt my heart leap with hope and fear as he swatted at the shape, but it was too fast, shooting off the bed and onto the floor. I caught a glimpse of it then—mottled brown skin that seemed to glisten and a shape that reminded me of some prehistoric creature. I looked it up later and from the brief look I got, it was similar to a trilobite.

But at the time, I was more concerned with killing it. I keep a baseball bat in the corner of my room, and I reached for it even as I saw with dread where it was heading. I grabbed the bat and flung it toward the air vent, trying to reroute it, but my aim was bad and the creature was undeterred. It seemed too wide and thick to fit through the vent slats, but somehow it did, and it was gone.

Tibbers went to the vent and peered down, giving a frustrated meow before looking back at me. I grabbed a flashlight from the kitchen and shined the light down into the vent, but I saw no sign of the thing. After a few seconds of listening for movement with no results, I gave up and went to the bathroom to look at my wound.

There was still blood on my side and my pajama shirt, but somehow the wound itself was gone. I considered if I had just been mistaken in my sleepiness and panic, but I knew I had seen a round bite mark there about the size of a dime. I shuddered remembering it, and I knew the memory was corroborated by the blood on me and the bed. Still, there was little more I could do for it now, so I washed off the blood, wiped down my side with antiseptic, and started patrolling the house for other signs of the creature.

I found none, but there was no way I was going back to sleep, so ultimately I closed all the vents and sat in my living room with the lights on until it was late enough in the morning that I could call a pest control company. The pest guy came out later that morning, and I described in vague terms seeing some kind of animal, but I wasn't sure what and it had headed into the vents. I stressed that I needed them to check everything from top to bottom and get rid of it. The older man nodded jovially, telling me it was likely a field mouse, and that he would track it down or at least find the way it had gotten in.

Four hours later and he had patched two holes in my ductwork, but said he saw no sign of any pests other than a few spiders under the house. He laughed, saying this was one of the cleanest houses he had ever seen, top to bottom, and he had no problem declaring it pest-free. I knew he was patronizing me, but I think it was well-meant, as he could tell how worried I was. My hope was that whatever that thing had been, it was gone and couldn't come back. After the pest guy was gone, I decided to take a long bath to try and relax.

I had been in the water only a few minutes when I felt a sharp pain in my side. It was the same spot where the bite mark had been. Sitting up in the tub, I felt the spot and the skin was unbroken but sore to the touch. As I ran my fingers over it a second time, I felt something beneath my skin move. I stifled a scream, feeling sure it was my imagination or a muscle spasm. I stood up and went dripping to the mirror so I could get a better view of my side. I rubbed the spot again, but nothing happened. Again, and still nothing. I was about to give up when I saw a ripple pass across my flesh as something shifted underneath.

This time I did scream.

I called Alicia, frantic and crying, and within an hour she was there and taking me to the doctor's office. I kept my eyes closed most of the way there, Alicia rubbing my shoulder and trying to calm me down. The only benefit to the state I was in was that I couldn't get in a panic about the traveling or the people when I was in a panic already.

My regular general practitioner wasn't in, so I saw a pleasant-looking woman in her fifties instead. She listened to what we told her, though Alicia had not seen any sign of it moving herself, so she was having to recount what I'd told her when I got too upset. Between the two of us, we got enough across for the doctor to look concerned and start physically examining my side. She gave no indications of what she thought, but said she wanted to get x-rays and blood work. Two hours later and she said there was no sign of anything showing up in imaging, and initial blood work showed no sign of an infection. She would call after the more detailed labs came back, and if I continued having problems, she could order an MRI in a few days.

"But," she said in measured tones, "Keep in mind that it might be anxiety-related or otherwise psychosomatic."

"I'm not crazy."

She shook her head. "I know that. Not saying you are. But the mind and the body are connected, and if you had a bad dream that stressed you out, your body can react to it in strange ways. Just keep it in mind as an option."

The ride back to my house was a quiet one. She would never say it, but I could tell Alicia thought it was in my head. When she dropped me off, she offered to stay awhile, but I told her I just needed to rest. In truth, while I was grateful for her help, I was hurt that she didn't really believe me. And I did need some peace and quiet after the commotion of the last day.

The problem is that now I jump at every sound. I don't know if the creature is hiding somewhere in the house or is going to come back. I don't know what it did to me, but I can still feel something moving on the inside.

And Tibbers won't come around me anymore. When I go near him, he hisses and runs. The first time it happened, I cried a bit, but now I think I understand.

This morning when I woke up, I heard soft singing. At first, I thought the radio was accidently playing music, but a glance at my nightstand showed it was inert and silent. No, the singing was coming from somewhere else. I stood up slowly, trying to pinpoint it. After moving around a bit I knew it always stayed with me, that it was coming *from* me.

It was my side. I could hear faint music coming from where that thing attached itself to me.

Since I realized that, I've mainly been sitting and staring out the window. I don't know that there's a place for me out there, and this house, my world, feels alien and unsafe now. Even my own body seems foreign and hostile. But I hear the singing clearer now—from my side, but in my head now too.

It washes against me like cool waves—calming me, yes—but taking parts of me with it as it rolls away, back into some unknown sea. I feel like sand crumbling and dissolving against a rising tide. I've written all of this because I can feel myself fading more and more, feel myself caring less that it's happening as the music in my head begins to swell.

I think I may go outside after all. In just a little while.

After I finish listening to this song.

My apartment has a roach problem

I grew up on a farm. Aside from the occasional field trip or family vacation, I rarely went to a big city as a child, so like many, the idea of living in a metropolis held a special mystique for me. From early high school I made plans to go to college somewhere big, and I wound up going to Tulane in New Orleans. I managed to get a partial scholarship, and between that, student loans, and working most of the time, I managed to make ends meet. And I loved my time there. While New Orleans has its problems, I still think it's one of the most beautiful and interesting places I've ever seen, and my apartment was cramped and dingy, but I still loved it.

I graduated last May and things have been going downhill. I've had a hard time transitioning from college jobs to some kind of better-paying career, and the lack of money and looming shadow of deferred student loan payments has caused me to realize I couldn't afford to stay in N.O. any longer. So I started applying for jobs all over, eventually snagging one outside of Houston with a big company that manages websites. The pay wasn't great, but more than I had ever made before, and the cost of living in the area I work is actually a bit less than New Orleans.

To save money and because I didn't know the city at all, the day I arrived I started looking for a place to rent near my work. The company set me up in an extended stay room for a week while I got settled, but I didn't know how long it would take for me to find a place I could afford, particularly when I had very little for a deposit.

My first few days of looking was depressing. Every day at lunch and after work I would hit several different places, spiraling out further and further from work as my desperation grew. The company building was in an older office park, and the apartments in the area weren't especially new or nice. Honestly a lot of them were fairly rundown, not that I minded. I wasn't used to fancy, and all I cared about was cheap and available.

But having just moved to town with no local references and little money, I was not a prime choice most places. The couple of apartments I had found that seemed willing to consider me were so far out of my price range that I would starve before my lease ran out.

That Friday I sat in my car, eating a pack of crackers and anxiously scanning the classifieds for any new listings. My supervisor was already starting to ask how I was settling in and did I think I'd be out of the extended stay in the next couple of days, his wet, fishy lips smacking discontentedly when I said I sure hoped so.

Suddenly my heart leapt as I saw a new apartment listed. It was on a street that sounded familiar, even close by. I pulled it up on my phone and saw it was less than three miles away. Throwing the newspaper in the passenger seat, I put the car in drive and headed over right away.

I remember having the irrational fear that there would be a line of people already there to claim it before I got there. I turned onto the street and felt my stomach sink slightly. The buildings here were in worse shape than most in the area, but more concerning was that all the parking spaces were full. I circled the block and finally parked half-ass in a nearby alley before walk-running up to the front door. I hit the buzzer labeled "Mgmt" and an older female voice answered, buzzing me in.

When I walked into the front foyer, my first impression was of how dimly lit it was. To the left and right there were small mail boxes for the tenants, and beyond that there were three doors that appeared to lead to apartments and one door in the back that was labeled "Maintainence". I noticed it was misspelled, but decided it was better to find it charming than concerning. Looking up the stairs that ran along the right wall, I saw it curved back on itself as it continued up to the second floor and beyond. The carpet runner on the stairs looked old and stained, but not in terrible condition, and aside from a faint mustiness, the building didn't seem to have any weird smells.

The door to "Mgmt" opened and a gaunt woman in her fifties stepped out in a pink housecoat, giving me a shrewd look before nodding and beckoning me inside. Her apartment was neat but cluttered, smelling of stale coffee and old perfume. She took me over to a small kitchen table and gestured for me to sit. Then she began, her tone stiff and her words clipped as she spoke them.

"The rent is $700.00 a month. Can you afford that?"

I swallowed. "Yes. I think so."

Her eyes narrowed but she went on. "The deposit is also $700.00. Can you afford that?"

I felt my stomach clench. "I don't have that much right now. Not to pay the rent and the deposit."

Her lips pursed and she nodded. "Then your rent is $800.00, no deposit. Agreeable?"

I nodded. "Yes, thank you. I won't cause any problems."

She raised a bony finger. "I'm not done yet, hun." I nodded silently and she looked mollified. "No pets, no roommates, you got a boyfriend?"

I shook my head. "I just moved to town. I don't know anybody."

She raised an eyebrow and nodded. "No boyfriends staying over. If you get behind on rent, you have to go. This place isn't fancy, but it's what I've got, and I aim to keep it. Understand?"

"Sure, I understand. I'm just happy to have a place to stay."

She smiled, her teeth long and yellow behind her thin and cracked lips. "Good. Glad to have you." She reached forward and patted my hand. "I think you'll like it here. Quiet street, quiet neighbors. We have some bugs around here, but absolutely no mice or rats, don't you worry. And I find if you don't mess with the bugs, they won't mess with you." She gripped my hand tighter. "But no pesticides in here, hun. Absolutely none. We have a couple of tenants that have conditions that are severely aggravated by them."

I found this last part of the conversation more than a little odd, but I didn't want to make her angry or offend her, so I let it go. Later that same night I was already unloading my car and toting my stuff up to my new apartment on the third floor.

The apartment was actually larger than the one I had left in Louisiana, and in some ways it was nicer too. I did hear what seemed like a stealthy scuttle of legs when I opened the door and turned on the light, but I tried to ignore it. I would just keep things clean and washed down. The odd roach or spider wasn't going to keep me from enjoying my new place.

And that held true for the first few days. I cleaned the apartment from top to bottom and while I was tempted to get some bug spray, I held off out of fear that a stray whiff might hurt another tenant or bring the ire of the landlady. In writing this, I realize I've never even learned her name, but that is the least of my worries at this point.

I had been in the apartment for just over a week when I decided to go out on Sunday afternoon to explore more of the neighborhood. Between work and apartment hunting, followed by getting settled in the new place, I'd had precious little time to get to know the area I was living in. I was heading downstairs to the front door when I saw one of the first floor tenants heading back into his apartment. Even though it was May and very humid outside, the large man had on long pants, an overcoat, and a hat. As I drew closer, I saw he even had a scarf on. He turned at my approach, and I saw most of his face was obscured, but his eyes looked terrified and frantic.

I had been about to say hello, but seeing those eyes I asked if everything was all right instead. He didn't answer, but instead wrenched the door to his apartment open and lurched inside. I considered walking closer and asking again, but the door was already slamming shut. Figuring it was none of my business, I tried to put the thought out of my head and went on out.

When I came back later that night, I noticed something strange in my apartment. Several items were in different spots than where I had left them. Most of them were small things. My toothbrush. My watch. A pair of socks I had thrown on the floor. Nothing was missing, just moved somehow. What's more, it made me realize that it had happened before during the week. Nothing as obvious, and I had been exhausted and distracted, but hadn't there been a few times when things weren't where they should be?

I tried to make excuses and convince myself I was wrong, but as the days went on, I noticed it continued happening. A ponytail clip here, a pencil there. Never taken, just moved around. I also was beginning to wake up at night, perhaps out of growing nervousness, and I would hear scuttling in the dark of the apartment. I never saw anything, but I could tell something or many somethings were in the darkness with me.

I finally went to the landlady and asked her if anyone had been in my apartment. She acted shocked and said absolutely not. She had the only other key and she hadn't been in there since before I moved in. I then asked about the possibility of getting some roach traps or something to cut down on the bug situation, and her expression soured further. No kind of pest control could be risked because of tenant sensitivities, but as long as I kept my space clean it shouldn't be a problem. And if I decided this wasn't the place for me, I was welcome to go.

I quickly apologized, assuring her I meant no offense and that yes, I was keeping my apartment spotless. She gave a thin smile and nodded, shutting the door without another word.

When I turned around, I saw the door across the hall belonging to the overcoat man was open a crack. I almost ignored it, but I could see a flicker of movement through the small opening and I found myself approaching the door before I realized it. Looking in through the crack, I could see the man inside. He was still wearing the same outfit—overcoat, hat and all—and I watched as he stumbled around scratching at himself erratically, soft mumbles that resembled some kind of plaintive cry seeming to issue from him as he moved unevenly around a filthy living room. I almost pushed the door further in and asked if I could help again, but that's when I saw his coat move. In two different spots on his back and one on his arm, I saw the fabric rise and fall, not from any movement of the man, but seemingly from something else inside the coat with him. I felt my scalp begin to itch as a buzzing filled my ears, fear climbing up my spine as I stepped back quietly. When I got back into my apartment, I turned on all the lights and stayed awake the rest of the night.

Over the next few days I avoided the apartment building as much as possible. I was starting to get more duties at work, and I took the opportunity to dive into my job and try to get my mind off what I had seen in the man's apartment. I would get there early and stay late, but even then there was only so much time I could kill. I found myself slipping into the habit of going to the local shopping mall and public library, and when they closed, I'd go to a late-night dinner, nursing a glass of water and some chicken noodle soup until close to midnight, when I would finally force myself back to the apartment.

I was keeping my lights on all the time now, so when I opened the door I didn't hear little rustlings of movement too frequently. Still, I could feel them there, hidden in shadows and tucked into unseen cracks. Tiny eyes watching me, weighing me. I would practically run to my bed, checking all the sheets and pillows before climbing in for the night. To say my sleep wasn't restful would be an understatement, and by the third week in the apartment I could barely stay awake at work.

Last night, I woke up in my car. When I looked at the clock, I saw it was after 9, and I vaguely remembered going to my car at 6 when I left the office. Looking around, I saw I had never actually left the parking lot. I must have fallen asleep—thankfully before I could drive off and have a wreck. But it was a wake-up call. I needed sleep and I needed to get out of that place, cheap or not.

Trying to wake up enough to think and drive, I formulated a very basic plan. First, I was going to go to the apartment, try to get a good night's sleep if I could manage, and get up early to start packing. Second, I was going to ask my boss about using the extended stay room again for a few days until I found a new place. Third, I was going to find a new place and hopefully never have to think about that awful apartment building again.

The first part was the hardest. I went back to the building, and as I went inside it struck me again how quiet the place was. I never heard any televisions or doors slamming, and I had only heard muffled voices a few times. I knew there had to be other tenants because there were different voices and they came from different apartments, but I had never actually seen anyone other than the landlady and Mr. Overcoat. The thought of him gave me a shiver and pushed away any thoughts other than getting to my apartment and shutting the door. Running up the stairs, I unlocked the door quickly and stepped in, turning to lock it behind me.

It was only when I turned back around that I noticed how dark the room was. A single lamp next to my bed was the only light that shone, and in the dim light that trickled into the living room, everything was cast in shadowy gloom. In a mild panic, I reached for the light switch near the door, which was still in the up position from days ago. I flipped it down and back up with no response. I started to make my way to the kitchen to try the light there or at least open the refrigerator for its illumination until I could find a light that worked, but then I noticed the low, sneaky noises in the dark around me.

Individually, the tiny scrapings and scuttlings would probably have gone unnoticed. But not so many, not all at once. What was worse was the idea that struck me next. They weren't trying to be quiet or hide any more. And the noise was coming from all around me, headed in my direction. I had to decide quickly whether to make a dash back into the dark for the door or head for the island of light in the bedroom. It only took a moment for me to run towards the lamp.

I had a moment of relief when I reached the bedroom, my eyes scanning around for possible sources of light or new threat. When my eyes landed on my bed, I was momentarily confused. Laid out neatly across my bed were some of my clothes. There was the long raincoat my grandmother had given me two years earlier—a nice coat but two sizes too big for me. There was a knit cap and scarf from an old boyfriend that I did still use some times, but not in May. A pair of gray sweatpants and some old wool gloves. And then on the floor at the bed's edge, were my red galoshes.

None of this stuff had even been unpacked yet, much less seen use. Yet here it all was, and something about it was setting my scalp to itching again. My first thought was that it was another example of someone messing with my belongings, but then I realized there was more to it than that. Someone or something was making me an outfit. An outfit like Mr. Over…

That's when the lamp went out and I started to scream. I turned and ran blindly towards the door, but in the dark I hit the bedroom doorframe and went down. I awkwardly tried to scramble to my feet as I remembered my phone and pulled it out to use the flashlight app. What I saw set me to screaming again.

There were millions of roaches over every surface in the dark. The ceiling, the walls, the floors—nearly every surface was awash with such a mass of crawling reddish-brown bodies that it looked more like some kind of obscene tide as they shifted and flowed towards me. I heard myself screaming "Oh God!" over and over at this point, hysterical to the point of insanity as I flung myself at the door and fumbled with the lock.

I felt the first of them reaching my feet and crawling up my legs as I got the door open and stepped out into the hallway. Looking down, I saw hundreds were already on me, but they began to jump off and fly away back into the dark as I stepped into the sullen light outside my apartment.

I was still screaming my frantic refrain as I danced and shook my legs, and I realized after a moment that I was hearing it echo. From behind the closed doors of two of the apartments on my floor I could hear my screams of "Oh God!" being mimicked, one by what sounded like an old woman and one by what seemed to be the voice of a young man. On the floors below I could hear more of the same drifting up, following my words and terror exactly.

I considered other people could be getting attacked at the same time, but I realized that when the last of the roaches was off and I stopped screaming, all of the screaming stopped. And while I had slammed my apartment door shut when the last of the bugs were gone, after a moment I saw they had regrouped and began pouring under the door towards me again, light or no light.

"Fuck no! Fuck, fuck, fuck!" I started running for the stairs, the cacophony of mimicking screams of "Fuck, fuck, fuck!" rising on all sides as I took the steps two at a time. It was more than I could take, and my screams and curses devolved into a terrified, inarticulate wail as I ran, the sound doubled and redoubled by voices around me and growing louder as I started hearing doors opening simultaneously on every floor.

As I reached the bottom, I saw Mr. Overcoat was standing before the front door, massive arms outstretched as he let out a rough, wet version of my own screaming cry. His eyes were duller now than before, but they still held the terrible insanity of some kind of trapped or wounded animal. There was no other way out of the building, so I would just have to be faster than him.

I acted like I was going to his right and then cut back to the left at the last moment, my need for concentration silencing my voice and thankfully his own. I felt the knob in my hand as I ducked past him, and then one of his massive hands gripped my shoulder and spun me around. I tried to back away, but it was too late. Staring at me without sound, he began dragging me towards the open doorway of his apartment. He wore ragged cloth gloves, and I could see the fabric moving and bulging as he pulled me along. At this close proximity I could actually see movement all over him, even under the skin of the narrow swath of face that was exposed.

I started screaming and he screamed right along with me, his grip and strength never faltering.

A moment later and we were in his apartment. He took the time to issue a shambling kick that closed the door before dragging me onward. Stacks of moldy clothes and newspapers lay in every corner, and there was a rancid almost dusty smell permeating the air that made me choke. How I had never smelled it from the outside was beyond me. He continued dragging me across the living room towards some back hallway, and I knew I had no chance of escape unless I surprised him.

Without warning, still coughing and screaming, I shifted direction suddenly and launched myself at him. The change in momentum worked, freeing his grip long enough for me to grab the lapels of his overcoat and tug it down past his shoulders. My idea was to partially trap his arms for a moment and use the second it gave me to run out of the apartment. It somewhat worked, but the problem was he was still stumbling backwards, beginning to fall, and as he went he grabbed hold of my arm again, taking me with him.

He landed with a wet, squelching thud with me on top of him, my face buried in a decaying sweatshirt that writhed against my cheek. I pushed away immediately and his grip was weaker this time—just enough that I could yank my arm free. I started to stand up, and as I did he started screaming again, his own scream this time—a strange, almost musical sound that sounded angry and painful. As I made it to my feet, he began rolling around on the floor, yanking and tearing at the clothes he was wearing. Walking backward so I could keep my eyes on him, I quickly glanced back to make sure the door wasn't blocked or that I wasn't about to trip on one of the mounds of trash that littered the room.

Reaching the door, I found it had somehow automatically locked when he closed it and there was no latch or button on this side to unlock it. Yelling in frustration and fear, I cast my gaze about for a blunt object of some kind to batter the knob itself with. I found an old umbrella stand that seemed caked with what I assumed was roach droppings, but I was past caring. I just wanted to escape and live, whatever it took.

I began striking the knob, and after the fifth blow I felt it beginning to give way. I looked back over my shoulder to see if he was up and heading back to attack me again. It was a mistake.

He was standing again and still making that strange, rage-filled wailing sound, but he had completed his task of stripping away his clothes. He stood, staring at me as he screamed, his body a ruin and a horror. Small dark bodies swarmed over him and under his skin, nestling in his hair, mounded up like a clutch of bees at his groin. His lips and ears were gone, long eaten away, and as he bellowed I watched several of the roaches traverse between his mouth and one of several holes in his cheek and gullet. Under his armpits were large brown growths that pulsated slightly before beginning to rupture, spilling forth new hordes of baby roaches from the deflating egg sacs to replace those crushed by his fall.

As I continued to stare and take it all in, I saw that not all of the roaches were crawling. At various points of his body, half in and half out of his flesh, there were roaches that barely moved at all. They kept to stations at his knees and elbows, hands and feet, neck and shoulders and jaw. Suddenly they started moving more vigorously, their heads and front legs undulating underneath his skin, and the man began to lurch forward once again in his ungainly way, his tendons and ligaments, or perhaps his nerves and pain receptors, being plucked and controlled by this orchestral horror.

I let out a fresh scream and slammed down on the knob again, popping it off. Yanking the door open, I bolted out into the front hall and almost ran into the first of the tenants coming from upstairs. In the brief glimpses I got, I saw robes and nightgowns, parkas and hoods, all with gloved hands reaching out for me. I ducked past the closest and flung the front door open. Running to my car, I leapt in and peeled off. I didn't start crying until I was twenty minutes away.

I drove on for another hour, finally stopping in the parking lot of a 24-hour grocery store. I wrote most of this in the parking lot there. I couldn't sleep, and after I calmed down I wanted to write up an account of everything while it was fresh and before the morning light could make me doubt myself.

But then I started hearing rustling in my car. It was after four in the morning by this point, and the shadows felt very dark and deep. I shined my phone's light around and saw nothing, but I couldn't quite convince myself it was just my imagination. So I went into the store and managed to find a bug bomb to buy. I've set it off now, and after killing time wandering around the store until the sun came up, I've now set up camp on the bleachers of a small softball field next door until my car can finish airing out.

I don't know if I'll find dead things in the car when I go back or not. I don't know if it would be more of a relief to find them or not. But I know sitting here, even in the sunlight, I keep hearing small rustling noises. I wanted to tell myself it was the wind, but it's not windy today, and it's still early enough that the world is still quietly waking up. No one is around that I can see, and I don't know where the noises would be coming from.

Well, except from the shadows, of course. Even in the middle of the day there are so many shadows. And I know it's impossible that those things followed me here. Impossible that they are pooling in the dark corners of this ballfield and inching silently up these bleachers, waiting until their strength and numbers are such that they can pull me off into a forgotten corner and make me into…

But I've seen impossible things already. And I don't know where is safe. I have this document periodically saving automatically to a cloud account. And without going into specifics with her, I told one of my friends from college to check the cloud account if she doesn't keep hearing from me and to post whatever I've written in this document on the internet wherever she thinks it might be seen and understood.

I think I just saw something move near the closest dugout, and I don't think I can stay here anymore. I hope my car is okay to drive now and I hope they can't really follow me. Fuck, it just moved again. I have to

A thing called Candleheart killed my brother.

My brother is dead. As I sit looking into the tattered brown box that sits in my lap, I know that now. And while I know the thing called Candleheart is to blame, I still feel like it's really my fault. It was my suggestion that put us in it's path in the first place.

Two years ago, our father passed away. He was only 61 years old, but he'd had a bad heart for a number of years, so when I got the call that he had died in his sleep, it was terrible news, but not really a shock either. I had gotten on a plane the next morning, and when I arrived, Michael picked me up from the airport. He was a good little brother as little brothers go, and while he was ten years younger than me at 24, we had always gotten along well and remained friends even when I moved across the country after college.

We talked on the trip back to the house, alternating between catching up on the latest happenings in each other's lives and talking about our father. That rhythm continued over the next few days when we had time alone together, which wasn't much between helping our mother and dealing with friends and relatives. But after the funeral was done and the last of the mourners had left, our mother had announced she was going to go sleep for a good long while, no doubt aided by the pills I had seen our Aunt Clara pressing into our mother's palm after the graveside service. So me and Michael decided to head into town and get something to eat.

It was while we were eating hot wings and reminiscing about our dad that the idea of taking a camping trip came up. Our father, who was no real outdoorsman, had always enjoyed camping for some reason, and when we were growing up he would always try to get us to go out camping with him. In truth we only went a few times over the years, but I still remember how happy it seemed to make him. Those camping trips seemed part of some idyllic familial fantasy to him, and no matter how much our mother protested the bugs or me and Michael argued, he would always bring it up once or twice a year like a car salesman trying to entice us into another test drive.

Looking back on it now, I admit to feeling some guilt that we hadn't gone more when he suggested it. And I know that guilt is part of what prompted me to ask Michael if he wanted to go camping that weekend.

I expected him to laugh or make an excuse why we couldn't do it, but instead he started nodding right away. He still lived at home, and he said that a couple of days away from there, assuming Mom was doing okay, would suit him just fine. We started making plans, and when we got back to the house we found enough camping gear in decent shape that our costs aside from gas and food would be minimal. So after talking it over with our mother and making sure she was good for the next few days, we headed off the next morning on our camping adventure.

I had wanted to go to an established camping area with designated campsites and a building containing toilets and showers, but Michael convinced me that it wouldn't be in the spirit of things to half-ass it. We needed to go somewhere off the beaten track where we weren't surrounded by people and had to squat to take a dump. His argument was less than eloquent, but I got his point. We wanted it to be a trip our Dad would think was really cool.

So he found us a large state park covered by forest about a hundred miles away. After downloading maps and considering our options, we settled on a loose plan that involved parking on the west side of the park, hiking in about ten miles to a smallish body of water called Winter's Lake, and then setting up camp. Day two would be hanging out, hiking around a bit more, and then heading back out.

We got to the large gravel parking lot by ten that morning, and after adding the food and water we had bought on the trip up to our backpacks, we headed east into the forest. Despite it being a bright and sunny day, parts of the forest were surprisingly dark, the large hardwoods that loomed overhead blocking out much of the light as we traveled along what looked like some kind of pig path in a generally easterly direction.

I had some concerns with us getting lost, but Michael did a surprisingly good job of keeping us on course, periodically checking the compass he had brought and calling out a couple spots where he could see what looked like landmarks from the map. The past few days, seeing him help our mother and remain patient and kind with all of the other mourners, had helped me appreciate how much my brother had grown up. He could still be immature at times, and I knew he still relied on me for some things because I was his big sister, but he had become a man, and a good one at that.

I was thinking about that and looking off into the trees when I ran into the back of him. He stumbled a step forward and then turned to look at me. "Watch it. Gave me a flat tire." He shot me a mock frown before grinning as he pointed. "Look over there."

I followed his finger and saw that fifty yards to our left there was what looked to be the ruins of some old, large house. It was surrounded by trees and bushes so thick that it was easy to overlook, and if we had been a bit further away I doubt we would have seen it at all. I would have preferred that, because the place

"Looks creepy. Looks like the start of a horror movie." I glanced at Michael, seeing the look on his face. "No sir. No way. We're not going to be the dumb bitches that go explore the abandoned house to get eaten by the hillbilly zombies that live there. We're going to be the smart bitches that keep moving and go eat smores."

His frown was genuine now. "But it looks badass." He pointed at it again as though to drive home his point. "Look at how badass that is."

I shook my head. "You know what's not badass? Snakebites. Falling through rotten floorboards. The aforementioned hillbilly zombies. Let's go."

"Fine. You suck. Robbed us of a really cool story and pictures too. I hope you're proud of yourself."

I nudged him forward. "I think you'll survive."

Another half hour and we were at Lake Winter. It was actually a bit bigger than I thought it'd be, and while calling it a lake was still somewhat grandiose, I had to admit that there was something striking about it. The shore was made up of small gray rocks that we had not seen anywhere else in our walk here, and the water itself was a placid, steely blue. Compared to the brownish green ponds I was used to seeing growing up just a hundred miles south, it seemed almost like the rocks and water had been plucked from another continent, maybe one with Vikings.

Turning to Michael, I gestured towards the lake. "See? This is cool."

He looked skeptical. "It's all right, yeah. It's kinda weird. Do you think it was man-made?"

I shrugged. "I guess it's possible, but it would cost a ton for something this size, and given that it's a state park, wouldn't there be some kind of sign up or some marker saying who donated money for it or something? Either way, let's get back up on the grass some to set up the tents. My ass does not need eight hours of sleeping on those hard little rocks."

We set up camp and got a fire going, and after taking a long walk around the oval perimeter of the lake, we settled in to cooking hot dogs as twilight began to darken into night. While I was tired, I wasn't ready to go to sleep yet, and I was having to fight the urge to pull out my phone and start playing a game or watching a video. I heard Michael grunt and looked up from my plate to see he was already poking at his phone discontentedly.

"I have like one bar. My browser has shit on itself and died twice."

I scowled at him. "Good. We're supposed to be out here camping and having family bonding time." He flipped me off and stuffed the phone back in his pocket.

"Okay. Well, I have to take a piss. So don't do any bonding without me while I'm gone." With that, he jumped up and headed back off toward the trees. When I saw him continuing to go the hundred yards or so to the edge of the forest, I thought about yelling that he didn't actually have to piss on a tree. Instead I just shook my head and went back to eating my hot dog.

About a minute later, I heard Michael yelling something to me. I looked up and I saw him at the edge of the trees, shifting from the ball of one foot to the other as though trying to get a better look at something with his flashlight. I yelled back and asked what he had said. Faintly I heard him respond.

"I think I see something. A light or something? It's closer now than it was."

For whatever reason, I felt my stomach go cold. Sitting down my plate, I stood up and walked a few steps away from the campfire, my eyes locked on Michael's barely illuminated form.

"Michael, come back from there. Come here, please."

I saw him turn towards me, and then something made him turn back to the woods. I heard him yell, "What the fuck…Oh God. No, fuck!", and started running to me. I was going to ask what was wrong, but then I saw the figure stepping out of the brush.

At that distance and in the dark, I couldn't make much out. The only light that touched it came from the partial moon glowing spectrally above the lake and some kind of flickering light on the shape itself. But from what I could tell it looked like a large man, and my desire to encounter some large stranger in the middle of the nighttime woods was less than zero.

As Michael made his way closer to the firelight, I could see by his face that he was terrified. I was going to ask who it was or what was wrong, but he was already yelling again.

"We've got to go! Run, leave everything, just run!" He grabbed my arm and started pulling on me, but I resisted for a moment, wanting to understand.

"What? What is it? What's wrong?" I glanced back at the approaching figure and I could only make out slightly more detail. His feet seemed abnormally large and strange, and it looked as though he was wearing a hood or cloak, as I could see something billowing behind him. But the oddest thing was the light he was holding. It was flickering like a flame, and I guessed it must be a lantern of some sort, but in the dark it almost looked like it was a part of him.

Michael yanked my arm again. "It's some kind of monster. I don't know. But it looks fucking real. Let's GO!" This time he pulled enough to propel me forward and I started running with him. I still had in the back of my mind it might be an elaborate joke, whether Michael was in on it or not, but he looked scared enough that I wasn't taking any chances.

We ran towards the woods, Michael moving his grip down to my hand as we hit the brush at the edge of the clearing and kept going. I glanced back and saw the figure had changed course and was heading towards us, but at a measured, almost leisurely pace. *Good*, I thought, *Please let him keep going slow*. We ran a few more yards before Michael looked back and came to a stop.

"He's gone."

I looked around panting and saw he was right. In the span of less than ten seconds, it had gone from walking towards us across the clearing to vanishing into thin air. That didn't do anything to make me less afraid.

"Keep moving, Michael. Let's get out of here."

We started back running, trying to strike the right balance between speed and not breaking something in the dark. We only had the one flashlight between us, with mine having been left back in my tent near the lake. The blackness of the woods felt like a palpable thing, a thick, cool liquid with a weight and viscosity we had to push against as we made our way forward. Michael would periodically stop and glance at his compass, and both of us were constantly scanning our surroundings for any sign of an approaching shadow or the strange glow of firelight.

We made the journey back to the car in a fraction of the time it had taken us to leave it, and when we stepped out onto the gravel, I stopped to catch a few lungs worth of gasping breath. Still bent over, I started fumbling in my pocket for the keys when I heard Michael screaming. My head snapped up and I saw him trying to backpedal from the thing that had somehow pursued us across ten miles without being seen.

At this distance, and with the parking lot illuminated by the pale moonlight, I could see the creature much better. It looked like a man, or at least the crude, monstrous approximation of one. It stood around seven feet tall, its head and torso partially covered by some kind of thin and rotting shroud. The skin underneath looked like dark stone or clay in the darkness, with arms and legs of the same material, but bearing the appearance of hard, twisted appendages like the branches of some sinister looking tree dwelling deep in the heart of a forgotten and decaying swamp. It reached one of those arms out and grasped Michael's arm in a clawed hand that turned his screams of terror into screeches of pain.

"He's biting me! He's biting me!"

I was already in motion to pull Michael free, but his words sunk in enough for me to find them strange. I could see little of the thing's face, but I didn't see its mouth anywhere near my brother. I grabbed Michael's other arm and pulled, afraid it would do little good. To my surprise, I saw the monster let go as I tugged, and in the dim light I saw something my mind didn't want to accept. The palm of the thing's hand was filled with a black void that dripped with my brother's blood. When I thought about it later, I realized there were silvery teeth retreating back into that oval hole in its hand. Small and sharp, I had seen the glittering of two rows in the moment before I turned away and pulled Michael with me toward the car.

I expected to be caught at any moment, that horrible biting grasp falling onto my shoulder or the back of my neck. But nothing came. When we were inside the car and I turned the headlights on, I could see that the creature was still standing where we had left it, silently staring at us. The lower half of its body was illuminated by the lights, showing thick legs that ended in something more akin to roots than any kind of feet. And above the line of the car's lights, the fire flickered on.

The monster wasn't holding a light. It was the light. In the left upper part of the thing's chest, where a heart would lay beating in a man, there was a hole over half a foot wide that went all the way through its body from front to back. In that hole, a large yellowish-brown candle burned brightly, illuminating whatever material made up the surrounding flesh and a portion of the tattered shroud that draped down the creature's back.

I found myself growing transfixed by that flame, and it was a shove from Michael that woke me out of it. Nodding, I threw the car into drive and spun out of the parking lot.

Michael was understandably hysterical, and I was too, though I tried to keep control for both our sakes. We debated going to a hospital, a hotel, or home. We both quickly ruled out home until we had some time to calm down and make sure we wouldn't be followed further. I pushed for the hospital, but Michael said he just wanted to get a room some ways away from the park and look at his arm before we made a decision on that. I thought about arguing further, but given his state, I relented.

I drove another thirty minutes and then pulled in at a decent-looking motel. When we got into the room, I took him to the bathroom and we looked at his arm. I knew immediately we had made a mistake and he needed to go to a hospital. It looked like a small chunk had been ripped out of his arm, the edges of it ragged with small holes as though the thing had been biting and raking its teeth into his flesh trying to find a good purchase to tear a part free. The perimeter of the hole was also looking darker than it should, with several sinister-looking lines starting to push out from the wound itself.

"We have to get you to a doctor, now." He was already starting to shake his head, and I stopped him. "No. Not a conversation. You could have an infection or be poisoned. And we'll be as safe or safer at a hospital than we are here."

As the last words left me, I heard the front door of the room swing open. Leaning and looking out of the bathroom door, I saw the thing standing in the doorway, the lights in the room showing me more of it than before. I let out a scream and shoved the bathroom door shut, keeping my weight against it, but I knew it wouldn't be any real barrier to that thing. I knew I had locked the room door and put the chain on, but it had somehow walked in like those locks didn't exist.

I searched for a bathroom window, but there was none. I had time to look into Michael's terrified eyes and see that he knew what was out there before the door was flung open and I was shoved out of the way and into the wall. Michael began to squeal like some kind of caught animal as the thing reached into the tiny room and grabbed him by the forearm, casually dragging him out despite my brother's desperate attempts to hold onto the sink and then the doorframe.

I got back up and launched myself past Michael and onto the creature's back. I tried to find purchase on it, digging my fingers into its flesh and finding it to be somewhat yielding even as I gagged. The smell as I broke the surface of its skin was like that of rotten meat, and the texture of the material itself seemed like hard wax.

Pausing for a moment, its free arm bent backwards and grabbed me by the neck, pulling me free from its back. It swung me around until I was facing it. I could distantly feel the hard rasp of teeth scraping the skin on the side of my neck eagerly without actually biting down, but my thoughts were preoccupied by its face.

Any crude shapings or strange, blunt lines of its body did not carry over into that face. There was a well-shaped, long curving nose over thick, batrachian lips that tipped upward at the ends as it looked at me. Its eyes were some sort of glowing stone, almost like large fire opals given some inner iridescence, flaring in time with the terrible sound it made deep in the black hollows of its throat.

It was chuckling at me.

I was barely able to breathe, but I was going to try and plead for my brother and myself, despite the cruelty and malignant pleasure I saw etched across its features. But then it flung me aside, sending me crashing through the front window of the room a moment before dragging Michael out the door.

For a few seconds my world was flashes and noise and pain. I knew I needed to pull myself together, to try again, but I couldn't make my body work right. Rolling over on my side, I saw the thing pulling Michael with him, the keening animal wail having dwindled to a defeated muffled groan. As I watched, I saw the thing and Michael sinking into the earth as they proceeded forward, almost as though they were walking into the tide of some earthen sea. I let out a scream, and I saw Michael reach out his hand to me feebly a moment before they both disappeared into the ground.

I lay on the concrete outside the room, broken and bleeding, for some time before anyone came out and called 911. I went to the hospital, and the next day I had to tell my hysterical mother that I had somehow lost her son. I tried to tell people the truth of what happened, but they looked at me sympathetically and talked about head trauma and shock. So then I told a more palatable version of a man attacking us at our campsite and then the motel, and that got some level of search parties and investigation, but of course nothing was ever found.

Two years have passed since that time, and despite my own efforts, I've never found my brother. I've been back to those woods a dozen times, but things are never as they were on that trip we took. I never see the ruins of that old house, and Winter Lake is a small, yellowed pond, not what we camped near on the night Michael was taken. And I've never seen Candleheart again.

I know he's called Candleheart by some because of the research I've done. There are very few references, even in the darker and more eccentric corners of the internet, but I found a forum post that described the legend of a monster with mouths on its hands that abducted and sacrificed people. The comments were rife with more random speculation and odd tales about rituals and what the motives of the monster really were, but no one had anything verifiable or frankly very credible sounding. But there was one brief reply that caught my attention.

Its name is Candleheart. It feeds the dark things of the earth for its own profit and waits for Winter's return.

I tried to contact the poster, but I never received any response, and while the name Candleheart makes sense, I've never found another reference to it in relation to the monster. After a year of trying,

I'm ashamed to say I gave up. It was too hard to keep living every day reliving what had happened to Michael, looking for some clue or sign that might help him, lying to myself more as time passed about the odds that he could still be okay or even alive.

Within the last couple of months life has started to feel less terrible. Not like it used to be, but somewhat better. Therapy for me and Mom has helped, but most of it has been time. I realized last week I had gone an entire day without thinking about Michael, and it made me both relieved and terribly sad.

Then this morning I opened my door to go to work and found the box. It was of thick, high quality cardboard, though it was ragged in spots and had several stains along the top. A little larger than a cake box, it was tied with a rough twine string that I had to saw at to cut off with a kitchen knife. There was no writing or label, so I was slightly leery of opening it at all, but my curiosity and growing dread told me I had to know what was inside.

When I took off the top and looked inside, I stopped breathing. The box contained Michael's face. Not his literal face, but a yellowish mask of it. A death mask.

My skin crawling, I reached out and touched its surface, already knowing what I'd feel. It was made of wax. And my God. It was screaming.

Everyone in my town has vanished except for me and the demon.

"Just let me in."

When I hear the rasp of the thing's words, I have to fight the urge to run back out of the church, to keep running until I find help. It looks somewhat like an old man, though something is off about him. His skin doesn't fit right, and he looks more like a younger man that has been somehow worn out or used up than a man who has just gotten old.

I hold my ground for the moment, and my brief courage seems to amuse it, a rattling laugh hitching out of his chest. He can't move much because of the silver chains that bind him to the altar, woven thrice-thick, blessed thrice-strong. There are seven chains and seven locks, each line of restraint terminating at two opposite points of the floor of the sanctuary. Those points are punctuated by iron circles bolted to the floor and serving as anchors for running the chain through on one side and locking the ends together on the other, so that all told, he has fourteen lines of holy encumbrance bearing down on him at all times.

I know all of this just like every child of Emberton knows this. We are taught the nature of the demon, of our duties to confine it, and the tools we have to maintain its imprisonment, from our earliest days. Before a young boy or girl learns to read, he or she can perfectly recite the sunrise and twilight prayers. Before I ever had a bike or went camping, I knew how to check the chains for weakness, how to replace and repair corrupted links, how to care for the locks and ensure their inner workings never fail.

Even at a distance, I can see the chains all appear to be intact. I need to go closer and inspect the locks, but I don't want to. I was taught to fear the demon, but not to let that fear control me. I was told to cling to the rules and the safeguards and I would remain safe in my holy duty.

But that was before today. Today I woke up, and my parents and little sister were gone. The neighbors were gone. Cars are running idle in the street, which is doubly odd, because I'd think they would have crashed if the drivers suddenly disappeared. I explored the town and the woods surrounding it for over four hours, and I haven't seen a single soul or any sign as to where they went.

From the start, my assumption was that the demon was somehow behind it. I kept hoping it was some kind of mistake or practical joke, but that made no sense, and the last few hours had proven the pointlessness of that hope.

No, the truth was that the rules and safeguards had somehow failed. Somehow the thing that was snickering at me, its lips stretched tight against its clenched yellow teeth as it ticked its head back and forth like one of those piano things…a metronome, I think…it had…

"Just let me in."

****

I want to be a filmmaker. I wanted to make great documentaries that would move people and change the world, but a year after graduating film school, the only thing I had accomplished was recording hours of boring footage and developing a profound sense of self-loathing. So I set that aside and tried to become an internet personality. I've been making videos and posting them online for the past two years, but nothing has really gained traction yet. I tried video game lets plays, movie reviews, and even a prank channel, but my subscriber base has never gone above 12. My parents keep gently suggesting I should try and find a way to put my film degree to some other, more lucrative use, or in the alternative, just get a steady job that pays more than minimum wage. I'm starting to agree.

I had come back to my hometown and moved back in with my parents when my small documentary grant had petered out, and it was excruciating. They were sweet people and tried to be supportive, but I could feel them judging me every day, and every day I could feel myself getting closer to giving up on any semblance of the life I wanted just so I didn't feel like an embarrassing burden any more.

So this is my last attempt at this. I'm going to try and make a semi-professional video about something potentially creepy and hope people give a fuck. Doubtful.

After trying to find some angle for several days, I went to the local library in Ash's Hollow. The library was small and depressing, and after a couple of hours of looking for any books on local myths or legends, I had started staring morosely at an old map of the area, more out of boredom than any hope of finding any inspiration in hundred year-old roads and land borders. But then I saw it. A small town forty miles away I had never heard of. Emberton.

I felt a small thrill of excitement, but I figured it was just a gap in my knowledge rather than an actual forgotten town. Pulling out my phone, I googled the town, but found nothing aside from an Emberton in Colorado and Maine. When I pulled up a current map, no matter how I zoomed, I found no sign of it either.

Now I was really excited. It wasn't unheard of for towns to die off, and after a few decades, most people wouldn't even remember it. But to find one this close…it was clearly destiny, or at least really good luck. And if I was super lucky, there would be enough of the old town left behind to make for some really good footage. Urban decay and abandoned streets…people eat that shit up. And I was from a town with Ash in the name, searching for a town called Emberton…there had to be some kind of fancy artistic throughline there I could use. Something about the town burning out early or something. Fuck, I really suck at this. But got to try and stay optimistic.

The next day I was heading out. I took off from the yogurt shop I had been working at lately, not telling them or anyone else where I was going. If it wound up being a wild goose-chase, I would save some embarrassment. And if it was badass…well, that would make for a great story when I returned.

I traveled by interstate for ten miles, then a state highway briefly before turning onto a barely maintained county road. This stretched on for nearly fifteen miles before just ending. I sat staring glumly at the stand of pine trees pressing in all around me, wondering if I had somehow missed a turn-off along the way. I turned around and started back down the road, going much slower this time.

I slammed on the brakes as I saw the remnants of a dirt road on the left less than a mile from the dead end. Trees and bushes had overtaken it almost entirely, so there was no chance of getting the car through there, but I hadn't come this far to just give up. I got out my camera, locked the car, and headed out.

I had only walked for a few minutes when I saw something bright white through the trees. I started the camera rolling, and as I moved closer my heart sped up as I saw it was the Emberton town limits sign. Just sitting in the middle of these woods, bright and perfectly preserved like it had been painted the week before. And behind it, a well-paved road stretched up and over a hill.

"Holy fucking shit."

****

I woke up to see that my hands were raw and bleeding a little. I was sitting on one of the few pews we kept in this church. There were never any services here unless you wanted to count the morning and evening prayers, and it was rare that anyone wanted to sit near that thing for longer than necessary. At the thought, I raised my eyes and saw with horror that the chains were laying discarded on the floor. Still sitting on the altar, the demon sat staring at me with a small smile on his face.

"Just let me in."

It said it almost casually, its gaze shifting from me as it looked down at its clothes. They looked old and faded, but still in good condition considering how long he must have been wearing them. The demon's hair was long and fell into his face as he looked himself over with an expression that looked like mild irritation, and as the fan of black hair swept down, I caught a glimpse of the large scar on the thing's neck. I had seen it before, but never well, and I still didn't know what it was from. When I asked my mother once, she had just given a nervous look to my father and told me to keep my thoughts from the wicked thing unless I was doing one of my duties.

Its eyes cut back to me and narrowed. "Just let me in."

****

This place was a fucking gold mine.

I didn't know how this place was even possible, wasn't even sure it *was* possible, but I was walking through it and recording just the same.

It was a fully preserved, fully functional small town. Not some ancient, grown up ruin. Not even a slowly eroding spot in the road that had a handful of houses that no longer qualified it for town status or a dot on the map. No, it was a decent-sized small town with working street lights. Cars on the streets. Dogs in the yard. And that, I shit you fucking not, was not the best part.

There were no people. None.

I don't mean that I was catching the sleepy town at its sleepiest. It was eleven in the morning, and there was not a soul in sight. Even better, everywhere there were signs that people had been around until very recently. Cars were left running in the street. Televisions were on in a nearby store window. I saw food on tables in a diner, and when I went in, while the food wasn't warm, it wasn't dried up and gross either.

I already had over two hours of footage, and I just kept finding more weird shit. Yet the weirdest part was what I didn't find. No signs of violence or disturbance. No indication of people being sick or part of some weird townwide cult. Still, the longer I stayed, the more uneasy I was becoming. It was great that I was getting legitimately creepy footage, but I was just about ready to call it and start heading back before I wound up getting abducted and fed to a corn god or something.

Then I saw the church.

****

I sat paralyzed on the bench. I was eleven, almost twelve, and I was strong and fast. But I knew I was no match for that thing. I didn't understand why it hadn't killed me or taken me over already, but I guessed it was just playing with me. It could have left at any time, and it clearly had the ability to mesmerize me or something, as I had every idea I had hurt my hand taking those chains off of it.

But it just sat there, smiling its smile and staring at me.

Deciding I had to try something, I started saying the evening prayer. Immediately, the demon started clutching its head, a sour hiss escaping its lips. Then it turned back to me, openly laughing now as though it had been told a good joke. Wiping tears from its eyes, it eased off the altar and came to stand in front of me in one fluid motion that was impossibly fast.

Crouching down, it held its face just inches from my own, and I gagged at the hot, rotten smell that emanated from it. Its eyes were almost human--a deep blue and still shining from its tears of laughter. It raised a yellowed nail in between us and tapped my nose with each word as it spoke, its voice jolly and low.

"Just. Let. Me. In."

I was ashamed, but I started crying then. I was shaking my head, my lips trembling and my hands growing cold. I knew I was about to die or something worse. As if reading my mind, the demon suddenly shot out its hands and gripped me, and in the span of two terrified heartbeats it had lifted up my shirt and bit down into the meat just below my armpit.

Just then, I heard the doors to the church opening.

****

I felt my heart thudding as I approached the church, my eyes constantly scanning in every direction for some sign of danger. My fear was approaching real dread, and that only increased when I thought I heard something move inside the building. I almost broke and ran right then, but it was my parents' faces that stopped me.

This was my chance. I had so much great footage, but the church would be a great ending even if it was empty. I just had to not be a coward. For fucking once in my life, I had to see things through.

So I threw open the doors, and at first I didn't know what I was looking at. There was a boy, maybe twelve, chained down to the altar at the other end of the sanctuary. He watched me silently as I entered, a strange smile on his face. I looked around for anyone else, but there was no one.

"Kid? Are you okay? What happened?"

He said nothing, and considering his condition, it wasn't surprising. As I got closer, I saw that he was far from well. His skin looked thin like yellowed crepe paper, simultaneously too tight and too loose in the wrong places. He almost looked like a little old man. And his clothes seemed worn out and dirty, an old dried reddish stain blossoming out from under one arm of his t-shirt. Deciding my best bet was to try talking to him again after he was free and he knew he was safe, I started inspecting the chains.

They looked like they were made out of silver, and at first I thought they were all locked to eyebolts embedded in the floor, but then to my relief I saw the locks were all sprung. After a few moments I had the boy free and I pulled him off the altar gently.

"Is that better?" The boy had continued looking at me silently as I had freed him, but now he finally spoke, his voice deeper and rougher than I expected.

"Just let me in."

He opened his mouth wide, and what I saw inside started me screaming. His mouth was full of black worms, each of them writhing and fighting for the opening, their own mouths open with hunger and yearning, the black needles within each clicking together with a musical tinkling sound as they reached the edge of his lips. Then he was burying all those terrible mouths into the side of my neck.

****

The demon was falling away as the people approached, its body limp as it tumbled to the floor. I looked up and saw with confusion that I knew these men and women, that my parents were among them. My head was swimming, and I was trying to form some kind of question, but my tongue was somehow too thick. Then my father was thrusting a pen and pad of paper into my hands, telling me to write what happened and do it quickly.

I wanted to complain, but I felt a strange urge to do as he asked. I started writing this slumped down on that same pew, my mother propping me up and crying, her tears and my father's worried looks seeming farther and farther away as I tried to remember everything. I think I'm done now. I'm feeling different now. Better, but different. I can see my sister helping the adults to ready the chains around the altar again.

****

Report Cycle: 47B

From: Town Council of Emberton

To: Town Council of Ash's Hollow

Summary: The cycle was completed within normal parameters. Elder Steven took the seat while Younger Steven was returned to his home with his "parents" and was exhibiting no physical or mental signs of past occurrences by the following morning. Alternate memories of his past appear to have fully reasserted themselves, although he now says he had a dog. A dog matching his rough description of the pet will be arriving this afternoon.

Elder Steven is tolerating captivity per usual, having reverted back to the expected docile primary behavior of the Entity within minutes of Elder Steven completing his written account.

Written accounts are attached per protocol. Based on my review of past accounts, they are growing more detailed and fanciful over recent cycles, but nothing else of note.

"All is well in the two towns, and as go the towns, so goes the world."

****

Addendum to the report re: Cycle 47B

I understand this goes against protocol, and I have been warned by my own Town Council to not step outside the normal chain of command or communication, but I feel like I have no choice.

I understand all of the history and tradition that have led us to this point. When the Entity first appeared in 1923 in Emberton, it possessed and consumed nearly two dozen people before the Divide occurred. Even now, I know that when they are being honest, our own historians aren't in agreement on whether the Divide was caused by some holy ritual of ours finally taking effect, some kind of Divine intervention, or if it was the intention and design of the Entity itself. I suspect you have these same concerns.

But what is known for certain is that on August 27, 1923, eleven year-old Steven Pemberton was the current host for the Entity. During a feverish battle outside of Sacred River Baptist Church on Burch Street, that little boy was in the process of killing two grown men when he suddenly stopped. He began to levitate, rising as high as five feet by some accounts, and then there was a terrible flash of light and sound. The poor souls that were observing from nearby were instantly and permanently blinded and deafened.

Those that approached from a distance found the little boy laying on the ground, apparently unconscious. Laying nearby, was a naked man in his mid-twenties. A stranger at first glance. As we all know, subsequent investigations showed that this was somehow an adult version of Steven. While it was now strangely docile, it became evident that the Entity was still in Younger Steven. It also became clear that while Elder Steven should not exist, he seemed largely normal and was confused by how he got to Emberton at all, as he remembered growing up and living his life as a type-setter in a nearby town called Ash's Hollow.

This was found to be especially odd because Ash's Hollow did not exist at that time. Given the circumstances, the Town Counsel decided that both must be confined in the sanctuary of the church until some more permanent solution could be found. But Elder Steven escaped, and for two long years the town of Emberton kept watch over the monster residing in the little boy they all loved, hoping for a miracle and praying that their lapse in letting the older anomaly escape would not bring ruin to them or others.

And then one day, Elder Steven returned. He went to his younger self, but was stopped by guards at the church. They began dragging him in, intending on finally binding him as well, but then the child was free of his bonds and on them, ripping them in half before they could even cry for help. Instead of going on a further killing spree, the child bit his older self and then bound Elder Steven to the altar himself. He then went home, knocking on his parents' door with tears in his eyes, wounds healed, and no apparent memory of what had occurred.

This cycle continued every two years for the next decade until Joseph Mire, head of the Emberton Town Council at the time, declared that something must be done. While efforts had been made to keep Elder Steven in town when he would somehow free himself, it only led to needless death and he would still disappear, only to come back after two years had passed. Mire determined that if they gave him a place to go, a place that was controlled and provided a fabricated life that matched his recollection, it would give at least some degree of knowledge of his whereabouts during both phases of the cycle.

Others argued against it, saying that the Entity would not be controlled or fooled by setting up some fake town Elder Steven claimed to be from. Mire pointed out that Elder Steven's memories were largely consistent, but they also always remained current. He would always seem confused when he was done biting his younger self in the side, but he would always be from Ash's Hollow and have the same parents and live at the same address. Yet smaller details would change. He always knew the current year, was roughly aware of recent events, and even his supposed life would include new elements like different jobs and new hobbies. What purpose would any of that serve if the Entity was just making it all up? What logic was there in trying to fool people that it clearly could eradicate at any moment?

"Of course, the rest of the Council didn't care for discussion of that point. It was an unspoken reality among the council itself and some of the townspeople that very little, if anything, that they had tried actually had any effect on the Entity. Even its supposed incarceration was largely a farce based on past events.

So in the end, they relented and agreed with Mire that they needed to found Ash's Hollow and attempt to make it a place that

Elder Steven could stay during his times away. And as we all know, it actually worked. It has seemed to work for over 80 years.

And that's the problem. It's seemed to work, and people are satisfied with appearances. On the day of the Divide, Emberton was somehow wiped from the collective memory of the rest of the world. People could leave town of course, but if they went to Memphis or wherever else and said where they were from, they would typically just get a confused smile, and the people they met wouldn't remember the name of the town even ten minutes later. It was disturbing at the time, but it was the least of the town's worries during the aftermath of all that slaughter, and in the years since it's been decided it's actually a blessing designed to keep Emberton safe from the world and vice versa. We get everything through Ash's Hollow, which isn't afflicted by the same strangeness, and everything is just fine.

Except it's not. We are not in control of any of this. We now have generations of people in this town that honestly believe that the thing we have here can be contained by silver chains and prayers made up by Mire in the late 30s. They devote their lives with a religious fervor that borders on fanaticism to the rituals and rules that have been set up for them. I know, because I was much the same before I was appointed to the Council last year.

But the truth is, they are in a zoo with a tiger. They think there are bars between them and the tiger, but they are mistaken. They think they are keeping the tiger, but it's the tiger that is keeping them.

We don't know what the Entity is. It may be that it is a demon, or an alien, or something else entirely. But what is clear is that it has all the power. It has all the control. It is allowing us to live, letting us put on this little stage play day after day, year after year, because it finds it funny.

No, that's wrong. How do I know what a tiger finds funny? That's the mistake we've all been making. We think we can know that thing's mind. What's to say that it thinks and feels as we do, that it uses human logic to guide its course?

I have read the accounts of what that thing did before the Divide, and it was truly terrible. I understand why you are all afraid. But the people here are prisoners and don't know it. They are in far more danger than they can appreciate, and the world at large is and has been in grave danger ever since we first decided to keep this all a secret.

I hope and pray you see the sense in what I'm saying. We have to find another way or warn the world. Just because the Entity has gone along with all of this for so long is meaningless. Maybe it finds it entertaining.

What happens when it gets bored?

****

Internal Action Report: 19-012 (Cycle 47B)

Action Summary: Councilman Jefferson has been removed and silenced. Investigation shows no cohorts or information leaks prior to apprehension. Action is complete and case is closed.

"All is well in the two towns, and as go the towns, so goes the world."

I helped pull a dead girl's body out of thin air.

Since I was a kid, my dream was always to be a magician. I grew up watching David Copperfield specials and reading books about Houdini, but I also devoured fantasy and horror books dealing with their versions of real magic. Like lots of children, I got a little magic kit for Christmas one year, full of sponge balls, a wand that would push out silk flowers, and a small stuffed rabbit that would hide in the inner pocket of a small, collapsible polyester top hat. Unlike most children, I stuck with it, and any family vacation led me to begin meticulous research of any magic shops on the route, followed by a campaign of whining and extra diligence in my chores to ensure I got the necessary detours to pick up some new book or item.

Even at 35, I still truly love magic. Believe in magic. Want to hone my craft as a stage magician, which has been my trade for the past few years, and still hold out some dim hope in the deepest recesses of my heart that one day, just maybe, I'll see real magic instead of the illusions I perform. But I know that's not realistic or likely, so I practice stage magic in its place. Pick up new tricks where I can by working as back-ups and assistants to more well-known and experienced illusionists. And that's how I got here. Holding a noose out for this fat, drunk fuck known on stage as the Great Sadir.

It's very much up to debate if the Great Sadir was ever actually great. From what I hear, he was never very original or talented, but early in his career he had a whole Indian mystic theme going that was unique enough to draw in decent crowds. Then he got bit by a snake, spent a week in the hospital due to infection, and after that he apparently pretty much said "fuck it." Good-bye cool turban with mysterious sitars playing in the background, hello cliché top hat and weird 80s synth music blaring like A-Ha and Depeche Mode on a slow train to hell.

When I got to him, he was a bad alcoholic and a worse stage performer, but the tragic thing was that he did have a lot of knowledge and some talent. I saw an opportunity to learn, so I joined up with him. And he has taught me a few things, though he doled them out with agonizing slowness to ensure my continued indentured servitude.

But fuck me. I think I've learned all I can and I'm at my limit. He is half in the bag already, and it's the early show. When I finally cinch the fake noose around his fat neck, I find myself wishing he didn't have the harness.

Afterward, I hit the alley behind the lounge we're playing at full speed, still trying to decide if I'm going to get dinner or to pack my shit and head out. That's when Johnny Quick comes up to me. If you don't follow magicians closely, or didn't a few years back, you probably don't know who Johnny Quick even is. But there was a time where he was a BFD in certain magician's circles. He was never flashy and he never played big venues, but he always had money and he could do tricks that other magicians couldn't spot. People just chalked it up to how fast and nimble his hands were, which was where his name came from. It stuck, and he started using it as his stage name until he suddenly fell off the map a couple of years ago.

I knew all this because I'm obsessed with magicians, not because I've ever met him. And meeting him, dirty alley or no, was a huge deal for me. After a moment of stunned, idiotic silence, I stepped forward and shook his hand. I was about to launch into some embarrassing gushing about how awesome he was, when he beat me to it.

"Hey, I'm Johnny. Your name is Keith, right?"

I nodded, beaming like the girl with the bedazzled head gear who just got asked to prom.

"I saw your show. Christ, Sadir really is shit, huh?"

I laughed. "You have no idea."

He grinned. "Well, your stuff was good. Especially your close-up work with that woman from the audience." I felt myself flushing at the compliment, but he was already moving on. "Good, but not as good as it could be. I can help you get better. Way better."

I felt light-headed. Was this some kind of prank? "Um, really? You'd do that?" He nodded, and I went on. "Well, sure. That'd be awesome. What did you have in mind?"

He glanced up and down the alley with a theatricality only a magician can muster before leaning in towards me. "How would you like to learn real magic?"

****

Over the next week, Johnny taught me what he knew. And what he knew, surprisingly enough, was actual real magic. Specifically, two tricks. He could make things appear and make things disappear. At first, I thought it had to be an illusion, of course. But over time, as he showed me how to increase my speed, the proper angles to hold my hands, the images and words I had to hold in my head depending on the object I was working with, I realized it was real. It was actual fucking magic.

The funny thing is once you know how to do it, it's easy. It really just feels like a natural extension of normal legerdemain aka slight of hand. But instead of palming an object or pulling it from a hidden pocket, you were literally pulling it out of thin air. Within some limits, you could pull any object you could clearly imagine into the world and you could make most objects you could lay your hand on disappear.

I asked Johnny how he had learned how to do it, and he was always vague, but after I had it down, he told me a bit more. He said he had used to run with a "pretty eclectic crowd". Magicians tend to draw some odd birds from time to time. He had a buddy that was in some kind of secret society or cult supposedly, and whatever bullshit that might have been, he had apparently picked up some real power along the way. He wouldn't tell Johnny much, but he did teach him how to make things appear and disappear.

Johnny said the guy had told him that you weren't really conjuring new objects or destroying old ones. You were just pulling them from or sending them to a different plane of existence he called the Nightlands. He never told Johnny more about the place, but he did say there were rules to using that kind of magic.

First, if you make something disappear, you need to make it or something of "similar value" reappear within an hour. Second, if you make something new appear, you needed to make it or something else of "similar value" disappear within an hour. When I asked what he meant by "similar value", Johnny shrugged. Best he could tell, it didn't have anything to do with the size of the thing or how much money it was worth. He said you got a feel for what was needed over time, but when in doubt, just keep your mind blank when you were doing the balance and the trick would bring or send something that was appropriate on its own.

That's what he called it. Doing the balance. He said that you always had to do the balance or it created problems. When I asked what kind of problems, he looked at me for a long time.

"Let's say you pull a coin and you just say fuck it, I'm not doing the balance. Well, a few hours later, your car keys might disappear. Or your cat. Now let's say you make something disappear once or twice without doing the balance. Maybe you find a random shoe that doesn't belong in your house sitting in the middle of your living room. Or a tree. Or something that looks like a spider mated with a mole rat. These are all real examples I'm giving you from times I decided to test the limits of not doing the balance. It's a bad fucking idea."

"Okay, got it. Always do the balance."

He nodded. "Exactly. Which brings me to my next point. I need your help."

****

Two hours later we were standing on the stage of the Burnt Rabbit, an industrial music club that had become some kind of neo-goth grotesquerie before finally going bankrupt a few months earlier. Unbeknownst to me, when it was still open, the Burnt Rabbit used to host underground magic competitions. Most of it was more shock magic and body horror spectacles, but occasionally you would get a real artist like Johnny to show up as well.

Unfortunately, Johnny, who through the smart use of his magic and diligent doing of the balance had amassed a small fortune, had also amassed a large heroin addiction. When he showed up the night of the magic competition with Juliette, his girlfriend/assistant of the month in tow, he was high as a fucking kite.

But that didn't stop him. He leapt up on stage to thunderous applause and screams, going through a series of small tricks with such ferocity and speed that the crowd continued cheering like it was a rock show. This only encouraged him, of course, so he decided to up the ante.

Swaying on his feet, he swirled his hands around and then tapped Juliette on the head. She popped out of existence like an overripe soap bubble. The crowd fell deathly silent, and then they began to roar. He turned to face them, his arms raised in triumph. The plan was he would pump the audience up for a few seconds and then bring her back. Instead, as he started to yell out to the people packed into the small club, he distantly felt himself stumble and then fall.

When he woke up, it was two days later and he was in a hospital room. He learned he had almost died of a heroin overdose. Police had asked him a few questions about Juliette, but given that nearly a hundred people had seen him collapse and be put in an ambulance, there was no real suspicion he had anything to do with her disappearance.

I asked him if he tried to bring her back and he lowered his eyes. "I...no. I didn't. I'm a piece of shit, and I know it, but I felt sure there was no point. We had done it before, see. Twice before I had disappeared her and brought her back a few seconds later. The place she went...she said she could breathe there, but the air was bitterly cold and stale, and everything was dark except for lights far away in the distance. The first time she handled it okay, but the second time she had come back terrified, saying she'd never do it again."

I shifted uncomfortably. "Did she say why she was so scared?"

He glanced up at me, his face drawn. "She said she heard things in the dark. She wouldn't say what, she just kept saying "I could hear them in the dark, Johnny. Bad things. And I think they were reaching for me." His face crumpled. "Shit, how the fuck could I have left her there? I figured she would be dead after two days, that's what I told myself at least, but who knows? I left her there to die because I'm a coward and I didn't want to deal with the consequences."

His eyes were red-rimmed and fiery as he went on. "Well I'm dealing with them now. I didn't do the balance on this. I can't. I've tried sending different things over, but nothing works. And I think the magic has sent something over to balance it for me."

"What do you mean, 'sent something over'?"

He scrubbed his hand through his hair. "Just what it sounds like. Something has been stalking me the last few weeks. I get glimpses of it sometimes, and I don't know what it's waiting for, but I think maybe it's just playing with me. From what little I've seen, it's not something I want to play with." He gestured around at the stage. "I came back here the night before I met you and tried to bring her back, tried to do the balance. It sometimes works better in the same spot if you're trying to bring back or send the same thing, so I thought it was my best shot. But I couldn't get it to work. I don't know if it's because of how much time has passed, or what the problem is, but I couldn't pull her back."

I was going to ask why not when I heard thunder coming from outside.

"Oh, shit fuck. That's it. It's here." His eyes were stretched wide with fear. "You have to help me. We have to try again. I think if we both do it together, we can pull her back through."

BOOM

He looked across the darkness of the club to the far end, where I could barely make out large double doors jumping inward from some massive impact outside. If not for the chains run through the handles, they would have burst open already.

"Okay, okay. Fuck. Let's try."

BOOM

He nodded and hurriedly we got into position. Johnny had never showed me how to pull something with another person, and I wasn't sure he knew how either, but after a couple of false starts I felt it starting to work.

BOOM and then a metallic wrenching sound as the doors finally gave way. I glanced up to see a large silhouette framed in the dim light filtering in from the lobby windows. I couldn't see much, but it was enough to know I was giving this five more seconds and then I was gone.

I turned back to the task at hand and felt something give, our combined efforts finally synchronizing to pull the poor girl back.

Her body thudded to the floor like a carcass on a butcher's floor, and I felt my gorge rising at my first glimpse of her. I remembered the thing approaching us and looked back up, but it was nowhere to be seen. It seemed like bringing her back had done the trick, and I felt a surge of relief mingling with my fear and disgust.

Johnny was on his knees beside her, weeping. He reached out as though to cradle her head, but half of it was gone, along with a good portion of her left side. It looked like it had been torn away by something large. As for what was left, her flesh was torn and cracked in various spots, patches of her skin various shades of light blue veined with bruises and lines of black. I saw something gleaming on the patch of shirt that was left to partially cover her remaining breast and I felt my anger building when I saw what it was. It was a cheap little brass pin that showed a lightning bolt with three stars around it, and in the center it said "Johnny Quick, Master Magician".

I took a couple of steps back. "You're a fucking asshole."

Johnny said nothing. He just kept crying, his thin hands, usually so supernaturally sure and fast, fluttering back and forth over her ruined body like troubled birds looking for a place to light. I wanted to feel sorry for him, but I didn't. I wanted to thank him for what he taught me, but I wasn't sure it was much of a gift.

****

That was all six months ago. I have my own stage show now, and I'm doing really well. At first, I swore I would never use what Johnny taught me. I told myself it was tainted, and far too dangerous. But then I had a really bad set. The crowd hated me, and a group of drunk college kids were down front heckling. I just needed to shut them up.

So I pulled a sword out of thin air. Then I pulled a suit of armor to go with it. I sent it back--got to do the balance--but the roar of that audience had told me what I already suspected. The next night, the audience was twice as large, and by the end of the week my shows were sold out.

Everyone has their addictions. And I've found mine. I can't stop using it, and I'm trying to do the balance, but sometimes I'm not sure what that even means. Just because I can use magic doesn't mean I understand it, and just because I try to balance things doesn't mean I really know the price to be paid.

I heard last week that Johnny was found outside his condo, his head caved in and his chest ripped apart. They have no suspects of course.

I keep telling myself that he was self-destructive. That he probably couldn't live with what he had done to that girl, so he brought something over or didn't balance again just so he could die. And maybe that is what happened.

Or maybe I'm standing at the edge of a black pit, pretending I know something that is unknowable. And as I look down into that darkness, reaching out my hand to touch that wonderful magic, something is crawling up to meet me and take my hand in kind.

I have to go. There's a knock at the door.

I convinced my friend that I'm a vampire. Now he's hunting me.

To: Det. R. Kraftman detkraftman#scpd.com

Date: June 21, 2018

Re: My recent phone calls

I am writing this out to send to you as I have been unable to reach you by phone or visiting the station, and the amount of info I need to give you is more than I can fit into a 30 second voicemail. My understanding is that you are the detective assigned to the murder investigations of Clint Perkins and Milo Foster. I read today that you have arrested a suspect in connection with both of these murders. I do not know anything about Milo Foster or his murder, but I can tell you I have clear evidence that Clint Perkins was killed by a man named Peter Barker. I am attaching a video to this email that might be self-explanatory, but I will provide a detailed account below of what I know and what I'm afraid is going to happen next.

Peter, or as we always called him, Petey, was a friend of mine and Clint's since we were all 8 and in third grade together. Me and Clint were best friends pretty much since birth, and from the outside it probably looked like we weren't friends with Petey at all, but that was just because we were always picking at him. The thing was, he was always so gullible. He wasn't stupid, not exactly, but he just seemed to fall for everything we told him, and we could get him to do most anything.

For example, Clint once convinced him that Clint's father, who was a drunk who had left town when we were infants, was actually a deep cover CIA operative in Moscow. Another time, we convinced him that my cousin had sent a new kind of chocolate pop rocks that were being sold in England. It was rabbit shit. After just a couple of minutes of convincing, Petey ate it down with a grimace.

I know that sounds bad. And looking back, especially now, I wish we had never treated him like that. But he made it so easy, and we were kids. And I will say, when he left town at twelve, we really did miss him. That's what made it so hard when he came back our senior year of high school.

Petey had been a jolly, nervous kid with a high-pitched laugh and too much baby fat when he left. When we saw him sitting in homeroom the first day of 12th grade, we didn't even recognize him at first. He had shot up to well over six feet, with thin, pale features and a perpetually somber expression. When we approached him between classes though, he brightened up and gave us quick hugs. He told us that he thought we'd forgotten about him, his voice deep and rumbly in a way that made it even harder to associate him with that little boy we had last hung out with.

But, he was still Petey, and between missing him and feeling some guilt over how we had treated him before, we tried to restart our friendship. I want to stress that we really did try. But it seemed like everything about him that had been weird or off-putting before had just been magnified in the intervening years.

He was very socially awkward. That was nothing new, but now it took the form of him alternating between being sadly creepy and aggressively rude. We took him to a couple of parties, and aside from scaring off every girl in a 100 yard radius, he almost got his ass kicked for talking shit three different times.

And it wasn't like we could just drift off and leave him to self-destruct his social life either. He would glom onto me or Clint any time he was around, following us relentlessly and bringing down our own stock by association. We started trying to just ditch him and avoid him, but he always managed to hunt us down. That phrase…"hunt us down"…has a different meaning for me now. That crazy motherfucker.

Sorry, I'll try to edit this before I send it if I have time. Just very upset right now. Anyway, when we realized that ditching him wasn't the answer, we started trying to come up with some way to make him want to not be around us. No idea seemed good enough, and we knew we would likely have only one shot before he caught on. For a normal person, figuring out your "friends" are trying to drive you away would do the trick on its own, but as we were figuring out more and more, Petey wasn't normal.

Then the murder happened. When Milo Foster got killed, it was big news in our town. Not that we don't have murders, as you well know, but it was just the weirdness of it. The neck wounds, the blood being drained…hell, even the newspaper was calling the unknown murderer "the Vampire Killer", although I guess that sounds more like someone who kills vampires really.

In any case, it gave me an idea.

We had avoided being mean to Petey or trying to trick him since he had come back to town, and it was hard to say if he was as gullible as he had been when he was younger. But one night when we were drinking and avoiding Petey's texts, Clint and I were talking about the murder and it suddenly hit me. We should convince Petey that we killed the guy.

Even drunk, we knew that was potentially dangerous. We didn't want to get in any actual trouble with the law, so we needed to either have proof we couldn't have done it or make up such an outlandish story for Petey that no one else would believe it and we could play it off as either a joke or a lie if Petey tried to go to the cops.

I remember Clint busting out laughing when I suggested we convince him that we were vampires and that Milo Foster was our latest victim, and it started me cracking up too. But as we continued to talk and drink, the idea hung around, and over the next few days we kept talking about it, less and less as a joke and more as the beginning stages of a plan.

This is what we did. Stage One was smaller stuff in front of Petey. Clint made a point of having a bad reaction to pizza with garlic on it, saying he had developed a bad allergy. I made veiled statements to Clint in front of Petey about how my mother was still pissed that I wouldn't try going to church any more since I had gotten so sick walking in last year. And both of us made a point of letting him see these silver pendants we started wearing, making a big show of trying to hide them after he had a chance to spot them. This was all stupid, obvious shit that wouldn't work on most people, but if the obvious stuff wasn't going to work on him, the whole plan was fucked anyway.

But it did. It took a couple of weeks, but Petey started acting different. He was still glomming hard, but now he was more quiet and he seemed to be watching us a lot more closely. We had a big homecoming party coming up in just over a week, so we decided it was time to escalate things into Stage Two and see if we couldn't get rid of him for good.

After a lot of debate, we decided that Stage Two would be all me. We arranged for Petey to come over to hang out at my house, that I needed to talk to him. I then told my mother to just send Petey up to my room when he got there, but to please not disturb us after that. Petey was going through some stuff, I told her, and we were going to talk it out.

When Petey walked into my bedroom, the shades were drawn and the only light in the room came from my bathroom. I sat up in bed, trying to act surprised and sleepy, yelling for Petey to come in and shut the door in a hushed, nearly frantic tone. I leapt out of bed and slid home the deadbolt I had just installed on the door that morning and which would have to go as soon as he left, as my parents were really serious about their "no locked doors" policy.

I made a big show of looking upset and telling him that I had overslept and I didn't want him to find out about it this way. I said I'd had a plan as to how I was going to tell him today and not make him scared, and fuck, now it was ruined. I said this as I was trying to gather up a bottle on my computer desk that was half-filled with pig's blood. I was doing a terrible job acting—way over the top. But while I was busy internally cringing, he was eating that shit up.

He put his hand on my shoulder and told me to calm down. Told me he was my friend and that we could talk about whatever had me so upset. The poor, creepy fucker. I actually felt bad for him. But it had to be done, so I sat down and started.

I told him that close to a year earlier, Clint and I had gone up to his Uncle Mark's cabin for the day. We were just planning on fishing and hanging out, but then a little after dark, Mark had shown up. He was acting weird, but it was his cabin, so we tried to play it cool. Cooked some fish, played some video games, and we were getting ready to leave when he locked the door. I didn't go into the gory details (which I didn't have because it was all made up), but Mark wound up attacking us and we woke up with bite marks on our neck. We had thought about going to the police, half convinced he had drugged and sexually assaulted us, but embarrassment and the family relation led us to keeping it quiet.

Over the next few days, we started noticing changes in ourselves, and then on the third day, the sunlight began hurting us. That night, an envelope was slid under our doors with our names on it. Inside each was a silver pendant that contained what appeared to be a patch of dried blood—we assumed Mark's, but we didn't know. There was also a slip of paper that just said "Wear it and it will protect you against the light and the hunger."

And the necklace had worked. By the end of the week, we had developed a hunger that food couldn't satisfy, and while the urge to attack people was strong, wearing the necklace usually controlled it enough that we could get by on pig's blood. At this point I had gestured to the bottle, feeling compelled to use the prop after the hassle involved in getting it in the first place. And while direct sunlight made us uncomfortable, as long as we had the necklace we wouldn't burn.

Now during all of this, Petey is just staring, taking it all in like it's the most important thing he's ever heard. Hell, to him maybe it was. But at this point he did ask why he hadn't seen us wearing the necklaces in the gym locker room. The truth was because this was all pulled from our asses within the last couple of weeks and he had been in gym class with us for months, but thankfully we had thought up a response to that already.

I told him that we didn't want to get made fun of or draw attention to ourselves, so we would hide it in our underwear or a pocket during gym. As long as we were touching it or it was in our physical proximity, it would work. That lead into my next thing, which was the part we had worked the hardest on to get ready.

I told him that mirrors worked fine for us, but video cameras would only see us if we were wearing the necklace. I knew this was a lot for him to take in and try to believe, and so I had set up a safe way for him to see proof. I led him into my bathroom, where I had a computer monitor sitting on the counter. I showed him that it was connected by a long hdmi cable to the laptop on my bed, and the laptop had a camera.

Because I wanted him to be safe, I explained, he would lock himself in the bathroom and watch the monitor. Once I knew he was secure, I would take off the necklace while he watched, and he would see what happened. Trying to sound worried, I told him that I thought I would have enough self-control to get the pendant back on without any problem, but he was not to come out until I said it was okay and he could see me again on the monitor.

I expected to get some kind of argument or complaint. For him to start laughing or get mad at me for trying to trick him like the old days. Instead, he just looked at me silently for several seconds. When he spoke, his deep voice was grave.

"You sure you want to keep doing this?"

I was momentarily confused. "Well, yeah, man. I want you to see proof so you know I'm not joking around. And I have more I need to tell you."

Again he was silent for a few moments, and his expression looked a little sad as he nodded. "Okay. Show me then."

I took him back into the bathroom and shut the door. Once I heard him lock it, I went back in front of the laptop and started the video.

The key to the video was keeping it short and consistent. There was no sound, mainly to avoid him yelling something and it not showing up on the video. And I had recorded the entire thing just the day before at the same time of day, making sure that the lighting and position of things in the room were kept close to identical. In the video, I strip off my clothes except for the pendant—I really hated that part, but Clint said it would help sell it and make it a lot easier to do the special effects that were needed. Since I was the one doing the special effects, I saw his point.

Basically, I just used software to wipe myself from part of the video, so that what you see is that after I make a big show of taking off the necklace and throwing it on the bed, I disappear for about fifteen seconds until I suddenly reappear as I'm bending down and touching the necklace again. Then I put my clothes back on and turn off the camera before yelling that it's okay for him to come out.

Petey came out immediately, and I expected a big reaction, be it fear or anger or excitement…but he looked pretty much as he had before seeing the video. It was odd, but I decided to just push through to the end.

I asked him if he believed me and he nodded that he did. I told him that the reason I was telling him all this, trusting him with our secret, is because we cared about him too much to put him at risk any longer. That we knew that the pendants worked most of the time, but we knew that occasionally they were overpowered by our evil, vampiric hunger.

Six months ago, I had woken up covered in the blood of a poor homeless woman. When I had talked to Clint about it, I found out he had attacked someone the month prior. We were disgusted by it, but we just pledged to help each other stay strong and not hurt anyone else. But then…as Petey had probably heard…Milo Foster happened. I told him that I would spare him the details (which I honestly didn't know beyond that one article), but that we had been the ones that killed him.

Again, no real change in his expression. I wasn't sure if he was buying it or not, but I was in the home stretch. I told him that we were coming to accept that we were dangerous to be around. We still didn't know what we were going to do, but we couldn't keep putting him at risk. Clint and I were in agreement that after he left my house today, we weren't going to have further contact with him other than saying hello at school. I told him that Clint was too broken up about it to be here in person, but he could call and confirm everything with him.

He didn't look upset by any of this really, but when he spoke, his voice trembled. "I...I understand. I appreciate you thinking about me, and I'll respect your wishes. I really do hope the two of you find a way to control it or reverse it. I'll miss you a lot." Suddenly I saw a trace of tears in his eyes, and I was afraid he was going to lose it. But instead, he just backed away from me slowly, unlocked the door, and left.

That was on a Sunday, and I found out later that he had called Clint briefly, who told him it was all true. Clint told me he had been afraid he was going to mess it all up, but he managed to keep from laughing and hung up quickly. The following day Petey wasn't at school. We found out later in the week that he had transferred across town, and before the school year was out he had moved away again. We felt bad, but we were also relieved, and if I'm honest, a little proud that we had pulled it off.

That was over three years ago, and I haven't thought much about Petey since. I've just finished up my Junior year of college, and while Clint stayed back in town to work at his mother's store, we still kept in touch. He still was one of my best friends.

When I found out on Monday about Clint's murder, I was devastated. Not just because he was killed, but that he was killed in such a savage and bizarre fashion. I had no idea who would want to do something like that, and when his mother texted me that you had caught his killer, it made even less sense. A random junkie just happened to kill Clint in his own home? No sign of a break-in or anything stolen, and the killer had come prepared with not only some object to stab him repeatedly in the chest, but a can of gasoline as well?

I didn't express my doubts to Clint's mother, but when she then texted that the man was also being charged with Milo Foster's murder as well, I felt a chill. First, because it made so little sense. Meaning no disrespect to your investigation, but it's fucking stupid. Second, because it made me think about Petey.

I tried to find Petey on the internet. Social media, address lookups, you name it. No sign of him at all. I tried to tell myself that I was being paranoid, that my guilty conscience and my grief were making me crazy. Then two hours ago I got an envelope slid under my door. Only this time, it wasn't a pendant from a made-up vampire. It was a USB drive containing a single video file.

Petey had clearly set up the camera before Clint came into the room--the angle was high up and showed everything clearly. I recognized it as Clint's bedroom, and while I had known Clint was killed at home, I didn't know exactly where until I watched it. I felt dread crawling up my spine as I watched Clint come in and flop down on the bed. After only a few minutes of shifting around on the bed, he looked like he was asleep.

I wanted to scream a warning as I saw Petey slowly come out of the closet and inch closer to Clint. Suddenly, with alarming quickness and grace, he leapt on top of him. Clint woke immediately and began yelling, but Petey remained silent. While he tried to struggle and get Petey off of him, it was no use. Petey was much bigger and stronger, and it didn't take long for him pin Clint's arms underneath his knees. That's when he pulled out the wooden stake.

I couldn't see Clint's face well at that distance, but I could hear him screaming. "Oh fuck! Oh no! Shit! Petey! No! I'm not a vampire! It was a fucking joke, man! Please don't do thi-" He was cut off as Petey began to slam the stake into his chest once, twice, five times. At first there was wet gurgling, but by the third blow Clint was silent.

When he got up off the bed, Petey turned to the camera, his face still solemn as he spoke. "Better safe than sorry." Then he goes back to the closet, pulls out a gas can, and starts soaking Clint's body with gasoline.

That's where the video ends.

My hands are shaking as I write this. I'm about to attach the video and send it on to you. Not trying to be a dick, but if I haven't heard something from you by in the morning, I'm going to the newspaper. You'll have all the evidence you need to lock that sick fuck up when you find him. I don't know if he really thinks we're vampires or if this is all some sick revenge for him. Either way, he's extremely dangerous.

After I send this, I'm leaving town for a few days. Please try to find him soon. Maybe it's my imagination, but the last few days I've been feeling like I'm being watched, and he clearly knows where I live. If you have

****

He stopped writing the email there because I interrupted him, and it doesn't feel right trying to guess at how he would finish it, so I'll leave it at that. I felt like I needed to post this somewhere to honor what was his final wish, his final word, etc. I changed the names and a couple of details, of course, so it can't ever be traced back to me. I'm trying to do the right thing here, but that doesn't mean I want to go to jail for it.

As for the truth of what he was saying, whether they made all this up or whether that was just a palatable version for law enforcement, well, who's to say? As to whether I think they were really monsters or not? It's a complex answer, and the best response I can give is that there are many kinds of monsters and not all vampires feed on blood. Some feed on hope and self-respect and dignity. So either way, yeah, I think they were vampires. And I loved them, but they needed to be put down. I hope they have found some rest now.

-"**Petey**"

I survived a stay at the Apocalypse Hotel. At least so far.

My name is Lisa Montgomery. The reason my name is important is because for the last three years I've gone by Janet Matthews and have lived in an entirely different part of the country surrounded by people that have never known my real name or past. I didn't have a choice.

Three years ago, when people still called me Lisa, I was a sophomore in college on the east coast of the U.S. Like many college students, I was always strapped for cash. My mother had left when I was a baby, and my father had passed away during my senior year of high school. Aside from some distant relatives I had never met in another state, I was all the family I had.

While I had a hard time when my Dad died, by the time I got to college I made fast friends with my roommate and some of her sorority sisters. But missing my father aside, having no family meant I didn't have anyone to call if I ran short on cash. Which, being a dumbass, I inevitably did.

I was moving past the ramen and cereal phase of frugality and into the water and crackers phase when I passed one of those tables you always see on college campuses. You know what I'm talking about. The metal folding table with the weird sign/tablecloth that is telling you to sign up to protest this or support that, or maybe just join a weird club dedicated to some obscure interest. After nearly two years of college life, I typically just blocked them out. But the sign on the front caught my eye.

On the left side there was a logo of some kind. It was a short triangle atop a square that was missing its bottom side, and inside that shape was what looked like an arrow pointed down. Underneath the symbol it said "Markley Research Group: A subsidiary of Tattersall Global". Okay, so far, so corporately creepy and off-putting.

But the right side of the sign said, "Be evaluated for participation in a two-week clinical trial. Stay in a luxury hotel for 14 days and nights. Leave with fond memories and $5,000.00."

Holy Shit.

I would like to say that there was some major thought process or weighing of options that I went through at that point. In reality, the speed with which I rushed over to the table was akin to how quickly and instinctively I would take my hand off a hot stove. Even though it was early in the morning, I saw other people drifting up to the table too. I felt a nervous fear that someone else would get the open slot or slots before I could, so I stuck out my hand awkwardly and introduced myself to the smiling woman sitting behind the table, thinking to occupy her attention before someone else could.

She shook my hand with a quick laugh and told me to have a seat. Introducing herself as Margaret, she told me to fill out the forms she was handing me, and after she reviewed them she could ask follow-up questions and answer any I had as well. I took the clipboard from her gratefully, trying not to stare at the scar that ran past her left eye and back into her hairline.

The questions were extensive, but nothing that seemed overly weird for some kind of scientific experiment. Age, weight, health conditions, mental conditions, phobias, genetic ancestry (if known), family health and mental conditions (if known), that kind of thing. I did notice that there were a lot of questions that boiled down to how crazy was I and any genetic problems I might have, but there was also what seemed like a small personality test and a section on food allergies.

And for the most part, I was honest. Look, I'm generally a very truthful person. But I really was desperate for money, and I didn't think one little lie on the questionnaire would be a big deal. Under "known genetic disorders" I checked no.

I have what is called minor thalassemia. It's inherited, though my father didn't have it and I don't know if my mother did or not. Basically what it means is that some of the hemoglobin in my red blood cells is abnormal. Some people have a really hard time with it, but mine has always been very mild thankfully. I really didn't think it would be a big deal, and I didn't want to get kicked out of the running for something so stupid.

Margaret reviewed my answers and asked a few more questions. She was an attractive woman in her late forties, and her tone and the scar made her seem severe but not unkind. When she finished her questions, she asked if I had any. Trying to be charming, I jokingly asked, "When do we leave?"

She smiled thinly and gave a low, throaty laugh. "How's tomorrow sound?"

****

The next day I was on a small jet along with eight other students from my college. Based on the orientation we had before we got on the plane that morning, we were going to a secluded "resort" that was really a highly sophisticated testing facility. We had to sign paperwork agreeing to not leave the resort until the end of the week or we would forfeit our money and be liable for the expenses incurred by our inclusion in the experiment up to that point. A couple of people raised concerns about that, but Margaret was quick to allay them.

She said that for all intents and purposes, we were just getting two weeks of paid vacation at a deluxe hotel. The main differences were that we would be under surveillance at all times and that there would be a low-level infectious disease introduced at points around the hotel throughout the week. This, of course, raised more questions.

Margaret smiled and nodded as she listened, and she responded with the smooth and placid tones of a polished politician. She understood the worry, but that was the entire point of the experiment. They were using a very mild form of the cold virus and just needed to track its spread throughout the hotel over the course of the two weeks. Very slight symptoms that would be a runny nose and slight cough at most. They would start introducing the virus after the first twenty-four hours, and they would stop introducing it after the first week, so that by the time everyone left, they should be "fit as a fiddle and $5,000.00 richer."

This calmed people down some, but you could still feel a palpable tension that hadn't been there before. Margaret went on to say that this experiment could give her organization vital information to help see the effects of a terrorist biological attack on a populated area and how such an attack could be combatted. That by participating, we would not only be helping ourselves and their research, but helping our country as a whole. They never specifically said they were working for the government, but you could tell they wanted us to have that impression. Anything to make it look and sound official and safe, I guess.

In the end, the sales pitch worked, and we all got on the plane. Three days later, the killing started.

****

The first couple of days were weird but fun. The hotel really was great, and while I got a very strange feeling when I first saw the twenty-foot security fence that surrounded the edge of the grounds, you kind of got used to it after the first day or so. The thought occurred to me more than once that I really had no idea where I was, which meant no one else did either. There were trees all around, and I know we were on the plane for several hours, but beyond that I had no clue. Still, I told myself, there was too much going on here for it not to be legitimate.

We get into the mindset that if someone is open about something, it is likely safe. That if something is backed by a lot of money and planning, it is going to stay within certain guidelines. Because they have too much to lose, right? If you're in a strange city, you go to the franchise restaurant or store that you know. Even if it's not somewhere you like to shop, there's a comfort in knowing they have established products from giant corporations and uniform ways of treating their customers. If you go to the hospital for surgery, there's that part of you that eases your worry by the idea that if they messed up somehow, you could always sue them because they have so much money. But the real point of that thought isn't the money. It's the idea that they are established, they are authority. They have too much to lose and they know better than you what you need. So you trust, and the world goes on.

It's the same way with the hotel. They don't hide what they're doing. They go to campuses, talking about the hotel and the organization they work for. They have the resources for jets and staff and this wonderful hotel that would probably cost a grand a night in many parts of the world. So they have to be on the up and up, right?

But what if they're crazy? Or what if they have enough money and power that they just don't give a fuck?

These are the questions I started asking myself when Sam, a freshman who wanted to become a political science major, started laughing uncontrollably at the poolside restaurant, slamming his head repeatedly into the bar where he was eating lunch.

I had heard him laughing for a couple of minutes, but I tried to ignore it. I was reading a book while I ate a delicious club sandwich and drank a mimosa, just enjoying the sun and the relative tranquility only slightly broken by his increasingly loud titters. There were a total of thirty "guests" at the hotel, and over the last two days we had mingled enough for me to know that they had recruited from three other schools like ours. I had hung out with larger groups both evenings, but during the days I planned on just sticking to myself a lot of the time. Even with spring break taking care of the second week, I was missing a week of classes for this trip, and I wanted to make the most of my break from real life. That didn't include getting caught up in reality show friendship drama with people I didn't know and would never see again in a couple of weeks.

Still, Sam was one of the people I had actually talked to a bit. He was from Arizona and seemed like a very nice, normal guy. So it was weird when he started laughing like that, but I just tried to tune it out. Then I heard the first loud thump and somebody started screaming.

When I turned and looked, I could only see part of his face from my angle, but it was already a bloody ruin. He was leaving teeth imbedded in the wooden bar with each hammer fall of his head, and his laughter had become a wet caw that sounded more like raw hamburger meat thrown against a sidewalk over and over again. After a few more seconds, the bartender and one of the other guests tried to stop him, but it was too late. He was already dead.

The next few hours were a blur of fear, anger, and panic as word spread and we tried to find someone to talk to. There were a handful of "hotel staff" present, but we quickly found out they were recruited just like we were, except their recruitment had been done more selectively from a variety of resorts and cruise ships around the world. The bartender that had tried to stop Sam from beating his own brains out was named Jeff, and he was clearly just as shit-scared as the rest of us.

Administrative offices, security office, outbuildings, all were empty beyond the normal "staff". No phone calls outside the resort and no internet. And we figured out quickly that the fence that surrounded the resort was electrified with just enough juice to make you piss yourself and black out for a few seconds if you tried to climb it.

There was no one in charge, at least that we could find. And there was no way out. We were trapped.

Over the next few days, people fell into three camps. There were the doomsday preppers. These were the ones that had decided this was some Lord of the Flies shit and they weren't going down like that. They stockpiled some supplies and holed up in a couple of spots in the hotel the rest of us avoided. Then there were the ostriches. We just kept our heads down and pretended like everything was cool. It was just an experiment, and we just had to play our part and it would be okay at the end. Nevermind that we had just watched a man murder himself.

Then there were the crazies. Sam was the first of these, but he was far from the last. On the fourth day, Jeff the bartender stabbed a girl from Louisiana he had been hanging out with a lot since we all arrived. He used a small knife he had been cutting limes with, and as far as we could tell, he did it without any warning or provocation. We didn't get to ask either of them though. They were alone at the other pool's bar when it happened, and Jeff had followed three deep stabs into her neck with another two into his own. By the time anyone noticed, they had been baking in the sun for half an hour and the pool had taken on a pale, pinkish tint from the blood that had sluiced across the patio from their dead bodies.

The small wooden house that housed twenty bikes for riding around the resort had now become where we hid the bodies, and half the ostriches became preppers overnight. That wouldn't have been so bad, but by the end of the fifth day, seven more people had gone insane.

Between "guests" and "staff", I think there were a total of 53 people staying in that resort. By day 12, there were 4. For the last week I was there, I stayed holed up in a room on the top floor, barricaded in with a croquet mallet and a dwindling supply of candy I had swiped from the gift shop. I slept very little, and every scream or thud made me jump, but I was left alone for the most part. The crazies didn't seem to be hunting for other people to hurt as much as just taking targets of opportunity. If you stayed out of their way, they left you alone.

Still, I wasn't taking any chances. I stayed in the room, ready to fight someone off if I had to, and I had a makeshift rope out of bedsheets already tied to the balcony railing if I needed to escape to the next floor down. I was holding onto the dim hope that when day 14 came, I would somehow be freed, but I knew it was highly unlikely. Despite my fear and worry about getting sick and going insane, I seemed fine so far as I could tell. But that just meant they would kill me at the end, not free me.

But I was wrong. On day 12, I heard a new sound. Gunshots. Going out on the balcony, I saw several people in black biohazard suits standing in the middle of the croquet field. Two of my fellow guests already lay dead on the ground, and as I watched, they put a bullet in the head of the last as she charged them with what looked like the two-prong fork from the roast beef station in the dining room. Then they looked up at me.

The one who had fired final shot had an electronic bullhorn in the other hand. She raised it to her mouth and called for me to come down, that it was over and I wouldn't be harmed. I couldn't be sure between the suit's microphone and the bullhorn, but it sounded like Margaret.

I debated my options. I could refuse, and they would just come get me. Possibly they could just gas me up here. I had tried to destroy any cameras I saw in the room, but I felt sure there were others that were better hidden. Who knows what other nasty surprises they may have for non-compliant guests?

My other choice was to obey. It was very unlikely, but maybe this time they would keep their word, and I had no better options. So I went down. Margaret met me with the others in the lobby and congratulated me on surviving. She said that they were going to take me now to get tissue and blood samples, decontaminate me, and then send me back home on the jet. And, she intoned with all the patronizing mirth of a game show host, a suitcase containing $50,000.00.

It only seemed fair given all I had been through, she said, and I nodded numbly. I didn't care about the money or anything else other than getting away from these people. I went with them into a part of the hotel I had never known existed, through several metal doors to an elevator that took us deep underground. I was poked and prodded, given an extremely thorough scrubbing and chemical bath, and then Margaret was back before me, a clipboard in hand.

"This is a NDA. A non-disclosure agreement. By signing it, you agree you will never discuss any aspect of your time here. Standard legal stuff, and I think we both know you're smarter than to talk to anyone about this anyhow, right?" She gave me a thin smile and I quickly nodded, my stomach in knots as I signed and initialed next to little yellow tabs at various spots throughout the thick document. "Good girl. Off you go."

I was dropped off outside my dorm building, and I didn't even bother going inside. There was nothing in there I couldn't replace, and I dreaded running into my roommate or someone else that might ask me questions I would have to avoid or lie about. Better to just make a clean break of it.

I had already decided on the flight back what I needed to do. I ran to the parking lot, pulling the suitcase full of money behind me. It was the only suitcase I had left. Margaret had said that the rest of my belongings had to be left behind and burned, including my old suitcase, but they had furnished me with clean clothes and shoes in my size before having me sign the stupid NDA. Tossing the suitcase in the trunk, I headed for the bank.

I deposited $45,000.00 into my bank account and kept the other $5,000 out in case I need cash, which I would. I threw away their suitcase and drove to the airport where I said good-bye to my car in long-term parking and got on a plane to Cincinnati. I paid cash for an extended-stay room there and a rental car, and over four weeks I used one of the local branches of my bank to take out various amounts of cash until I had the money back. Then I bought a cheap car for cash and drove southwest.

From the time I made my last cash withdrawal from the bank, I never went by Lisa Montgomery again except for when I filled out the paperwork to legally change my name in Nevada. I answered only to Janet Matthews, and those first few months were terrible. I was super-paranoid, always looking over my shoulder and waiting for a van to pull up and snatch me or to wake up to someone standing over my bed. But that faded some with time, and over the next three years I built a new life. I have a good job, a boyfriend who loves me, and I'm looking at buying a house in a few months.

A lot of times I eat lunch in a park near my office. This past Friday, I was walking to my favorite spot, a bench frequented by curious squirrels and hungry geese from the nearby pond. That's when I saw the table.

It was set up along one of the main paths through the park, but was near a curve thick with shrubbery from the direction I was coming. When I rounded the corner, I was only thirty feet from it, and I felt my body wanting to freeze like a deer scenting a hunter. I forced myself to keep moving, trying to look normal and avoid eye contact. It was probably just some random cause or sales pitch, but I wanted no part of it either way.

"Hi there, Lisa." It was Margaret's voice, and now I did freeze. I cut my eyes toward the table and saw the woman smiling at me. "Good to see you. Hope we see you again soon."

****

I'm sitting here writing this, less to try to save myself and more as a cautionary tale for others. I don't have it in me to run any more, not that it would do any good. I'm going to post this and then talk to my boyfriend Nick about it. Tell him that I love him, but that he may not want to be around me anymore. They could leave me alone forever or come get me tonight. I just don't know.

In some ways that's the worst part. Whatever immunity I had to their murder virus, they infected me just the same. I can see it every time I look in the mirror. I can feel it whenever my heart stops at a sudden noise. They've infected me with this fear and dread, and I don't know how much longer I can take it.

So I'll end with this. Don't take your life and your safety for granted. Don't trust people just because it's convenient to do so. And if you get an offer to go stay at a luxury hotel for a couple of weeks as part of some mysterious experiment, don't just say no. You fucking run.

Someone replaced Independence Day with a snuff film.

One of my favorite movies growing up was Independence Day. I know there are better movies, but the combination of actors and special effects made it just about perfect in my young brain. I used to drive my parents crazy not only wanting to watch it, but wanting them to bask in the glory of Randy Quaid in a jet *with* me, so they finally settled on a compromise. We would watch it together every 4th of July if I would shut up about it the rest of the year.

And so we did. During the years I was 8 to 14, we watched it religiously somewhere between afternoon hot dogs and evening fireworks every year. And it was awesome. But as I got older, my interests changed, I was busier, and I just…forgot. Since I was 15, I don't know that I've seen the entire movie more than once, and I'm 29 now.

So when I found a box with old movies in the storage unit of my apartment building, imagine my delight upon spotting a blu-ray of Independence Day sitting right on top. I had moved into the apartment six months before, and part of the lease agreement was that each apartment had a little storage unit in the basement for excess stuff. It sounded far more grandiose than it actually was—each "unit" consisted of a cramped cinderblock room that was the size of a small walk-in closet. Still, it was handy if you had excess stuff. I just didn't.

I had moved to town for a job, and my furniture initially consisted of my mattress and television from home. Over the past several months I had accrued enough furniture that I didn't look like a serial killer any more, but I was still living very frugally. My first real splurge had been the week before when I bought myself a new t.v.

I was really pumped about it. 4k, HDR, and obscenely big for my smallish living room. When it got delivered, I started setting it up immediately, but that also meant moving my old t.v. I've had since college. It was one of those hulking "flat screen" televisions that had a *technically* flat screen, but also had a giant two-foot ass that weighed a hundred pounds. It wasn't awesome, but I admit to being a little sad as I waddle-dropped it to a piece of cardboard and slid it out and down the hall to the elevator. It was going to be my first deposit in the storage unit.

When I opened the door, I saw the box immediately. It was labeled "Private Valuables" in a spidery black marker scrawl, which struck me as slightly odd. But when I opened it up and saw Independence Day, I immediately drug the t.v. in and brought the box back upstairs with me. Feeling a wave of nostalgia fueled by a combination of putting my old t.v. to pasture and the anticipation of seeing evil aliens exterminated with a floppy disk, I pulled out the blu-ray, popped it in my console, and got ready to watch a modern classic.

The video was dark and grainy, and I could tell right away that this wasn't Independence Day. It looked to be in some kind of old, run-down gymnasium. I could see what looked like the weathered floor of a basketball court along the perimeter of the illumination provided by twin floodlights. In the center of the light was a thin, stained mattress and clear plastic tarps that covered the bedding and the surrounding floor.

The blackness outside this circle of light combined with the excited breathing of the person holding the camera made the whole thing feel claustrophobic, and the breath only quickened when a large masked man led the naked couple into view. They were bound at their neck and wrists, and it was clear that they had been beaten already. They looked toward the camera as the person holding it approached, and the man let out a terrible, low moan of despair. The woman's bottom lip trembled, but she said nothing as tears began to run down her cheeks.

I had a brief moment where I thought this was some odd, bootleg horror movie I had never seen before, but it didn't look right. Aside from no credits or music, the entire thing felt too *real*, even for a well-done found footage movie. And as the camera had approached the lit area, the picture had sharpened to an almost painful degree. I could see with agonizing detail the shape these two were in, the emotions they were feeling. They were genuinely terrified.

I won't describe the details of what happened next on the video. I lack the stomach or the words to properly convey the torture, cruelty, and depravity I saw inflicted on them over the next twenty minutes. I deeply regret continuing to watch it myself, and by the time I came out of my shock and horror enough to turn it off, they were both dying or dead.

I didn't know what to do. I thought about calling the police, but what could they do? For all I knew, those people had been killed on another continent ten years ago. I could just throw it away or destroy it, but what if it really was evidence of something? There was always the outside chance it really was fake, of course. A low-budget, edgy horror movie with wonderful actors and special effects. It sounded dumb as I thought it, but it was what I was hoping for in my heart of hearts.

In the end, I went down the next day to the office of the company that owned my building. They leased several apartments all over town, and the only person I was familiar with there, Vicki, was less a landlord and more a real estate agent with a side gig. Luckily she was in, and within a couple of minutes I was sitting in her office.

I didn't talk about the movie specifically, but I told her about finding a box of what I assumed was the prior tenant's belongings in the storage unit. I wondered if she had any information about him so I could contact him about getting his stuff. In truth, I had no intention of contacting him, but I wanted to know more about them before I made my final decision on what to do.

Vicki, a perpetually chipper woman in her mid-fifties with bright blond hair and an unnaturally dark tan, visibly paled as I started talking. Three sentences in, and she was already waiving her hand and shaking her head.

"No, honey. Don't worry with that. Throw that mess in the trash. No telling what kind of trash she had in there."

I raised an eyebrow. "So you know who the last tenant was? It was a woman?"

Her eyes widened slightly as she realized she'd said more than she meant to, and she leaned forward with a frown. "It was, but no one you want to contact. Look," she glanced around like she was about to divulge the location for a dead drop in a spy movie as she went on, "that girl was troubled. Very troubled. She had some rich family in another state that would pay her rent like clockwork, and for a couple of years everything was fine. She was some kind of computer something or other, and she kept to herself most of the time. Then she had some episode where a neighbor of hers went to the hospital and she got committed."

Vicki paused a moment as though gauging if she had said enough to satisfy me, and when she saw she hadn't, she went on. "She bit the woman, okay? Bit her thumb clean off. The neighbor was okay…mostly, but she moved away soon after, and as for the crazy girl? As far as I know she's still in a loony bin somewhere. Either way, we terminated her lease immediately and her family came and got her stuff." She sighed. "Well, except for this crap in the storage area I guess. Still, I'd just throw it out if I were you. She doesn't have any need for it, whatever it is, and trust me, that's a friend you don't want to make."

I was unnerved by what Vicki had told me, but at least it gave some explanation for that disc and whatever else might be in the box. I decided that I'd leave well enough alone. As soon as I got home, I'd carry the box down to the incinerator and try to put what I'd seen out of my mind.

Except when I got back to my apartment, there was a thick envelope waiting against my door. It had no writing on it, and once I got inside and opened it, I saw it contained a cell phone with no note or explanation. I felt a new wave of unease as I looked at the phone, weighing exploring the phone itself for clues versus throwing it away immediately like some diseased thing. When it suddenly lit up and started vibrating, I let out a high scream. I almost dropped it, and after several seconds of panicked fumbling, I opened it and answered the call it was receiving from a restricted number.

"Hello?"

There was silence, but I could tell someone was on the line.

"Hello? Is anyone there?"

"**Did you look inside the box?**" The voice was feminine, but with a strange, husky rasp that made it hard to guess the age or accent.

I almost dropped the phone again as my hands went numb. "Um, what? Who is this?"

"**Did you watch one of those movies? Did you explore what else is in there?**"

"N-no, I didn't. I didn't watch anything or even look in the box. It's not my stuff, and I'll happily…"

"**LIAR.**" The phone crackled slightly at the word. "**I know you watched one of the discs. It pinged off the server when you started it up. Why do you lie about it?**"

My mind was racing. Server? What was she…And then I remembered. Some blu-rays automatically connect to the internet. Usually it's to download new movie trailers, but this one had apparently been made to let someone know if the disc was being watched. Was that even possible? It didn't matter, I needed to deal with the nutjob first.

"Look, I'm sorry. I loaded the disc, but when I realized it wasn't Independence Day, I cut it off. So I don't know what you're talking about, and I think I should go now." I was edging further into my apartment now, and my hands were starting to tremble from the adrenaline. It seemed like a reasonable lie, but why wouldn't she just fucking answer?

Then finally, "**I don't believe you.**" She drew out the words like she was expressing some kind of corruption from a pregnant boil and savored the smell of doing it. She gave a short laugh, her voice crackling again louder. "**But that's all right, I think. We can work with this…I think, yes?**"

By this point I had moved far enough into my apartment that something caught my eye in my bedroom. Turning to look, I saw that the bed, floor, and walls had been draped in clear plastic tarps. I took three unconscious steps toward the room as my mind tried to reconcile what I was seeing with how the room should be. I felt the static buzz of panic rising in my ears, and as I approached I could see that a small black video camera sat perched upon a tripod in the corner of the room, its red recording light glaring at me like a baleful eye.

I was about to back away and leave the apartment when I heard two small creaks. One from the bedroom, and then half a second later, the other from the phone. I saw the plastic tarp on the left side of the room billow as my closet door was pushed open.

I dropped the phone and ran. I didn't stop running until I was three blocks away and safely under the fluorescent lights of a local pharmacy. I had dropped my own phone as well at some point in all of this, so I asked to use theirs and called the police. Twenty minutes later they pulled up, and after I gave an explanation, they went with me back to the apartment. The two officers went in first, and after they cleared the apartment, they came back out. Their initial expressions of mild interest and concern had been replaced with irritation, and when I went inside with them, I understood why.

The tarps and camera were gone, as was the mystery phone. Even the box of movies, which I had left sitting next to the t.v. in the living room, was missing. And no Independence Day box or snuff film disc. No trace that any of it had happened.

The police weren't rude, but they clearly thought it was either a dumb prank or I was on something. Either way, they left quickly and I could tell they wouldn't be writing a report on it. Not that I could blame them.

I spent the next week in a motel as I went through the process of breaking my lease and finding a new place on the other side of town. That was over a month ago, and since then, everything has been fine. Boring even. At first I dreaded every phone call, every visitor at work, every event that could potentially be her making contact again. But I was moving past it, and the new apartment was actually nicer with better security.

So when I walked in today and saw the box sitting on my sofa, I actually had a moment when I was confused. Then I saw the words written on the side in black marker. Private Valuables. I almost left the apartment then, but I saw there was a sticky note above the old labeling. When I was closer, I could see it was in the same handwriting, though this had been written in pencil. It said:

We still have much work to do, yes?

Ol' Mr. Horsehair

A couple of days ago my dad took me swimming at Shiner Lake. We hadn't been there since Mom left when I was ten, and if I'm honest, I was more excited about spending time with him than I was going to the lake for the day. It's not that the lake wasn't fun--it was. We swam, cooked out, and I got to check out several hot girls throughout the day. But I'm 16 now, and between my friends and school and my dad's work, we don't really see each other much beyond dinner and the occasional football game on Sunday. It was nice to have a full day together.

It sounds sappy, but my dad is a great guy, and growing up he was my best friend. He's always been smart and patient and kind, even when I didn't deserve it. That's why I didn't understand what was happening. That's why I didn't know why he tried to kill me.

It started yesterday morning. I got up and was eating breakfast in the living room, mindlessly flipping between internet videos while I munched on some cereal. When he walked into the room, I could tell something was wrong immediately. He was frowning terribly and wiggling his finger in his ear. At first I thought he might have an ear infection, particularly since he stumbled slightly when I asked if he was okay. But when he raised his eyes to meet mine, I felt scared. It was like he hadn't realized I was there. No, it was more like he was seeing me for the first time and he didn't like what he saw.

"What the fuck did you just say to me, you little shitterrrr?" He drawled out the "r" so long I would have thought it was a joke any other time. Instead I got up and started backing away toward the kitchen.

"Nothing, Dad. I was just asking if you were okay. Sorry." I had hoped me retreating and apologizing would calm him down about whatever this was, but it seemed to make him angrier instead.

"Sorry. Sorry. Fucking sooooorry." He shook his head twice and slammed the palm of his hand into his ear with a grunt. "You just think you-you're sorry. Coming at me with that sasssssss mouth."

There was a thin line of drool forming at the corner of his mouth, and a new thought punched through the thick layer of fear that was taking me over. A stroke. He might be having some kind of weird stroke.

The thought distracted me for a second, and that was all it took for him to surge forward and close the distance between us. He grabbed me by the shoulder and slammed his other hand into my stomach, knocking the wind out of me and sending me to the floor. I was so surprised and hurt that I could barely think at all beyond some dim expectation that he would start kicking or stomping me now. But there was none of that.

Instead, he just stood over me, staring. A large, humorless grin stretched his mouth wide, and that thin string of drool yo-yo'd above me before landing on my cheek and sliding into my hair. "Now you're sorry. Now you know what'ssssss what."

With that, he turned and walked away, heading back in the direction of his bedroom. I heard the door slam, but I still waited a few seconds before getting up and going outside.

I didn't know what to do. I could call the cops, but they might either blow me off or take it very serious, and I wasn't sure if either was what I wanted. I thought about calling the hospital, but my father has clout and money around here, and if he didn't want to go, they weren't going to push it unless, again, I elevated it to a cop situation. I wasn't badly hurt, just scared more than anything, and maybe it was just some weird fluke?

But that was dumb. He had to have something wrong with him. He was sick or something. I ran back inside and got my car keys, and I was getting in the car when I heard him behind me.

"Jack? Where you heading off to so early?"

I turned around and he was smiling confusedly at me, his face so different from the twisted, hateful mask it had been just a few minutes before. He looked like my dad again. I felt a sense of relief flooding through me, but I held it in check. I could still see the glistening saliva at the corner of his mouth, and for all I knew this was some kind of trick.

I got in the car and turned it on, rolling down the window before I answered. "Dad, you just attacked me. You remember that?"

The change in his expression broke my heart. I could tell he didn't know what I was talking about, but from how I was acting he knew I wasn't joking around either. He asked me what was going on, coming closer to the car. I asked him to stop, and he did, his face looking even more wounded.

When I told him what had happened, he started crying. He swore to me that he didn't remember anything. He said that he'd had a bad headache when he went to sleep the night before, but the next thing he remembered was getting up just a minute ago. I asked him if he could have just had some kind of bad dream and sleepwalked or something. He seemed to think it over for a moment and shook his head.

"I'd like to think so, but I've never heard of anyone doing anything like that when they were asleep. I need to see a doctor. I'd rather see Dr. Philips--he's discreet and knows his stuff, but I know he's out of town until tomorrow with Melanie." He paused, his eyes sad. "Are you okay with that? Are you okay with me waiting that long? If you don't feel safe around me I'll go to the hospital now or I can stay at a hotel overnight and see him tomorrow. You decide what will make you comfortable and that's what I'll do."

I wanted to tell him to go right away, but I knew he was worried about his reputation and work if it got out he was beating his son and not remembering it. And he seemed so much better, I really did hope it was just caused by bad dreams. I told him that I was cool with him waiting and staying in the house, but if we noticed anything else weird, he really had to go on to the hospital right away. He swore he would, and after an awkward silence I turned off the car and we went back inside.

We hung out some in the afternoon watching t.v., but it was painful. I couldn't help but be afraid of him a little, and I could tell it was eating away at him. That night he made us spaghetti for dinner, and we were in the middle of eating when he stopped mid-sentence and dropped his fork into his lap, noodles and all.

I froze, afraid to ask if he was okay or make any sudden movements. He shook his head twice, his eyes glazed and staring off at something I couldn't see. His lips started moving, and I could faintly hear him muttering from across the table.

"...pretty, yes...oh I think so...it's a perfect...thing..." Suddenly his eyes snapped to me, his mouth twisting into a grimace. He put his hands on the table like he was getting ready to either shove it towards me or come over it. So I ran.

I should have run outside, but I was panicked, and I thought if I could make it to my room I'd be safe. He caught me halfway up the stairs, dragging me back by the waist of my jeans as I scrabbled and screamed and begged. This time he didn't talk or threaten. He punched me twice in the face and started pulling me through the house by my armpits.

At one point, when we were nearly outside, I twisted away and tried to get up. He kicked me in the ribs and I fell back down, curling in on myself like a baby. He was still muttering to himself and smiling a strange smile as he took up his grip under my arms and drug me out to the car, this time dragging me on my belly.

That's when I first saw it. Out of the right leg of his shorts, trailing down to the back of his knee and curling there, was a thin brown strand of...something. It almost looked like a single long, very thick hair, but that wasn't right either. Even though my mouth was aching from being hit and my lips were starting to swell up, I still managed to let out a scream when it twitched twice and uncurled a little just inches from my face. That got me another, heavier hit, and after that I saw nothing but darkness.

When I woke up, I was being held underwater. My first thought was that my father was going to drown me, maybe in our own pool, and I started reaching back desperately, trying to claw at him. But his hand was on the back of my neck and his knee was bearing down between my shoulder blades. I tried pushing down into the sodden muck of the water I was in, but it was no use. A deep part of my brain was still screaming at me to fight, but I knew it was pointless.

Then I was being pulled back up. Not by rescuers, but by my father. He had the same insane glare as before, but at least he wasn't hitting me anymore. Instead he drug me silently back to the car and shoved me roughly into the trunk. I went willingly, knowing I had no real choice and terrified that whatever was attached to or protruding from his body might touch me.

I'd had a momentary idea that maybe I had imagined it or dreamed it while unconscious, but in the brief time between the water and the trunk, I managed to see he had taken me all the way to Shiner Lake and that the thing twitching restlessly against his leg was all too real.

Two hours later and I was out of the trunk. We were back at the house and he pushed me inside and up to my bedroom. I happily shut the door and locked it when I got inside, thinking I had finally managed to get some small window of safety. He didn't say anything or beat on the door, but instead went back downstairs. I started searching my pockets for my phone, but it wasn't on me. I grabbed my laptop to try and send a message out from it, but the internet was down.

By then my dad was back at the door. I heard loud thudding, and at first I was afraid he was trying to break down the door. Then I realized he was hammering in nails. He was sealing me in. I wasn't sure what to do. I was afraid he might try to burn the house down with me in it, but it was also possible he was shutting me up in here to try and protect me from himself. The only window in my room looked down to a straight drop onto the concrete patio around the pool. It was doable if I smelled smoke, but I would probably break something in the process.

I was still weighing my options when I realized he had stopped hammering and seemingly gone away. I went to the window to gauge the drop again when I saw my dad walking out onto the patio. He was walking stiff-legged, dragging his right leg as he went and shaking his head more and more. I saw that long dark tendril twisting this way and that as it wrapped itself around his leg and slid down toward his ankle.

He twitched more violently as he reached the edge of the water, turning enough to look at me for a moment. His eyes almost looked sad and familiar, but it was hard to say with the distance and the dark. Then he was in the pool, and a few moments later he was bursting apart.

The thing was much larger than what was on the outside. It was some kind of thick, brown worm, and when it touched the water it began thrashing about, ripping my dad apart in the process. Even in the dim exterior house lights, I could see the pool quickly turn from a dark blue to a darker red, and when I saw his chest coming apart underneath his shirt I just closed my eyes and screamed for awhile.

When I opened them, the water was calm again except for at its lower depths. I imagined I could see that long, thin monster swimming around near the bottom. And it looked as though it was coming apart as well. I swear I saw small pieces of it floating away, darker spots of black among the red. But then it was back at the surface, smoothly arching its body over the pool's edge and sliding into the shadowy hedges beyond.

I have been sitting here for the last hour writing this before I try to go down and find my phone. I don't know what that thing is, but if it gets me I want there to be some kind of record or warning for others. I don't know why it didn't get me the first time we were at the lake, and I hope the second trip doesn't mean what I think it might. My head is pounding and I'm so scared, but I have

****

I'm riting this later than now. Then then. I jest woke up. My head hurts so so bad now. I'm out of my room now? I woke up in the living room on the floor. I don't know how, but I brok the door down I guess. Fuk but my head. It's itching on the insid. So thirsty.

I can't find phone, but I got internet going again. I think I was blacked out for a long time. It's dark again. I can't figure out what to do, so I looked up giant worms. No luk. I tried paractes. I can't think right or rite good right noww, so I'm gong to paste it her.

The "horsehair worm" is a threadlike roundworm that derives its nickname from its resemblance to the hair of a horse's tail. The worm infests the body of an insect such as a grasshopper or beetle, growing fully inside the body. During its development, it affects the brain of the host, altering its behavior and ultimately controlling it so that the host finds its way to water and drowns. The worm, which often has already started protruding from the body prior to killing its host, then frees itself fully and begins its next stage of life.

I thnk something like that got my dad. I thnk it made him infec me too? So thirsty. I hurt al over now. Oh my hed. I feel it in me? I feel it insid and outside to? Oh no. I thnk Ol Mr Horsehair is crawlin all in me.

Stay away.

Pleas

So tirsty

Bye

Yesterday morning I found bloody teeth in my pocket.

I woke up early yesterday because of banging noises from next door. I figured that my neighbor, Jeff, must be doing some kind of renovation, and staring up at the waterstained crack in my ceiling, I found myself pondering if he was doing the work himself and how much he might charge to do some repairs over here if he was. I pushed the thought away as I shuffled to the bathroom, trying to focus on crawling out of the sleep fog permeating my brain. When I was done in the bathroom, I pulled on some jeans that were draped over the only chair in my bedroom.

Pushing my hands into the front pockets of the jeans, my left hand hit something hard and sticky feeling. When I pulled my hand out, I was holding a handful of broken, bloody teeth. I screamed and raked them off my palm onto the floor, going to wash my hands before coming back to examine them. There were 8 teeth, and judging by their size and condition, they were from a variety of people. At least two of them looked like they came from children.

I could hardly breathe. I had no idea or memory of where those teeth had come from. I checked the house for signs of a break-in, but there were none. I had only a handful of furniture and some clothes, so I was a poor target for a burglary, and I was new enough to town that I doubted I had developed a stalker already. Still, I was terrified.

I wracked my brain for any memory of how they could have gotten there or anything I might have done to hurt someone. I didn't even know anyone yet other than my neighbor Jeff, and I couldn't imagine one person—much less multiple people—doing something bad enough that I would want to hurt them like that anyway.

I didn't have internet yet, and when I tried my phone, I got an automated message saying it had not been linked to a cellular account. Weird. I went outside to get in my car, but halfway down the walk to where it was parked, I detoured on impulse and went up to Jeff's house.

It was a much larger and nicer house than mine and in much better condition, and that thought reminded me to ask if he did house repair work. If nothing else it would be a good excuse for coming over to ask him my more pressing questions.

When Jeff opened the door, I felt a small thrill at seeing him. He was handsome, with a face that was just worn enough to be interesting and a soft, deep voice that always sounded kind. He smiled when he saw me, and was about to say something when I blurted out my cover question.

"Do you do house work? I mean, like house repairs?"

Laughing, he looked back into his house, which looked very well-decorated and clean despite whatever construction might be going on in there. I found myself idly wondering if he had a girlfriend before pulling myself back to focus on his response.

"Well, I guess, if you can call it that. I can do some basic stuff, yeah. Why, you need something fixed over there?" He shifted his gaze to my house, his face looking concerned.

"Yeah, maybe. Just a few small things if you're interested some time. I'd pay you, of course, but I'm still looking for work, so I may have to do the repairs a little bit at the time."

"Oh, I'm not worried about the money. Just figure out what you need done over there and let me know." Turning back to me, Jeff had a slight frown. "Are you okay over there? Comfortable enough?"

It seemed an odd question, but he looked like he was legitimately worried, so I answered. "Yeah, I'm okay. Still settling in, but I'm glad to have a good neighbor at least."

He studied me for a minute before nodding. "You want to come inside?"

My heart sped up again slightly, but I shook my head. "I'd like to, but another time. I'm going to the library right now." I thought he was going to say something else, but instead he just nodded and said he'd see me later then. To come by whenever I wanted. Then with one last look that almost seemed sad, he went to shut the door.

"Hold...hold on, Jeff. I was going to ask you something else too."

He opened the door back. "Sure, what's up?"

"Well, have you noticed me acting weird in the last day or so? I know you don't know me well, but I was just wondering if you saw me doing anything out of the ordinary lately."

Instead of laughing or acting surprised, he just shook his head. "No, I can't say I have. I haven't seen you since yesterday, but you seemed fine then." He paused. "Are you sure you don't want to come in? Maybe if something is wrong, I can help."

I smiled, feeling embarrassed. "Later maybe. I need to get some stuff done first." He nodded and after saying goodbye again, he shut the door.

I considered whether or not I should have told him about the teeth, but what good would it have done? I think he'd have told me if he knew anything about it, and in the unlikely event he was the one that put them in my jeans, it wasn't like he would just tell me because I asked. I felt confused, and frustrated by my confusion, as I walked to my car, and my time at the library that morning did nothing to help my mood.

I tried looking up everything I could think of. Weird crimes where people left teeth behind. Stalkers or serial killers that took or hid teeth. Even myths and legends of supernatural creatures that could explain having a pocket full of ruined, sticky molars and incisors. Nothing really fit, and after a couple of hours of looking, I was growing increasingly convinced that I was either going crazy or had just been fooled by a very vivid dream.

Driving back home, I decided on a plan. I would go back to my house and see if the teeth were actually still there. If they weren't, I'd chalk it up to a nightmare and just keep an eye out for future weirdness. If they were, I was going to take a picture of them and call the police.

Despite my desperate hoping and praying on my trip back across town, when I got home I saw the teeth laying on my bedroom floor like discarded game pieces to some macabre board game. My stomach dropped at the sight and I started trying to come up with excuses as to why I shouldn't tell anyone and just flush them or something.

But no. This was serious and I needed help. The authorities needed to be notified. Trying to find my resolve, I bent down and took two pictures of the teeth from different angles with my largely useless cell phone. The pictures were for the police, but more so they were for Jeff so I could short-circuit any questions he might have when I asked to use his phone. I didn't want to spend twenty minutes on politely resisting his attempts to make me feel better or explain away what I had found. A picture was worth a thousand words.

I had a momentary panicked thought that he might not be home, but then I realized that I could hear new noises coming from his house. This time more of a scraping and a thud than rhythmic banging. Whatever he was doing, he was hard at it, but he'd just have to take a break for a minute until I could get the police to come.

When I went back to his door, he opened it right away. He was sweaty and looked tired, but he still smiled when he saw me. This time when he invited me in, I accepted.

Moving into the foyer and then on into the living room, I had the strangest feeling of familiarity. I didn't remember ever having been in his house before, but I would turn and know what was where before it actually passed into my view. When I sat on the large sofa in front of the fireplace, I unconsciously gripped the arm as though anticipating the deep sink of the sofa cushion before I actually sank down, as though I had sat there many times before.

Even the smells of the place. The room itself, the scent of food cooking in the adjacent kitchen, Jeff himself, it all seemed so known and so right. I realized I was looking around with something close to wonder and I forced myself to focus back on Jeff, who was studying me intently, his face neutral.

I pulled up my photo gallery app and awkwardly thrust the phone towards him. "Look at this. I found this in…" I realized with a mixture of embarrassment and dim horror that I was still wearing the same jeans I had found the teeth in. Who does that? Why hadn't I thought to change? "in my house. I found these bloody teeth in my house this morning."

His eyes widened as he looked at the first picture and swiped to the second. "Where did you find these? I mean, where in the house?"

Fuck. Well, I was going to have to tell the police anyway. "In my jeans. In the pocket. I swear, I have no idea how they got there. I don't know who would do this or why, and I…" I trailed off as Jeff reached forward and took my hand.

"I know why. I know we agreed I wouldn't say anything, but I can't watch you like this any more." He was staring at me with tears in his eyes, and I felt a stirring of new emotion as I looked at him and squeezed his hand. Then the banging started again.

Jeff stood up, his expression darkening. "Son-of-a-motherfucker. Can't give us a fucking moment's peace?" He was stalking out of the living room toward the back of the house when I heard a cracking sound like wood splintering, followed by a loud thud. I stood up and started out toward the hall myself, and that's when I ran into the naked, bloody man barreling toward the front door.

"Cas! Stop him!" That wasn't my name, but I felt myself responding to it nonetheless. With a swiftness and certainty of body that my mind didn't share, I shoved the man back. He stumbled, his eyes widening as he looked at me. He began to let out a strange, horrible wail, his mouth wet and wide as he screamed, and for a moment he seemed unsure whether to go backward to where Jeff was or keep heading toward me and the front door.

That was all the time it took for me to grab a hammer from the hallway table and bring it across his face. The man was a good foot taller than me, and the blow sent his head up and back at a sharp angle as I heard his jaw crack. Instead of feeling horrified, I felt a strange combination of joy and pride at what I had done. When the man tumbled back to the floor, he made a few more mewling sounds of fear and pain, his animal Os of panicked breathing having turned into lopsided ovals with his newly shattered jaw. Still, I could see well enough into his mouth to spot the toothless gums and tongueless root that lived there.

I looked at Jeff, who was walking toward me beaming. "Great job, sweetie. Really great job. I'm sorry, I think I didn't secure him well enough when you rang the door this time." He paused as he reached the man, giving him a kick in the head that sent him the rest of the way into unconsciousness. Looking up at me, his eyes were worried again. "Are you okay? Do you remember now?"

I realized I did. Or at least parts. Sitting the hammer back on the table, I folded my arms. "I think? This is my house isn't it? Our house." Jeff nodded, smiling wider. "And we're married. We've been married for eight years?"

He chuckled. "Nine last month, but close enough. What else?"

"My name isn't June, is it? It's Cassidy."

Nodding, Jeff stepped around the man and touched my arm gently. "That's right. June is actually your sister's name. Or was. She died when you were ten."

I frowned and nodded at the memory. He was telling the truth. "And we...we have people we take, right? We have a special room for them where we help them?"

He gave my arm a squeeze. "Exactly right. We help them by hurting them."

I smiled a little at that, but there were still things I didn't understand. "Why...Why was I over at that house?"

Jeff's eyes grew sad again as he looked in the direction of the house I had woken up in that morning. "That...well, we're trying that out to see if it works." He looked back at me. "Honey, you're such a wonderful person. So tender-hearted. And we *are* helping people, you've convinced me of that without question. But it's not an easy thing to do. We have to hurt people so much, take so many lives, and sometimes it just seems to overwhelm you for a little while."

He sighed and rubbed his hand through his hair. "About three years ago, I woke up one morning and you were gone. Not in the house, no note or sign of where you had went. You left your car and cell phone behind." His lips trembled as he went on. "I was terrified. I searched for you for two days with no luck. Then you called me. You were 200 miles away and had just remembered who you were. I went and got you, and we backtracked your route to try and figure out where you'd gone and why. We found out you'd walked to a bus station and travelled to the town where I picked you up. That you were looking for work and calling yourself your sister's name."

I was feeling relief as my memories returned, and his words were helping with that. It was like he was slowly turning on more lights in a vast room. But there were still patches of darkness, and it scared me a little. "Why did I do that? Did we figure it out? What's wrong with me?"

"It's called a disassociative fugue. As best we can tell, either due to the stress of what we do, or for some other reason maybe, occasionally you just…go away for a little while. The second time was last year, and it was easier to find you. The house next door wasn't occupied and I found you sleeping there. You still thought you were June, but you kind of remembered me—as your neighbor Jeff." He laughed ruefully and went on, "It was weird, but we dealt with it. I got you to come over to "visit", and after a few minutes here you came back to yourself."

"We talked about it, and took the chance you might go back to the house again if you knew it was available and it was separate from here. So we bought it, and you visit it once a week and I don't go over there often. What we do here," he gestured to the man at our feet, "that doesn't ever go over there. We hoped it would be a safe haven when you needed it, and its working. Well, pretty much at least."

He stopped and looked apologetic. "I know this is a lot."

I smiled. "It's okay. It helps." The man, a carpenter we caught working late and alone two states over last month, started to stir. "We better get him back." Jeff nodded and between us we started dragging him back into the inner chambers of the house. "I woke up this morning to banging. Was it him?"

Jeff shook his head as he reached back to punch the keypad lock on the door. "No, it was one of the girls. She had pried off part of the padding on the outer wall. I don't know if she was trying to get help or break through the wall, but of course she didn't make much progress before I stopped her. Poor thing." He looked sheepish. "Sorry it woke you though. And I can't believe I didn't think about you accidently carrying something over there with you. We were doing a shedding yesterday and I guess you just put some teeth in your pocket."

A "shedding", I remembered, was when we took one or more of our guests and stripped away parts of their bodies, be it hair and teeth or flesh and limbs. We had found that periodically doing several at the same time was not only a time-saver, but it maximized the fear and despair that was generated by them watching each other take part in the shedding. I now remembered slipping a few of the teeth into my pocket with the idea that they would make an interesting component of a craft project. Maybe even part of a baby rattle when the time was right.

We were going down the short ramp to the main room now, but first we had to get through two more locked doors. At the last door the man had roused enough to limply struggle, but I gave him a stern look and he settled down. I know it's not always true, but I like to think many of our guests come to see that what we're doing is for their own good.

This room was my favorite in the house. Thirty feet long and twenty feet wide, it had white tile floors and walls, though both the walls and ceilings had thick layers of heavy-duty padding like you find in padded cells at a mental institution. The padding was pricey, but well-worth it. They are made not just for taking away hard surfaces and sharp edges--they're excellent soundproofing too.

All told we had 9 guests currently, though two of those would soon be past further help it seemed. I saw the little girl he was talking about, Lisa, who had been prying at the padding. She tried hiding her bloody fingers when we drug the man by, and I gave her a smile and a wink. It was always a blessing to get one so young--before the world had a chance to put more obstacles in their way. I looked at the sigil I had painted on the far end of the room--it reminded me of a child's drawing of a house with a downward arrow inside, but its power and significance were never lost on me when I saw it. We were doing such good work here.

"You feeling okay? No weirdness or confusion?" Jeff was easing the man over to his spot along the wall, but his eyes were on me. "I might not should have pushed you to remember like I did. We had talked about letting it play out like…"

"…I was sleepwalking, right." I gave him a grin. "I'm okay I think. And I know it's hard on you when I get like that. Don't worry. You take good care of me."

He secured the man to the railing bolted to the wall and stood again, stretching his back before coming over to me. He gave me a warm hug and I squeezed him back tightly, my heart close to bursting. "We take good care of each other. And we always will."

We stood like that for a few seconds, our faces buried in the space between us. I felt so lucky. I have love and a purpose. I have…

I pulled back from Jeff a little to look down the room to where that same little girl was tugging desperately at the chains securing her to the wall railing. She really was a firecracker, wasn't she? Good for her. It was getting to be time for the girl's first shedding, and the strong-willed ones always benefited the most. Smiling to myself, I turned back and hugged Jeff again.

I'm home.

I keep killing my husband and he keeps coming back.

It was about a week ago when I first dreamed about killing my husband. In the dream, we were sitting in our little breakfast nook eating bagels and drinking coffee, which is something we typically do when we first get up on the weekends. I had gotten up to get the cream cheese out of the refrigerator and was coming back to the table, tub of cream cheese in one hand and butter knife in the other, when I suddenly dropped the tub and leapt onto my husband. My butt banged painfully into the table, shoving it back and sending coffee and bagels everywhere, but I didn't care. I was intent on driving the butter knife deep into the soft flesh of his abdomen.

It was surprisingly easy given the dullness of the knife, and when I woke up I remember feeling a dim sense of satisfaction at my bloody work. Then it transmogrified into horror and disgust as my waking mind surfaced from the black and murky waters of sleep, and I immediately turned and looked to find Ronald, my sweet husband of nearly 15 years, sleeping peacefully beside me unharmed.

I was initially shaken up by the dream, but out of some combination of guilt and wanting to share an interesting story, I told Ronald about the dream at dinner that night. He had listened intently, and I was worried it was going to hurt his feelings or be misconstrued as some subconscious sign of marital problems that weren't there. But when I got to the part about me waking up and checking on him, he just roared with laughter. Wiping his eyes, he told me not to worry about it. Dreams didn't mean anything and it was probably just a sign I was stressed or had eaten something that didn't agree with me. In the moment I had agreed with him, feeling a sense of relief after worrying about it all day. But then that night, it happened again.

This time we were in Ronald's car, though I was driving, and if I remember right we were on our way to go see a movie. One minute we are talking about reviews we had read about the thing we're going to see, and the next I'm repeatedly stabbing him in his left side with an icepick I had apparently hid in the driver's side door pocket at some point earlier. He was screaming in pain and I almost lost control of the car, the wheel jerking this way and that before I managed to get a decent grip with my blood-slick hands. I managed to get the car stopped half a foot from the ditch, and I looked over to see the ice pick still sticking out from under his armpit, blood squirting out around it in time with his dying heart. I started to yell, and then I was awake again.

This time I woke Ronald up, his expression confused and irritated as I asked if he was okay. He said he was, and I could tell he wanted to go back to sleep, but I insisted he stay awake long enough for me to tell him my dream. By this point I was so upset that telling the story felt akin to popping a blister. The pressure inside me had to be let out, and talking to him was the only way I knew how. So he listened groggily as I recounted my second time killing him, his expression becoming more serious toward the end.

"Look, Patricia. I can tell you're upset about it, but it's really nothing. People have repetitive or similar dreams all the time. And yeah, it'd be nice if you'd stop dreaming about murdering me," he chuckled at this part, but went on, "but it's not the end of the world or a sign that something is wrong. You probably just have it on your mind, that's all. Try to let it go and I bet the dreams go away."

That sounded good in theory, and I did try to not dwell on it throughout the day. That night, I took a sleeping pill in the hopes I would get a good night's rest and have a dreamless sleep. Instead, I dreamed that I shot Ronald in the chest as he was getting out of the shower.

By this point, I was pretty much a wreck. I made an appointment with a therapist for the following week and I kept quizzing Ronald on any strange behaviors he had seen from me. Any signs I was having mental problems or had some kind of brain tumor or something. That night, he finally just slid over and hugged me, holding me as I cried against his shoulder. I felt like I was losing my mind, and I loved him so much for being understanding. Looking back, I realize now I smelled the strange, waxy smell even then, but at the time I was too focused on my worry and guilt to realize it.

That night it was a thin, braided wire held tight against his neck as I kneeled on his back and sawed back and forth with all my strength. This happened in our bed, with him on his stomach and thrashing about for air as blood began to soak the sheets. I woke up in a cold sweat, and after checking on him, I went into the living room, my whole body shaking. I stayed there until he woke up and came down in the morning, and that's when I told him I was going to sleep in the guest room until this was resolved. I didn't know if it would help anything, but I had to try something until I could talk to a doctor.

Ronald didn't like it, but he agreed. He suggested I stay home from work for a couple of days and try to relax, but I couldn't. Work was the only real distraction I had. Besides, if it kept on like this, I might need any leave time I had accrued. I found myself googling the steps needed to voluntarily commit yourself. I didn't like the idea, but something was terribly wrong, and I didn't know if I trusted myself around Ronald with things as they were.

That night Ronald had a work meeting that was going to go late, so I decided to do some cleaning. I had all this nervous energy, and while the house was not that messy, my hope was that if I tired myself out maybe I could go a night without the dreams. I scrubbed down the kitchen and the bathrooms, and then I went to change the sheets. As expected, the mattress showed no signs of the bloodbath from the dream where I had garroted him in bed.

But that wasn't the only blood that was missing.

Back two years ago, I had a sinus infection that gave me terrible nosebleeds. One night I had bled onto the bed before I woke up, and when I checked the mattress later, there was a dime-sized circle of dried blood stained onto the edge of the mattress near the seam. I never mentioned it to Ronald, but I always noticed it when I changed the sheets.

Now it was gone.

I scoured the surface of the mattress, thinking I was either misremembering the exact spot or just overlooking it. Nothing. Then I flipped the mattress over, but it was clean as well. While it looked just the same, this was not the same mattress.

My stomach began twisting into hard knots as I paced around the house. I didn't know what to do. I knew something was going on, but I was afraid I didn't have enough proof to confront Ronald and learn if he knew more about it. When he came home, he seemed normal as always, giving me a sad look when I went to bed in the guest room.

That night I dreamed that I stabbed him in the back with a butcher knife, the handle partially breaking as I hit his ribs and spine. But I kept going, my hands still curled as though they were holding the knife when I woke up in a panic. I lay there sweating and crying for half an hour before I realized I hadn't checked on Ronald yet. He was sleeping soundly when I looked in on him.

In the last few days he had taken to wearing these high-collar, long-sleeved pajamas I got him for Christmas a few years back. This was different from the t-shirt and shorts he normally wore to bed. I hadn't thought anything about it at first, other than maybe he was trying to make me feel better by wearing an old gift he'd never really liked.

Now though, I wondered. The weather was warm and the pajamas covered more, not less. I started edging toward the bed, having some irrational desire to really check him out and make sure he was okay. As though he could be lying to me about having been shot and stabbed and choked to death. I was less than five feet away when the floor betrayed me with a wooden creak. I looked down at my feet for a moment, and when I looked back up, Ronald was looking at me.

"Another dream?"

I nodded, not trusting myself to speak.

He nodded back and began getting up. "I'm sorry, honey. I know it's hard on you. I think it'll be over soon, one way or the other, but just try to stay strong for now." He glanced at the clock, which read 5:32. "I think I'm going to go ahead and get up. I have some stuff I need to get done early at work." He looked back at me. "You okay?"

I cleared my throat and looked away. "Yeah, I think I'm going to take a mental health day today though. Try to figure some things out."

Ronald reached out and patted my shoulder. "That sounds like a good idea. Just try and relax."

An hour later he was gone and I was in the bathroom inspecting the shower.

It had occurred to me after I had woken up from the last dream. When I had shot him in the shower, I remember the bullet going through his arm and chest and hitting the tile wall of the shower, sending a spray of porcelain out at the impact. So I started looking at the tiles around the height the shot would have hit, and it didn't take long for me to find what I was looking for.

One of the tiles was new. It was a very close match, but you could tell it was slightly brighter than the rest and the grout around it was fresh, despite someone's efforts to make it look worn and discolored with age. I could barely hear my own thoughts for the static buzz of panic in my ears. I went to the breakfast nook and looked for any signs of that attack, but I found none. I guessed there would likely be something overlooked in his car, given all the nooks and crannies, but even if I could find it, I wasn't sure when I could get lengthy access to it without risking Ronald finding out.

I almost called him right then to confront him, but decided against it. First, I needed to check the house over for any other signs of what was going on. Really search from top to bottom before he or whoever was doing this to us knew that I had caught on.

I spent the next six hours going over the house, and I was almost ready to give up. Exhausted and smelly, I was doing a final sweep of the attic when I noticed something tucked away in the far corner. It was a small duffel bag I had never seen before. Inside it were some tubes and cases of make-up in brands I had never heard of before and two large jars of something called "restorative wax".

Carrying the bag downstairs, I got on the internet and looked up the items from the bag. The makeup was commonly used in funeral homes to prepare bodies for viewings. And the restorative wax was something undertakers used to cover up wounds on a corpse.

I ran to the bathroom and began to vomit. That's likely why I didn't hear Ronald coming in. He had taken off early to come check on me, and when I saw him standing in the doorway to the bathroom, looking down in concern at me huddled against the toilet, I screamed. Both from surprise and, for the first time since I had met him twenty years earlier, fear. I recoiled against the bathtub at the sight of him, telling him to stay back.

He frowned sadly. "I saw the duffel on the table when I came through. I guess you've figured some things out and I have some explaining to do." His expression was sheepish, as though he had stayed out late drinking with friends or forgotten our anniversary. I was at a loss for words. "See, I've been going through…a period of personal and spiritual growth of late." He raised his hand. "I haven't been trying to keep it from you, sweetie, but some of it…well, some of it is fairly out there, and I didn't think you would understand until I could show you results."

I stood up shakily. "Let me out of the bathroom." When he started to protest, I glared at him. "Let me out of this fucking bathroom. Then we will talk."

He nodded and stepped aside with a furrowed brow. I bolted past him, reaching the door of the bedroom before stopping and turning around. "Okay. You stay fucking there and you tell me what's going on." I was going to stop there, but then I heard myself blurting out, "Are you dead?"

Ronald let out a short burst of laughter before catching himself. "Shit. Sorry. No. I'm not dead. Not any more, at least. But that's what I'm trying to tell you about. You see.."

"Did I fucking kill you? Like, several times?"

He sighed. "Yes, technically you did. But it's okay. With this new thing I'm a part of, I come back. But still, I know how hard this has been on you. I've wanted to tell you so bad, and I swear, only a few more times and it will be finished."

I felt dizzy, like my head had been stuffed with cotton soaked in rum and cocaine. Putting my hand against the bedroom door for support, my teeth gritted from both my anger and the effort to stay in the conversation at all.

"A few more times? You fucking bastard. What are you talking about? How have you been getting me to do it at all?"

He raised his hands to me in a placating gesture, taking a step forward before retreating at my glare. "It's part of the process. My new friends, they have developed ways to facilitate all of this. You don't understand, it has to be you. It won't work nearly as well if I wasn't being hurt and killed by someone I love, and there's no one I love as much as you." When I just stared at him, he pushed on. "Look, they have been controlling you at times during the night. They told me you probably wouldn't remember, but when you had the dreams about what you did after we'd put you to bed, I figured we could just push through it. But you kept having them and getting more upset…and now I can see you've figured some of it out."

He rubbed his eyes. "Two or three more times. That's all we need. And you'll see what I become and you'll understand. You'll want me to do it to you, and I will, because you are my best friend and I want to share this with you."

I pushed down the urge to vomit again. "Just stop. I don't know what crazy, sick shit this is, but I want no part of it. I don't know if I even believe any of this at all."

He smiled sadly. "I understand. Let me show you." He started unbuttoning his shirt, but then he paused. "Now don't judge this too harshly. I know it will look bad, and this is largely because we're only part way done. But just try not to get too scared or judgmental about it. Work in progress and all that." Ronald continued taking his shirt off, and immediately I could spot a couple of different spots where the restorative wax and makeup were starting to slough off his multitude of wounds. At first, I thought it was just due to him moving around and sweating, my brain dealing with this impossible horror in a strangely detached and clinical way. But then I realized it was because something was pushing out the clay and makeup from inside the wounds.

Within a matter of seconds, several mottled brown tendrils ranging from one to three inches long snaked their way out of the wounds on his torso and neck. They glistened in the late afternoon light coming through the window as they whipped back and forth with a shared rhythm and cadence. I felt something start to give in my mind as I took them in. Then I realized Ronald was smiling, his arms extended as he started walking towards me.

"Aren't they beautiful?"

I ran. I flew through the house, snatching up my purse as I bolted for the door and out to my car. Ronald didn't immediately follow me outside, but as I was driving away I saw him walk out into the road. His shirt was back on and he was wearing a forlorn look as he watched me go.

That was two days ago. Since then I've been staying in a motel room over a hundred miles away, trying to figure out what to do or who to turn to. I've still been considering strongly that I'm insane, but when I listen to the voicemails that Ronald leaves, full of "I'm sorry" and "you'll come to understand", I'm not sure I'm hallucinating at all. I do know that I haven't had bad dreams for the last two nights.

But I'm not sure how long that will last. Two hours ago, there was a knock at the door to my room. It was Ronald. I didn't respond, but he still stood outside and talked to me through the door for over ten minutes. He was telling me how much he loves me, how he regrets not being more open from the beginning, how he will make it up to me. But he was also saying that he had to finish it now or it would go bad for him. Bad for both of us. That the people he was tied up with, they were wonderful souls, but they had a very low tolerance for mistakes and half-measures.

He said he could feel the things inside of him growing restless and unsatisfied. That they needed him to be complete, that they couldn't understand why there had been two days without any progress. He said he could tell they were unhappy because they had started to bite him a lot more often.

He left the door after that, but when I look out the window I can still see him sitting outside at the edge of the parking lot. He looks so sad and alone, and even from a distance I can tell he's lost weight. Every few seconds I see him grimace and shift uncomfortably, and I can only imagine what those things are doing to his insides.

If I try to leave, he may try to stop me. I could call the police, of course, but is that what I want? Or do I want to try to help him, despite all that's happened? I know I love him, and it's painful looking out there and seeing him waiting for me. And I know that I'm afraid. Afraid that if he comes back scratching at my door again, I might just let him in.

Come see what's in the tunnel.

When I was growing up, I lived in a small town called Coventry. We moved away when I was fifteen, but I always considered Coventry to be my hometown, and Mike Mattis was always my best friend. We moved to another state, so I only saw Mike a couple of times between the move and college, but we always stayed in touch and even wound up going to the same college the last two years when Mike transferred in from a junior college near Coventry.

After college, I went on to graduate school at Texas A&M for Architectural Design and Mike went back to Coventry where he started teaching at the local high school. Life went on, and we drifted apart some over the years, but when I got married, he was my best man. When we had our first child two years later, he was in the waiting room with me. We were best friends for life, regardless of how often we talked.

Maybe that's why it didn't seem strange when I stopped hearing from him for several months. Our communications had never been very regular—a text every few weeks, a phone call every couple of months, that kind of thing. And we tried to get together when we could, but in the two years since having our little girl, travel plans had slid to the backburner.

One day I was sitting in a meeting with a potential client, listening to him try to convince us that it should be possible to design his shopping center to be both a palatial shrine to wealth and comfort while still being buildable on a dismally low budget. I was about to tell him for the tenth time that he needed to get with his contractor to talk about the build costs when I heard my phone buzz. I picked it up and saw it was a text from Mike.

Up for coming back to Coventry for a long weekend?

I didn't respond right away, but the more I thought about it throughout the day and on the way home, the more appealing the idea became. It occurred to me that I hadn't actually been back to Coventry since we moved away over 14 years ago. More importantly, looking back through my call and text logs, I realized it had been nearly four months since I had talked to Mike. Feeling a stab of guilt and nostalgia, I talked to my wife Stacy about it and she was all for it. She'd stay back and take care of our little girl, and I'd talk to Mike about going and staying two or three days when it was good for him.

When I called Mike's phone, no one answered and it said that the voicemail box had not been set up yet. I was going to wait and call again later in the evening, but then my phone lit up with a return phone call from Mike.

"Hey, Parker. Sorry I missed your call, man."

"No problem. Just wanted to call after getting your text. How've you been doing?"

"Good, real good. Things have been real good here. Hey, you up for coming back to Coventry for a long weekend?" Mike's voice was slightly strange, almost like he was distracted or stressed out about something. And his question struck me as oddly awkward, mimicking the text message word for word and sounding almost as though he was reading from a telemarketer script and was new at the job. It was the opposite of the way he normally was—if anything Mike normally took things *too* easy, and I had never known him to be awkward talking to anyone, let alone me.

Still, it had been a few months, and maybe he had something going on. I suddenly worried I'd caught him at a bad time. "Hey…yeah I am, but we can do it later if things are too busy right now. It's up to you." I was barely done with the last word before he was talking again, his tone more strident.

"No. You should come right away." He paused and let out an uneven laugh. When he started back, he sounded like he was forcing himself to be slower and calmer, more laidback sounding. "It's all good, man. Miss seeing you. I'd like to show you around the town some too. A lot has changed since you were here."

Deciding I was overthinking it, I pushed on. "Cool, man. How's next weekend sound? I could fly in Friday morning and fly out

Sunday night. If you want to pick me up at the Glenville airport, that's cool, if not I can rent a car. What do you think?"

"Sounds great. Just send me the flight information and I'll pick you up."

When I got off the phone, I told Stacy about the weirdness of the conversation, but she agreed that he was probably just preoccupied or just woke up or something else innocuous. He was my best friend, and I should go see him, and it would be cool to see how the town had changed. She had never seen my hometown, so she made me promise to take lots of pictures. An hour later I had booked a flight for the following Friday morning.

****

The Glenville airport was tiny and dingy, consisting of a single brown brick hallway with a rental car kiosk and metal detectors on one end and the waiting area for the single terminal on the other. The small connecting flight had consisted of me and only a handful of other travelers, so there weren't but a couple of people waiting for the plane's arrival when I entered the building. Still, it took me a few seconds to recognize Mike.

As I said, I hadn't seen him since my daughter's birth two years earlier, but in that time he must have lost close to a hundred pounds, about seventy of which he didn't have to spare. He looked gaunt and sickly, and while I tried to not let it show in my expression, as I hugged his bony frame I felt a caustic mixture of fear and guilt curdling in my chest. My first thought was cancer or some immune disease. Clearly something was wrong. I had intended on waiting and broaching the topic more tactfully, but when I pulled back and saw his pale blue eyes in their dark and sunken sockets, watched his thin, cracked lips stretched over teeth that seemed too big in his now gaunt face, it just spilled out.

"Fuck man, are you sick? You've lost a ton of weight." I could hear the worry in my voice, but there was some accusation and anger too. Why hadn't he told me he was going through all this? I could have helped, or at least talked to him more. He was already shaking his head though, a deep laugh in his too pale throat.

"No, Park. Nothing like that. I have lost a lot of weight, that's true. At first, I was doing it on purpose. I was running a lot, trying to build up to do marathons. Then I got hit with this weird gastro thing for awhile. It fucked me up for about six weeks, and I only got over it last month. I had already lost about thirty pounds before I got sick, and I dropped another forty eating broth and crackers for so long." He grinned. "I know I still look like shit, but I'm on the mend. Just got checked last week and the doc said I've gained back 12 pounds so far. Trying to do it slow and steady. The healthy way."

I frowned, not sure I believed him, but desperately hoping that it was true. And I worried I'd hurt his feelings. "Look, you don't look like shit. You're just really skinny and it scared me for a second. If you say you're over it though, that's great. I just was worried."

Mike laughed again and gave me a light shove. "I appreciate it. I'm so glad you're here."

We headed out to his car—the same beat-up SUV he'd had since he crashed his old car the last year of college—and headed out of town toward Coventry. He asked a few questions about Stacy and the baby, and there were times during the drive that he almost seemed like his old self. But then he would suddenly trail off and go silent in the middle of asking a question or telling a story like a weak radio signal fading out as you drive along. Then right when I'd be on the edge of asking if something was wrong, he'd pick back up with something else, talking about the little shits in the classes he taught or how he was so ready to be living on his own again.

He warned me that we were going to his parents' house to stay, as he had been staying there since he was so sick and all his stuff was still there. He looked slightly embarrassed, but I told him I remembered that his mom was a great cook and I knew he couldn't cook for shit, so it was an upgrade. He laughed and shrugged.

"We'll see what you think of her cooking now. We're all on kind of a health food kick since I got so sick—all organic stuff, no meat, no gluten. You get used to it, but it might be a bit of a shock to your system."

I grinned, looking out at the countryside as we rode along. It really was good to be back. The country out here was beautiful, and I had a lot of good memories from growing up around here. "I'm sure I'll manage. So, what do you want to do while I'm out here? I'm up for whatever, or just hanging out with you eating kale."

Mike snickered and glanced at me. Suddenly his face grew inexplicably sad. "You really are a good guy, Parker. A good friend. My best friend."

I frowned. "Yeah man, of course. You're my best friend too. Are you sure you're okay? You can tell me if something else is going on."

He just looked at me for several moments, his expression still stricken, his lips moving wordlessly as though caught between a whisper and a sigh. Then his eyes cut away and back to the road, and when he spoke, his voice sounded strange again like it had been on the phone. "No, everything is fine. Just glad you could come."

We drove on in silence for several minutes, and I could see Mike's hands flexing as he clenched the steering wheel. Finally, his grip relaxed, and when he spoke next it was in a more conversational tone. "So, about things to do. I can show you around the town, of course. A lot has changed since you were last here. It's grown some, though its still small compared to something like Glenville. We can go bowling at the new alley that opened up a few years ago. It's a nice place and they have a tendency to hire hot college girls to work the counters."

I snorted. "Aren't you getting a bit old for trolling for college girls at a bowling alley?"

He shrugged. "Coventry doesn't have the largest dating pool, and while I admit this is a bit hypocritical since I live there myself, I find that women my age around here—that aren't already married at least—tend to not be awesome. At least with the college girls, there's a hope I can find a girl who is intelligent and ambitious enough to still get out while the getting's good."

Laughing, I shoved him in the arm. "Oh, so you're going to find some hard-working girl with a bright future and ride her coattails out of town?"

He started to respond, and then stopped, his expression darkening. "No, though that's a nice idea. But no, man. I'll never go anywhere else. I'm going to die right here in Coventry." I didn't know what to say. I was still trying to come up with something that could be encouraging without sounding patronizing when his expression smoothed and he glanced at me again. "One thing you have to do while you're here is go see the new tunnel."

I raised an eyebrow. "The new tunnel? What new tunnel?"

His lips stretched back in a strange smile. "Oh, its really something. Out on the north side of town where they used to have the big horse ranch? It's grown up out there a lot more now—they're even putting in a new Wal-Mart close by. But that tunnel…well, you just have to wait and see."

I was going to ask more questions, but I realized we were slowing to a stop. Looking up, I saw why. We were at his parents' house.

****

Mike's parents lived in an older ranch-style house. They'd lived there since I was twelve, and I remember always being amazed at how clean and well-kept it always was. Not that my family's houses growing up were terrible, but between Mr. Mattis keeping up the yard and the exterior and Mrs. Mattis keeping the inside immaculate, I always felt a little like I was walking into an idealized version of what a family home should be.

This extended to Mike's parents' themselves. His father was a kind-hearted man who ran a local hunting supply store and was always quick with a funny story or joke. His mother had been like a second mom to me growing up. She ran her own accounting firm and was always running around, but she was also one of the few adults that seemed to actually care what was going on in Mike's life and my own beyond the normal cursory check that we weren't being abducted or hooked on drugs.

Seeing the house now was almost as big of a shock as seeing Mike himself. More than one shutter was partially fallen down, and a ragged blue tarp was draped like a sash around the chimney, presumably to try and stop a leak. The yard was a thick mess of weeds, and as we entered the house, the sense of clutter and disuse only multiplied. It wasn't filthy, and I understood that people sometimes let their housekeeping slide as they get older, but it was such a sharp contrast from what I remembered.

Mike led me down the hall to the guest bedroom so I could put my stuff down, and as we passed the kitchen I saw his parents from behind. They were standing side by side, still and silent as statues, staring at the faded floral wallpaper on the far kitchen wall. I was going to say something, but there was something so unnatural about what I was seeing that an inner voice or instinct warned against it, and I wound up just moving on down the hall to where Mike was waiting.

After I put my stuff down in the guest room, I asked if we should stick around for a bit so I could say hey to his parents. Mike seemed to ponder it momentarily and then shrugged. "Nah, let's just catch up with them tonight. We can grab lunch out and then go goof off for awhile. I think Mom's planning on fixing a big dinner for us anyway."

I nodded and followed him back out, stealing a glance back into the kitchen as we passed. There was no one there now, and we saw no signs of his parents as we went outside and got in his SUV. I was still uneasy about how strangely they had been standing in the kitchen and how Mike was acting, but I tried to set it aside, deciding that I would chalk it up to an overactive imagination unless something else strange popped up.

The afternoon was actually good. Mike took me by his high school and showed me his classroom. School was out for the summer and all of the rooms were in disarray from the custodians re-waxing all the floors, but it was nice to see a part of Mike's life that was relatively normal. It was weird to think of him as a grown-up with a grown-up job, but he seemed to like it despite all his complaining, and I had no doubt he was a good teacher.

We then went to get something to eat, but the first two restaurants were closed despite it being early in the afternoon. We ultimately settled for a fast food drive-thru before heading to the bowling alley. The bowling alley wasn't in as good of shape as I had expected based on what Mike had said, but then the same could be said for much of Coventry.

It was strange—portions of town would be in relatively good repair while others seemed to be entering a sharp decline. This can happen in any town, of course, but what was odd was *how* it was happening here. There was no rhyme or reason to it, with a well-kept building side by side with those headed towards ruination. There were no "nice" or "not nice" parts of town, so far as I could see. There were still smaller houses in poorer neighborhoods and larger ones in wealthier areas, but the neglect and air of disuse was spread equally among everyone. When I mentioned it to Mike as we were getting out at the bowling alley, he just shrugged and laughed.

"Yeah, property values and stuff have been all over the place lately. I think it'll get better with time though. I think that new tunnel is going to help things a lot in the long run."

I almost stopped walking and forced him to tell me more about the tunnel. I should have. But I was enjoying being back around him, and it seemed like it was doing him a lot of good too. So I just smiled and nodded, pushing my worry down as we entered the bowling alley.

The place was relatively clean inside, though it was dimly lit in spots due to overhead lights that had gone out and not been replaced. Mike led me up to the counter where a young woman stood staring at us.

The girl probably was of college age, but it was hard to say for sure due to her appearance. Her curly brown hair hung in damp, tangled strings down the sides of her long, pale face. Her skin had an unhealthy, waxy quality to it, and the glazed look in her eyes made me think she was either high or suffering from a substantial fever. The worst thing was that she had these clusters of pus-filled sores festooning the skin around both nostrils. I had to fight from reacting as we approached, and when Mike asked for shoes, I echoed him dimly with my own size while trying to avoid looking at her further without being obvious. It didn't stop me from noticing that one of the sores was starting to drip down onto her lips as she handed me my pair.

When we were away from her and at lane 12 putting on our shoes, I whispered to him, "What is wrong with her? That's not acne."

Mike glanced toward the front counter and then at me. "Yeah, she's sick with something, I don't know. That kind of thing has been going around lately. Luckily my stomach problems didn't include killer pimples." He tried to smile but it faltered. "I do feel bad for her though. Poor kid." Glancing around at the empty lanes he let out a sigh. "I guess Friday afternoon is not the beehive of activity I was hoping for. Still, when's the last time you had a nice quiet bowling alley all to yourself?"

****

Dinner was surprisingly normal until the end. Mike's parents were older and a little odd, but more in the normal way you expect people to get in the last third of their life. They would talk over each other, repeat themselves occasionally, and take turns pelting me with questions about my life. It was kind of sweet, and it filled me with a profound sense of relief to just laugh and talk with these people that used to be a big part of my life without any of the disquieting strangeness I'd been seeing lately.

The meal itself was not great, but it certainly seemed healthy. Grilled artichokes and steamed kale along with a small cold salad that seemed to be a mixture of tomatoes, cucumbers, and some odd vegetable I couldn't identify. I took a bite of it and my mouth filled with a pungent, smoky-tasting liquid that I assumed came from the inside of the vegetable. Grimacing, I caught myself before I swallowed and spat it out into my napkin. I didn't know what that was, but I didn't want any. I could even feel a light tingling numbness on my tongue and lips from it.

After we had finished eating and the conversation was starting to die down, Mike's dad asked what we were going to do the next day. I shrugged and said I was up for whatever, with Mike adding in that he was thinking about taking me to the old state park west of town to go hiking in the morning. I remembered us camping out there with Mike's dad when we were twelve or so, and I was already nodding enthusiastically at the idea of visiting it again.

Mike's father smiled thinly as he looked at Mike. "That sounds just fine. Just make sure you take him to see the tunnel. It's really something." His gaze shifted to me. "You really won't believe it."

At this point I'd had enough. "Okay, what is it about this tunnel? Mike keeps talking about it, now you are too. Is it some kind of practical joke, or is there really a tunnel north of town?

Mike was looking nervous—possibly even scared—as he responded, his eyes going between me and his father. "No, it's there. And it is very interesting, but we can talk more about it later." Looking back at me, he added. "It's not a big deal and we don't have to see it if you don't want to." I saw his father staring at Mike out of the corner of my eye. I turned to face him while talking to Mike, catching the older man's gaze again.

"No, Mike. I'm fine to see it. But what is it? Why do we have a tunnel around here anyway? Most of the land around here is flat. Did we suddenly grow a mountain I'm not aware of?" Mike's father just stared back at me silently, his expression stony. When Mike didn't respond, I addressed his father. "What about you, Mr. Mattis? Can you tell me why there's a tunnel here and what's so great about it?"

The man's lips stretched tight across his face, slowly slipping back to reveal his gray, receding gums and his long, yellowed teeth. It looked less like a smile and more like a rabid dog bearing his teeth. He looked at me steadily, and I could see a trace of yellow around his irises that matched his mouth. He clicked his teeth together once, twice, and then turned his poached egg eyes back to Mike. "He'll understand better when he sees it, son. You make sure he sees it tomorrow."

With that, he stood up and tapped Mike's mother on the shoulder where she was standing at the sink. Without another word, they both left the kitchen and moved out of sight down the hall. When I felt they were likely out of earshot, I looked back at Mike.

"What the fuck was all that?"

He looked uncomfortable. "You know how it is. People get weird when they get older. The tunnel is just something that got made a few months back and it was a big deal at the time. Part of some new road development or something maybe? But everyone thought it was great at the time, and some people still do. Small towns fixate on anything new, I guess."

What he was saying made no sense, but he looked so desperate for me to believe him, for the conversation to be over, I just nodded. "Okay, man. Well, I think I'm going to get some rest if that's okay with you. Kinda beat."

He nodded, and I stood up to leave the kitchen when he caught my arm. "If you don't feel right about things, if you aren't comfortable here, it's okay for you to go. I mean, I would understand if you wanted to go. Right now even." His expression was sad and he was having trouble meeting my eyes, but as he said the last he looked at me clearly. "If you want to go, right now is a good time."

I considered it seriously. I didn't know what was going on, and I was feeling more and more like I was in the first act of a horror movie. But that was stupid. Things like that didn't happen in real life. There was nothing sinister going on in this town. It was just a rundown little community whose best days were probably behind it. It was just my best friend who had been sick, was lonely, and who felt trapped in the place he had never really left. My best friend who had finally worked up the courage to reach out to me. I wasn't going to abandon him just because I was a little uncomfortable and weirded out.

Shaking my head, I patted his shoulder. "No man, I'm cool. Just really tired. Let me get a good night's sleep and I'll be raring to go tomorrow, promise."

He nodded, the sad look still on his face. "Okay, Park. I...okay."

I gave his shoulder another pat and headed back to the guest room. I heard movement from one of the other rooms that I assumed was his parents' bedroom, but I quickly ducked into my room out of fear that one or both of them were coming back out. I wanted to avoid another run-in for a bit.

Laying down on the bed, I realized I really was exhausted. Without even changing my clothes or turning out the light, I soon found myself fast asleep.

****

I woke up to rough hands toting me by my shoulders and legs through the still-warm night air. I was disoriented at first, in part because when I looked up, I saw Mike's parents and two other people I didn't recognize were carrying me somewhere. Beyond them and between passing street lights I could see the blackness of the summer sky, and looking around I saw I was being carried up a street in a part of town I didn't recognize. I wanted to struggle, but I was coming to realize that I had somehow been drugged. Every attempt to move my limbs felt like I was fighting against quickly drying cement.

I heard Mike's voice a few feet back from the direction we were going. "Fuck, he's waking up! You said he wouldn't wake up before it was over."

One of the men I didn't recognize glared back in Mike's direction. "He has to be awake to appreciate it, doesn't he? He has to look to truly see it and understand." That's when we began to cross the threshold into the tunnel. We were moving at a distinctly downward angle now, and the air was growing cooler as they walked.

Looking at the walls of the tunnel in the fading light, I saw no signs of concrete or wood. Instead, every angle of the tunnel seemed to be made of a packed earth held together by clusters of ebony nodules and gray tendons rippling and twisting through the earth and connecting one group of black barnacle-like protrusions to the next. I redoubled my efforts to move, and while I managed to pull my arm free from Mike's mother's grip for a moment, she quickly regained control. I cast my eyes around for any other avenue of escape.

That's when I saw the stomach of the man who had yelled at Mike. His shirt had ridden up in toting me, and I could see what looked kind of like a handprint on his lower belly. Except the handprint was abnormally long and narrow, with what seemed to be six distinct and spindly fingers. And the print wasn't just some stain or even a burn. It was made up of the same fetid, blossoming sores that had been clustered around that poor girl's nose.

I began to scream then, and a moment later I was on the ground. At first I thought I was being dropped intentionally, but then I saw Mike had shoved down handprint man and then done the same to his father. I understood he was trying to help me, but there was only one of him and I couldn't fight. Just then, the thunder of gunfire echoed in the tunnel, the muzzle flash lighting up the darkness enough for me to see something moving towards us from further within the void.

I don't remember what it looked like now, or how we got out of that tunnel. All I remember is Mike helping me into the driver's seat of his SUV and pressing the keys into my hand. He was sobbing, and his left arm flopped uselessly by his side. He told me I had to go, I had to drive as best I could and get away. Drive back down away from the tunnel, keep going south until I hit the state highway and then pick a direction. Keep going until I got to a bus station or an airport.

I was more lucid now and interrupted him. "No, you need to come with me. I'm not leaving you here."

His shook his head. "I told you, I can't leave here." He reached out and grabbed the sides of my face. "Park, you listen to me. You need to get away now and never come back. I may call or text you, but you never answer, and you never come back."

I didn't fully understand, but I'm ashamed to say I didn't argue further. Whatever shadowy recollection I had of what was in that tunnel was more powerful that my love for my best friend. I drove away and made it to a bus station, then an airport. Mike must have been at least considering this plan for awhile, because I found my wallet in the glove compartment of his car, a new photograph tucked in with my cash.

I made it home eventually, and after some time just holding Stacy and our little girl, I told her what happened. Warned her that we could never go near that place or those people again, including Mike. I don't know that she fully believed me, but she agreed. Then we heard my phone buzz.

She picked it up off the counter and I saw her face pale. When she showed it to me, I saw it was a new text from Mike.

Up for coming back to Coventry for a long weekend?

I took the phone out to the garage and hammered it apart. Changed the number and got a new phone the next day. Less than a week later it buzzed with a new message from Mike.

Up for coming back to Coventry for a long weekend?

We've decided to move now. I'm writing this from a hotel room we're staying in until our new house is ready. The third phone, a burner, hasn't been tracked down yet, so hopefully we're in the clear. Still, I wanted there to be some record of all of this.

I'm holding the photo Mike had put in my wallet, and I'm trying not to wake Stacy with my crying. The picture is one Mike's mother took of us when we were fourteen. We were getting ready to go trick-or-treating despite Mike's father subtly hinting we were too old for it. I think we both knew he was right, but we also knew this was one of the few childhood things we had left. Besides, a week or two earlier my father had gotten notice that the local plant he worked at was closing the following year, which meant we were likely moving to another state in the next few months. So we were going to make the most out of the time we had left.

I look at that picture, reminded of all the memories and emotions I still have from my childhood and my friendship with Mike, and then I think about the last time I saw him in the rearview of his car. Standing on a lonely road, broken and terrified and so hopeless as he watches me go. Watches me leave him one last time. As I started to round the corner that took him out of view, I think he was turning to limp back to the tunnel.

I loved you, Mike. I'm so sorry.

On the Rooftop

You don't seem to understand. Taking you out of this... place...is a mercy. You sit there staring at me, fish-gasping in the stale air of this room and puffing out tiny particles of your decaying lungs. You fucking look at me with your meat, your fucking dying meat, and you think it'll compel me to show you mercy? It just reminds me how much I hate you.

When I came into your house tonight, I could smell you right away. Did you know that? I could smell your filth accruing at every orifice from your eating and shitting and pissing, your body a tomb for the beasts you've eaten, the bacterium you harbor, all dying every moment. You are a grave inside a grave inside a grave, and it disgusts me.

But I didn't just smell your meat. I smelt your sin. That internal corruption that makes you little more than an egotistical, vile monkey. I stand before you, eternal, and your presence offends me. It lessens me somehow. You make me lower myself by compelling such hate and disgust.

And this offering. Is this what passes for a boon? Is this a proper sign of supplication? Treats meant for dogs or peasants. In earlier times, you and your entire family would have been burned alive for even suggesting such an insult.

Stop your sniveling, cretin. I swear I'll cut your eyes from your head if you don't. There is work to be done in the long nights that requires no sight. Hell, blindness may be preferable. But nevermind. I'm tired of this and have far too much to do tonight to prattle on with you.

So get up there. Climb. Don't say you can't, that it's too hard or too narrow. If I manage so can you. And before you think of being pert, let me be clear. If you make another peep, I'll happily go and slit your parents' fat throats. Your little sister, good though she may be, will wake in the morning to find their bodies split wide like the disrespectful hogs they are.

That's right. Keep climbing. Watch their mouths, as they do love to bite. Get in. In the back, fool, and take this. Do not open it or stick your hand in or you will be even more lost than you already are.

Hmph. You look as though you think you are being wronged, when you're actually receiving a great gift. Extended life and purpose without end. Most of them thank me before they expire. Either way, your old life is over.

Shut up your mewling, child, the knife is sharp enough that you're speaking out of fear more than pain. Eat this and you will be healed. Your new life will begin.

That's right. Candy canes are good, right? Better than the tripe you would have me eat. This one is special, you know. Has a bit of me in it. Yes, I think you'll enjoy the work, given time. Don't look at me like that. If I take your eyes now, they'll only grow back, tempting me to take them again. And before you blame me for your lot, for losing the life you had, you need to remember—you've been complicit in your murder since the moment you were born.

That's better. Time to go now. There are a lot more houses to visit tonight. You get motion sick, you lean over the side or I'll skin you for a new belt. Just look up front. Keep your eyes on the one with the glow. I hear that helps sometimes.

Do not accept a download of the app called "Polterzeitgeist!"

I work as a clerk for a large northwestern law firm that is in the process of preparing a class action suit against the makers and distributors of a mobile app called "Polterzeitgeist! Find that ghost!". Due to false names and information being utilized in the initial distribution of the application, the search for the responsible parties is ongoing (so that the suit can be properly served on the defendants). In the meantime, I was tasked with going through the available materials and generating summaries and reports for the attorneys working on the case.

What I found scared me enough that I felt that I needed to issue a warning while attempting to maintain some level of anonymity. I will begin by giving a brief description of the app. "Polterzeitgeist! Find that ghost!" was originally distributed through various means online with the publisher listed as [null143325]. It was later discovered that this was not actually the name of any known publisher, but an error message generated when the required information was somehow removed from the databases of the platforms distributing the app. There is no known record of the actual name of the organization or the people behind the app, and as I said, that investigation is ongoing.

The app is described as a "ghost hunting tool" that uses "crowdsourced EVP (electronic voice phenomenon) and sighting reports to provide likely locations for paranormal activity" as well as "activity-driven and streaming rewards for investigations and live-streams". Basically, the app takes your data and that of others and uses it as a basis for suggesting places to look for ghosts. At the same time, it provides a form of metagame that rewards you with unlockable digital items, cosmetics for your "ghost hunter" avatar, and access to special forums when you post data and when you livestream your investigations through the app.

The livestreaming portion is wholly proprietary, and the app does not work or give any "ghost credits" if you are streaming through another service. Similarly, viewing of a ghost hunter's livestream must be done through the app itself for optimal results. Attempts to watch someone else's phone or tablet through a different streaming service causes severe degradation of video quality caused by what our tech guy is calling "intentional random-sequence frequency modulation". I don't know what any of that means, but the practical effect is that as of three months ago, there were about 3,000 regular stream viewers using the app in the continental United States. Out of that, nearly 600 were watching Sam the Spookhunter when he was murdered.

Sam "the Spookhunter" Morris was a low-tier internet celebrity for the paranormal investigator crowd before Polterzeitgeist!, but he found a much stronger following as one of the first and best streamers on the app. His first few weeks of in-app streaming were unremarkable by most accounts. Then, on June 29, 2018, he started his stream very excited, saying he thought he had just unlocked a secret location. Included below is my summary of this and subsequent streams that I prepared for work. I do not post this lightly or for entertainment value. But I hope it will serve as a better warning than I alone could provide.

****

June 29, 2018

Sam begins stream inside his apartment. He is clearly very excited. He says he has somehow unlocked a secret paranormal hunt called "The Dark Path". He shows the app on his phone, leading to the assumption that he is streaming from another phone or tablet. Given that the app screen is clearly legible, it is to be assumed he was streaming through the app on the tablet.

The app screen says "Welcome to the Dark Path. You have shown bravery and ingenuity in your past investigations, and as a reward, you will be given the opportunity to visit four secret locations that are known for supernatural activities and past atrocities. Are you strong enough to make it to the end?" Below this text, there was the low-resolution map used by the app to guide you to recommended locations. But unlike most users, Sam's map had a pulsing red star in one corner.

He manipulated the map, sliding towards the star and zooming in. He said that he guessed it was about forty miles away, and he was about to head out. Within ten minutes he was on the road, talking to viewers as he drove toward the destination. At one point he stopped for gas, and it was at this time he caught up on reading the chatroom attached to the livestream. Several viewers had searched online for information based on what his destination seemed to be, and no one had found anything remarkable. It was a quiet street in the suburbs with a small bus stop nearby. This didn't rule out something interesting being out there, but it was easy to see that Sam was starting to get worried his trip would be a bust. He begins to sing along with the radio and discuss possible fallback things to do on stream if the red star wound up being nothing.

But it wasn't nothing.

Based on the available information, Sam arrived at the marked location at approximately 10:41 at night. After driving around the area slowly, he eventually parked and tried to zero in on the red star's location by foot. It didn't take long for the young man to realize it was taking him to the aforementioned bus stop, which amounted to little more than a pair of metal benches and a small overhang enclosure to keep waiting riders out of the weather.

He entered the enclosure and panned the camera around, his forced excitement became more genuine as he saw something on the edge of one of the benches. Zooming in, there was a small toy skeleton sitting on the bench. Its white, plastic bones and skull had been smeared with something that looked like blood, and based on his reaction to it, it seems likely Sam truly thought it was blood as well. Next to the skull, a red word had been written on the metal:

What

The first video ends there.

****

July 3, 2018

This video begins with Sam explaining that he was somewhat troubled by what he had found, but he had decided to go ahead with the investigation, noting that a second star had popped up on the map since he found the bus stop. This portion of the video did not seem genuine. It seems likely that, as is a common cliche for both paranormal investigator performances and internet performances, Sam's fear and reluctance to continue were fake. The obvious reason for this is to generate dramatic tension and potentially make relatively mundane events appear more dangerous or interesting. This is in stark contrast to the earnest emotion he sometimes shows at other points in these videos.

Again, he drives to the location of the star while streaming. This point is closer to his apartment, but it requires him to go into a closed construction site to find the exact location of the star. He appears to be truly nervous about trespassing, but in a perceived attempt at false bravado, he makes a point of moving slowly and casually past several pieces of heavy machinery on his way to a office trailer that had been set up by the construction company.

Using his phone's light, he searches around the perimeter of the trailer to no avail. Sam then tries looking underneath it, but there was little access and nothing to be seen of note. At this point he seems close to abandoning the search, but after viewing several encouraging messages in chat, he opts to try the doorknob of the trailer instead.

It opens easily, and the interior is dark. Walking in slowly, you can hear his breath puffing nervously as he quickly shines his light around in a desperate search for whatever sign or clue might be there. It only takes a few seconds for him to find the small black cat toy nailed to the back of the door. Similar to the skeleton, it is covered in what looks like blood. Similar to the skeleton, there is one word written in crimson above the tiny stuffed feline:

does

****

July 5, 2018

This video is longer than the rest, as Sam spends some time at the beginning trying to explain and justify himself in reaction to several criticisms he had received after his earlier videos. Some people were complaining about him doing next to no "investigation" at the locations, likening it more to a televised scavenger hunt than the traditional ghost hunts his viewers were accustomed to. Others noted that he was taking unreasonable risks by following directions from an unknown source that clearly had been to the locations indicated. A handful just called the streams "lame" or hoped "you get your fat ass locked up for trespassing!"

All of this clearly upset Sam, and he awkwardly tried to take up for himself while placating his fanbase. He said that he was trying to play it safe, but that there also just hadn't been much to investigate other than the items and the words themselves. He did promise, however, that the first place he ran across that looked ripe for really exploring, he would do so.

However, it wouldn't be that night. The third star was only ten miles away at a public park. Sitting on the edge of a large stone fountain was a tiny clay pumpkin, and as expected, it was smeared with blood or something similar in appearance. This time there were two words:

the ghost

****

July 12, 2018

This stream also started with a kind of apology, this time for his absence. Sam explained that his father, who lived in the house next door, had recently had a severe stroke, so he had spent the last several days at the hospital and helping his dad transition to a nursing home for rehab. It appears that he is close to tears at this point, but he quickly turns it around by talking about the latest message he received in the app. As before, he shows the screen in the video so the audience can read it.

It said "Congratulations! You have made it to the final turn on the Dark Path. Your final red star location will appear at precisely 9:00pm PST. Good luck!" Despite his earlier sadness, Sam seemed truly excited and nervous about reaching the end of the strange game. He commented that he had twice as many live viewers as he'd ever had before, and it is clear from his conversation with people in his chatroom and his overall demeanor that he doesn't want to let them down.

He also discusses what the Dark Path could really be. It was clear it wasn't really a collection of traditional haunts, and Sam agreed with many of his viewers that it was most likely a promotional contest of some type to get the word out about the app. As 9pm came on, he excitedly showed the tablet's camera the appearance of the new red star. It was only after talking for a few seconds and studying the map that his enthusiasm faded.

The red star was next door at his father's house.

He gave a nervous laugh when he realized this, and there was a moment when he looked into the camera and you could see real fear in his eyes. But then he seemed to shake it off somewhat and started making jokes about how big a deal he must be if they set up the end of the contest this close to his house. He pauses again as he reads his chatroom, and that fearful, haunted look briefly returns to his face. He says several people are telling him not to go over there. That something wasn't right and he should call the police.

He seems to weigh the suggestion before rejecting it, smiling nervously into the camera as he gets up to go over to his father's house. "It'll be okay, guys, I promise. Besides, I have you all to protect me if it gets too scary, right?"

****

July 12, 2018 (Continued on second camera)

Based on the change in image quality and comments by Sam, it appears he abandoned the tablet and began using his phone as his primary streaming device for his journey next door. While not explicitly stated, it can be assumed from the circumstances and Sam's behavior that he wanted less restrictions on his attention and movement during this last leg of the Dark Path, and managing two electronic devices was too unwieldly.

He leaves his apartment and walks next door to a small gray house with peeling paint. After taking a moment to survey the empty street, he walks to the front door and lets himself in. He immediately attempts to turn on the lights in the front hall, but they don't work. You can hear him curse softly as his breath begins to pick up speed. "Things are finally getting really spooky, guys," he says with a shaky laugh. After a moment of looking around with the phone's small flashlight, he moves further up the dark hall.

At this point he has moved past a narrow set of stairs going up to a second floor and has reached the intersection of three doorways. To the left is an open doorway into what looks like a living room from the shadowy glimpses that the camera affords. To the right is a doorway covered by a long curtain—likely a closet or storage area of some kind. Straight ahead is a white door that Sam says leads into the kitchen. He is about to open it when he notices something above the kitchen door.

It is a small ghost that had been fashioned out of dried cornstalk leaves. It wears a tiny black velvet bow tie and would have been very cute if not for the blood coating both it and the wall around it. Written to the left of the bloody ghost is:

say?

What does the ghost say?

The phone is shaking some by this point, and it seems like Sam might be having second thoughts about being in the dark house by himself. He sits silent for several moments, shining his light around in the dark before muttering the completed phrase as though trying to solve the unknown puzzle of it all.

"What does the ghost say?"

"*Boo.*"

Suddenly a large form rushes out from behind the curtain to his right. There is only a glimpse of the figure as Sam drops his phone and starts screaming, but it appears to be a massive man wearing some kind of prosthetic or mask to make himself appear monstrous. When the video is slowed down, there is also some indication of a weapon, though it cannot be clearly discerned beyond appearing to be metallic and heavily serrated.

There is a moment of chaos as Sam's screaming, the sounds of a struggle, and finally a wet, tearing noise occurs off camera. Then the livestream is dead.

****

The audience of that stream had mixed reactions to what they had witnessed. Many thought it was a joke or a sham orchestrated by either Sam, the app developer, or both. Others were genuinely concerned and called authorities either in their own areas or Sam's. There was a brief criminal investigation, but no sign of Sam or his phone was ever found. The only reason we even have a recording is due to one of the viewers having figured out a way to record the streams directly from his phone. And Sam's father died from a follow-up stroke two days after the last video, so there was no one to even file a missing person's complaint on him. Officially, nothing has happened to Sam.

But how, then, did our firm get involved in it? We can't file a lawsuit on behalf of a missing or murdered man.

Because since the night Sam reached the end of the Dark Path, five more people have disappeared. Two of them caught on stream, the other three known users of the app but not streaming at the time whatever happened to them…happened. It was only after six people have been lost that it was taken seriously. Complaints were filed, the apps were removed from most platforms, and criminal investigations were started and then stopped again due to claims of insufficient evidence. After talking to three of the families of the missing, our firm started work on a class action lawsuit for any and all parties injured by the app and whatever lies behind it.

The problem is it's not really over. The app doesn't need to be widely distributed so long as some people continue using it. We starting getting in reports last week that it uses your contacts to email and text out links to new download sites for the app. As of yesterday, the usage rate was up to over 8,000.

So I'm posting this as a warning. Stay away from the app. Tell your friends and family to do the same. And if you get an invitation….well, I don't know what to tell you.

I got my invitation by text three hours ago. It was via a friend I haven't seen since college, but keep up with through social media. I didn't even know she had my phone number. But now I know she does. That they do. And they probably have much more than that.

I'm giving my notice tomorrow, and I think I'm going to use a burner phone for awhile. Unplug a bit, stay in with the doors locked. Not that I'm worried I'd ever go to visit the ghost. I've seen far too much to fall for that.

I'm just worried that the ghost may come to see me.

See you next October

"My mother used to think I was getting abused somehow. Back when it first started. I was only nine then, and the first time I woke her up crying, welts and bruises on my arms and back, she assumed her current boyfriend, Gary, had done it. Now Gary was a bit of a loser, but he wasn't a bad guy and he never laid a hand on me. He wasn't even there the night it happened. It was just that she refused to believe what I told her."

I looked at Rebecca and waited expectantly. We had been dating six months, and I felt like I knew her fairly well. When she had said with a worried expression that we needed to have a talk about something from her past, I didn't know what to think. My mind had spun wild scenarios involving an old boyfriend that had turned back up or a tearful recount of her secret teen years as a crack addict. Rationally I'd expected something much more mundane, and I never thought it'd be something about her being abused. I wanted to hug her, but I also didn't want to break her momentum if she needed to get it out, so I just sat still as a deer, waiting to see which way the wind blew.

"What had really happened is that I woke up in my bed one night—the night before Halloween, as a matter of fact—and there was a small, bald man standing by my bed. He was larger than a midget…or do they prefer little person? I never know. Anyway, he was very short and wide. I couldn't make out much detail other than moonlight from the window shining off his bald head and outlining his bushy facial hair in silver."

"I didn't really scream…I just whimpered a little. I was still half-asleep and my waking brain didn't know what to do. Then it was too late. He grabbed my arm and yanked me off my bed onto the floor. He started beating me with something…I never knew what." She swallowed, and I could tell the memory still terrified her. "I…I don't know how long it went on. Not long. He never said anything until he was done. Then he leaned over and whispered to me."

"See you next October."

"With that he stepped back into the shadows. I never saw him leave out a door or window—he was just gone. I stayed still, frozen in pain and terror, afraid that any movement would bring him back. After some time, I couldn't hold on any longer. I started to scream and cry for my mother. She came running in, and it went from there. She didn't believe what happened. Thought I was either lying out of fear of naming who hurt me or making things up to somehow block what had really gone on. I don't know. Her logic made no sense, but I know she wanted to protect me. The police were called, Gary was questioned, and my mother got investigated by family and children services. All for nothing. By Christmas things were somewhat back to normal."

Rebecca's lips trembled and she ran a hand through her hair. "Except it wasn't. Not for me. I knew what had happened, and I knew what that strange man had promised. I spent the next year dreading the return of autumn, and when October rolled around, I didn't have long to wait."

****

I was always slow changing after gym, and one day I was the last one in the locker room. It was the last class of the day, so I wasn't in a huge hurry. I had become paranoid and hypervigilant all the time since the first attack, but I kind of assumed that if the man did come back, it would be in my room in the middle of the night. Turns out I was wrong.

I was getting ready to leave when I sensed someone watching me. Looking up, I saw the man staring at me, his face half obscured by the bathroom stall he was standing behind. I felt a flood of panic and fear, but also like I was in some kind of nightmare. Because there was no way he should have been able to get in there like he did. There was only one door in and out of the place, and he would have had to go past me to reach the stalls. The idea occurred to me later that he could have just been hiding in there since before our gym class let out, but that didn't make sense either. Me and at least a couple of other girls had used those stalls after gym, and there was nowhere else he could have hidden. It was like he just appeared out of thin air.

At the time, all these things were just half-formed whispers in the back of my brain, unable to compete with the roar of fear that was driving me to run, to get away. I took one last look at his expressionless face, his black eyes, his pale skin, and I ran.

He let me get as far as halfway across the basketball court before leaping on my back, bringing me down and busting my lip in the process. This time he punched me repeatedly in the sides of my head. Hard enough to make me scream and bring blood trickling out of my ears, but not so hard as to kill me or do permanent damage. And as before, after a few seconds, it was over. His only greeting or farewell as he stood over me, looking down stonefaced, was to mutter the same phrase again.

"See you next October."

****

"Jackson, I'm 29 years old and this has happened to me nineteen times now. It's always the same man. Dressed in plain, normal clothes and looking like his face is carved from some white rock run through with black quartz for his eyes. I…Fuck, I don't really know what else to say. I could recount every time he's attacked me, but what's the point?"

A high static buzz had slowly filled my ears as Rebecca had told me her story. I could feel my breathing coming quicker as my chest tightened with fear—not of some mystery man that kept attacking Rebecca, but because I knew she had to be sick somehow. I'd never known her to be delusional or have any real mental issues, but there had always been a darkness about her. A part of herself she kept closed off. Now I knew why.

But it didn't matter. She believed it, and for the moment I would humor her. It was already Halloween, so when tomorrow passed without any attack, I could suggest she see someone and get the help she seemed to need. I loved her, and the idea she had been living with such terror for so many years...terror that could have been prevented if she had gotten help earlier...it saddened and angered me. I'd get her the help she needed though. I wouldn't abandon her the way her mother and friends apparently had over the years.

For now...For now I needed to act like I believed.

"So does the man ever age or does he always look the same? Do you have any idea who or what it is?"

She shook her head, eyeing me warily. "No, he always looks the same, and I have no idea where he comes from or why he comes for me. I thought over time he would move on to hurting me worse or doing something sexual, but he never has. The worst injury I've ever gotten is a fractured wrist once at 12 and a few bruised ribs last year."

I frowned, remembering her telling me before about having bruised her ribs a few months before we met. She'd never said how it happened, and I hadn't thought to ask at the time. "So how does he find you? It's not like you live in the same place any more. Hell, you're not even in the same state."

She shrugged, tears forming at the corners of her eyes. "I don't know. He always does though. When I turned 18, I ran away. Went under a different name, didn't talk to my mother or anybody else from my old life. Worked a waitress job for cash and was 300 miles away from my hometown. Not a soul knew where I was for over six months. Then one day I was in the freezer of the restaurant I was working in. I heard the door close behind me and turned around to find him looking up at me. I was a good foot taller than him by then, but it didn't matter."

"When he was done, I went back out and told the boss I needed to take off. That I was coming down with a stomach bug. It was close to the truth. My stomach was so sore I couldn't eat or sit down without crying out until the next day."

I frowned. "Why didn't you tell anybody? Why didn't you keep telling people until you found someone who believed you? Or some way to prove it was happening?"

She let out a watery laugh. "Oh, I tried. But cameras and stuff like that…they don't work around him. And he never comes when other people are around. And I learned early on what telling people would get me. It'd get me that look." She pointed at me, her face hardening. "That look that says that you're patronizing me. That you think I'm crazy. That I'm fucked up."

I reached out and grabbed her arm lightly. "No, baby. I…look, this all sounds bizarre. And yeah, being honest, I do have some worries that you could have something going on mentally. Not because I don't trust you, but just…it's so weird and hard to explain if it's true." She tugged away and I held up my hands. "But…but, I love you and I do trust you. So I'm going to keep an open mind and help you however you want me to. All I ask is that if we don't see any sign of this guy tonight, we talk again about what that means and what you want to do next. Fair?"

She nodded as her expression softened slightly. "Fair. But don't worry. I'm not crazy. And I don't think we'll have to wait too long. It's only three hours until midnight."

****

While I didn't expect us to have any late-night invaders, it seemed stupid to not try and prepare just in case, if for no other reason than to show Rebecca I was taking it seriously. So we double-checked all the doors and windows and set up in the living room. There was only one doorway in or out of there, and sitting together on the couch, we both had a good view if anyone tried to enter.

Before we had settled in, I'd found us both makeshift weapons as well. Initially I was going to give her a large knife from the kitchen, but—though I hated myself a little for having the thought—I had a flash of her suddenly deciding I was the attacker and stabbing me to death. So I took the knife and gave her a small hammer, figuring I could take a hit from it easier than a stab to the gut.

I know this sounds like I was afraid of her, but I wasn't. I trusted her, and I had no real concern she might hurt me. But I also didn't know what I was dealing with and wanted to avoid a bad accident if I could.

For the next hour or so we held hands as she flipped between channels on the t.v. It was Halloween, but my initial plan of suggesting horror movies seemed like a bad idea now, and this was confirmed by the speed with which she would move past channels showing some monster or killer terrorizing a hapless victim.

At first I was on edge, but as the minutes crawled by, I felt myself getting drowsy. I glanced over at Rebecca and she was wide awake—every few minutes she would look toward the windows or peer around the room as though searching for some sign of the strange man peeking at her from some shadowed corner. I gave her hand a squeeze and tried to focus on the latest thing she had flipped to, but it was some kind of infomercial and I felt myself jump as the knife began to slide out of my hand.

I had been dozing off. I blinked furiously and gave my head a slight shake. I had to stay awake. Not to protect her—because I felt more and more sure as time passed that nothing was coming—but to show her that she could rely on me to try. If she knew she could trust me, then she…

I woke up to Rebecca screaming.

The thing had her down on the ground and was sitting on her chest as it pummeled her thighs and groin with some kind of small cudgel wrapped in brown leather. It was just as she had described. A small, abnormally wide man with almost glowing white skin that looked carved from bright ivory. He wore a button down flannel shirt with the sleeves rolled up and cargo pants, but his feet were bare and terminated in strangely well-groomed obsidian nails. When he looked up at me with a yellow smile, I saw his eyes were two balls of shining black as well.

Standing up groggily, I yelled at him to stop as I started forward. He just continued to stare at me as he struck her, his blows falling accurately despite his eyes being pinned to the knife in my hand. His silent smile never faltered as I plunged the knife into his chest. I felt his powerful hand grip the back of my neck and the bones of my spine creaked in protest as he flung me away, the knife still protruding from his chest.

I slammed into the coffee table and felt pain flare across my left shoulder. Ignoring it, I rolled back to my feet and came back at him, this time aiming a kick at his grinning face. His head rocked back when my foot landed, but the only thing that changed was that the smile left his face and he returned his entire focus to her. He was working his way down her legs now, striking her knees hard enough to cause fresh wails of pain from Rebecca as she struggled feebly.

Regaining my balance after the kick, I leaned forward and pulled the knife free from his chest. I had half-expected him to grab me again, but he didn't even acknowledge I was there as I retrieved the weapon from the bloodless wound in his chest and moved to his back. Using both hands, I started plunging the knife into his back again and again. It wasn't until the fifth blow that he started to show signs of faltering. It wasn't until the tenth that he stopped still.

As I pulled the knife from him the final time, he toppled over, his body shattering as it struck the floor. Rebecca began crawling out from under his debris and I reached down to help her, my eyes still transfixed on what was happening to the man's body. It was continuing to shatter and crumble as though being ground down to dust by some invisible giant. In a matter of seconds it was no more than a white dusting over the clothes the thing had worn; and then even that dust was gone.

I looked down at Rebecca, ready to console her, get her to the hospital, whatever she needed. Because I was looking at her upside down, it took me a moment to realize that she was smiling at me. That was all the time she needed to grab my legs and pull me down.

Then she was on me, crawling on top while pulling me toward her with tremendous strength. She didn't make any sounds, and as she settled atop my chest, her knees pinning down my arms, even the smile fell from her face. I realized with growing horror that the small brown cudgel had not dissipated with the man's body. Instead it was in Rebecca's right hand.

The next few minutes were a confused haze of pain, anger, and terror as Rebecca beat me savagely. The initial flashes of white as she struck my head and face shifted to red and then grew speckled with black as I teetered on the edge of unconsciousness. My ears rang and my nose bled, and I could barely see at all when she stood up.

For a moment I just laid there, too hurt and in shock to know what to do. Then I felt something brushing my face. I jerked back, blinking, afraid that another attack was coming. Hesitantly I touched my swollen face and felt what had fallen onto it.

It was hair. Rebecca's hair.

I blinked again, trying to clear my vision enough to see her standing over me. She was taking off her clothing, but that was the least of it. Her hair was falling out in thick locks even as her skin grew ghastly white and took on an unnatural sheen. As impossible as it was, she was changing shape as well. Getting shorter. Wider. And her face was slowly shifting into a closer approximation of the man that had attacked her minutes before.

Then she was naked, and looking from her new and unfamiliar face down to her body, I saw that her breasts were gone as well as her more feminine shape. Lower, just inches from me, I saw that her groin no longer had genitals. Instead, the smooth, hard ivory skin was interrupted by an irregular patch of tiny glistening black stones that spread out from where the genitals should be to create an uneven fan across the bottom of her stomach and the top of her inner thighs. The pattern of it looked like some kind of rash or rot, but I also thought of miniscule volcanic pebbles scattered like beads across a starkly white patch of hard earth.

That's when I realized those pebbles, those stones, were watching me. Blinking occasionally and considering me with a thousand dark gazes, weighing me with endless inhuman glares from a sea of black pinprick eyes. Looking back now, when I force myself to remember, I could sense intelligence in that multitude of eyes that pockmarked her once beautiful skin. Intelligence and ill will of a magnitude that made me feel like a crude and frightened ape as I tried to shuffle back and away from the horror.

I was stopped by her foot on my stomach, bearing down enough to hurt and stop me, to bruise, but not rupture, my organs. I forced my gaze back up to her face—well, to his face now, as there was no trace of Rebecca left, and the blue-black shadow of his facial hair was already starting to grow in at his mouth and on his cheeks. But I found its eyes and went to speak. To try to plead with her, reason with her, get her back somehow. Even though I knew it was impossible in my heart, maybe even more impossible than the rest.

It stopped me, putting a finger to my lips to silence me as it bent down to pick up its old clothes. The way it touched my lips caused me to choke back a sob. It was something Rebecca would do to me playfully when we were joking around. I felt hope and sadness rising in my chest at the gesture, and I was going to try and speak again, to reach her somehow, when it spoke in a rough, male voice.

"See you next October."

And then it was gone.

Have you ever heard whistling on a lonely road?

Last week I was driving back home from my grandmother's birthday party. My family all lives close to each other, but five hours away from me, so my plan had been to spend the night and leave the next day around lunch. But then I got into a big fight with my brother—the worst we've ever had. My parents took his side, like they always do, and I decided I needed to go ahead and go.

It was about ten at night when I left their house, and by midnight I was starting to regret my decision. It was so far to drive that late and I was really tired. I'd have considered just stopping at a motel, but the route I always took consisted of tiny towns connected by long stretches of wooded roads, and I didn't think there was a single place to stay along that entire journey.

I was on the longest, darkest part of the drive—a stretch of nearly a hundred miles without any real signs of people other than the occasional farmhouse or closed country store. I began toying with the idea of just parking and taking a nap as my fatigue worsened, and when I woke up starting to veer, I knew it was a necessity. I would stop to sleep, but only when I reached the next semi-populated spot in the road.

I know the tricks to stay awake. I rolled down the window. I tried to sing along with the radio. I rolled the window back up and cranked up the air. I even slapped myself hard enough to make my face tingle.

The thing is, these are all half-measures. They're sandbags against the rising tide of sleep, meant to delay the inevitable for a few minutes. Getting out of the car, caffeine, actual sleep, these were the only things I knew that could really roll things back once you were truly on the edge of falling asleep on the road.

I had no caffeinated drinks with me and I had no real idea how many more miles it would be before I saw street lights again. But rightly or wrongly, if I was going to sleep in my car, I wanted at least the suggestion of civilization and order surrounding me.

So that left getting out of the car and walking around. I didn't love the idea of stopping at night on some dark and lonely country road, but it seemed a better option than risking a wreck when I finally fell asleep for a second too long.

The part of the road I was on was winding, with thick stands of ancient-looking trees looming over the road on both sides. It was nearly a full moon, but the shadows of reaching branches covered the road in an endless silvery tiger stripe of alternating light and dark. I drove on, looking for a straighter, brighter patch of road, but none came, and with each mile I felt myself drifting deeper and deeper.

Muttering under my breath, I pulled the car over on a semi-straight section of road that was maybe 100 feet long before it snaked off in new directions. I hit my emergency lights, hoping to keep any late-night drunk drivers from plowing into me or my car, and got out.

The air was colder than I expected, even for October. Colder than it had seemed when I'd rolled the window down earlier while driving. It was weird, but I was also half-asleep and didn't necessarily trust my logic at the moment.

I moved in front of my car and began walking in a circle within the glow from my headlights before transitioning to jumping jacks. I knew I looked stupid, but a glance at my surroundings made it clear there was no one around. Aside from my car's lights, the only source of illumination was the intermittent glow of moonlight from above the rustling trees. The only sounds aside from those shivering leaves was the low purr of my car's engine and my own puffing breaths as I went through my midnight calisthenics routine.

But then I heard something else. I stopped at the noise and listened, but there was nothing. After a few seconds, I decided it was my imagination and was about to head back to the car when I heard it again.

It was whistling. Not the cry of some bird, but the high, clear notes of some unfamiliar tune. My skin began to prickle as a low buzz of fear joined the music in my ears. It went on for at least ten seconds this time before stopping, and it was enough for me to tell it wasn't a recording or some scrap from a distant radio carried to me on a tide of nighttime air.

No, someone or something was whistling a song in the dark. And they were close.

Trying to keep myself from breaking into a panicked run, I went back to my car and pulled on the handle. The door was locked. I had locked it as a precaution when I got out because I had the image of someone sneaking into the back seat while I was outside with my back turned. The irony wasn't lost on me now, but my main focus was on getting out my key and unlocking the door.

I fumbled desperately in my pocket as the whistling started up again for a few moments—much closer this time. It seemed like a different part of the same song, though I couldn't say for sure. I yanked the keys from my pocket and started jabbing it shakily at the lock when I heard my car's engine shutter to a stop. A small whine of terror escaped me as I tried again to find the keyhole, this time successfully. Turning the key, I froze as the whistling began a third time, now directly behind me.

I could smell something now. A mixture of several strong smells, like someone was mixing cinnamon, garlic and rotten eggs in a hot skillet. I gagged slightly and was readying myself to try to yank the door open when the whistling stopped again.

The smell grew stronger. Then I felt a small, burning kiss on the back of my neck.

The next few seconds were a panicked blur. I yanked open the door and got in, slamming it shut without daring to look out to see what might be looking in at me. Locking the doors with one hand, I cranked the car with the other. I almost cried with relief when it came back to life immediately. I thought I heard light scratching at my window as I threw the car into drive and sped off into the night.

I had no trouble with drowsiness the rest of my drive home, and it wasn't until the next evening that I finally fell into an exhausted sleep. I don't have any explanation for what happened out on that road, and as the days have passed, I've found myself rationalizing it more and more as some kind of waking dream or false memory brought on by my brief moments of sleep as I drove home that night.

But then last night I woke up to a terrible smell in my room. It smelled of garlic and cinnamon and sulfur. I sat up in bed, my eyes wide and my heart hammering as I stared into the dark.

Then I heard it. The whistling. And it was coming from underneath my bed.

I bolted from the room and my house, running next door in my underwear and hammering on my neighbor's door until they warily agreed to call the police. When the officers came, they found nothing. No signs of a break-in or anything stolen. No trace that any intruder was ever there.

And for the most part they were right. When I returned home in the early hours of the morning, I did my own search for signs that some person or thing had been there. At first I saw nothing out of the ordinary. But then I looked more closely under the bed.

There was a minuscule amount of dirt there—strange greenish-gray dirt unlike any I had ever seen. And mixed in with the dirt was what looked like small patches of dried skin. As though something was…molting.

I don't know what to do or if I'll ever have another chance to write this down, so I'm taking the time now, mainly so my account is known if something happens to me. I don't know what this thing is, but I feel sure it will find me again soon. The thought of that terrifies me, but it's not the worst part.

See, the more I think about it, the more certain I am that every time it whistles, it's a different part of the same song. Almost as though it wants or needs me to hear the entire thing. Since I realized that, a single question has been haunting me. It casts its shadow over everything else, like the twisted, reaching branches of an ancient tree darkening some lonesome midnight road.

What will it do when it finishes the song?

Something came back with us from the woods.

I'm part of a writing group that meets once a month. We typically meet on a Saturday afternoon and spend several hours hanging out and discussing ideas, talking about problems we've been having, and helping each other with feedback from reading each other's stuff. On the "holiday months", which in our case has typically meant October and December, we try to make the meeting a bit more festive and it becomes more of a party than anything else.

That's why when Colby suggested we do an overnight camping trip this October, complete with a spooky ghost tour and scary stories around the campfire, it sounded like a great idea. More of an expansion of what we normally would have done around Halloween rather than any real departure from the past four years I had been part of the group.

I was excited for it, not just because the activities seemed like they would be fun, but because these people are my friends. Sure, we don't see each other as often as some friends, but I feel like I've gotten to know each of the five other members of our group pretty well over time, and I've reached the point that I look forward to our meetings more for the social aspect than for any help or support it gives my writing. So last Saturday we gathered up at Colby's house and headed out in his SUV to Winter Falls wildlife preserve.

Colby said he knew one of the guys that administered the property and we had the greenlight to be there, which was cool for two reasons. First, only a handful of people were given permission to camp on the property every year, so the likelihood of running into loud, drunk teenagers camping too close for comfort was very low. Second, there was an old abandoned place on the land that was rumored to be haunted.

Now I assumed this second thing was likely bullshit, and if it had come from Alan or Janet, our two horror/paranormal writers in the group, I would have said they were just making up stuff as part of some elaborate Halloween story or prank. But all this information came from Colby, and he didn't like horror. Couldn't stomach it, really. He mainly wrote poetry and character pieces that were so dense with historical detail that you felt like you'd been through a class on the given period before you reached the end of the story. He was sensitive and delicate and…well, it seemed odd he'd be the one to suggest going there in the first place, but it somehow made it more believable too.

We rode with Colby onto the property, past two gates that he had the keys for and on up a winding dirt road that finally petered out into patchy grass and hard scrabble before being consumed by brush and deeper woods. I made the suggestion that we just camp in that open area near the car, but Bonnie and Susan, who were both allegedly romance novelists (but who spent more time flirting with Colby than working on their writing during our get-togethers) giggled to each other and suggested to Colby that we needed to go deeper to find the right spot. I rolled my eyes and sighed as he awkwardly smiled at them and nodded. Although it hadn't been said, Colby was the de facto leader on this little trip, and without another word we pushed into the woods.

After the initial few feet, the walk actually became fairly pleasant. There was a cool breeze in the afternoon air, and a small, crooked path had opened up as we went past the first few trees and bushes. We walked for probably thirty minutes before coming to a clearing that Colby suggested was a good spot to set up camp. Looking at his watch, he said if we could get our tents and stuff set up quickly we'd have around a hour of daylight left to start heading to the haunted building he was starting to tell us more about.

He told us that at one time, it had been a private home owned by a family known for their strange ways and practices. He said this last part with a theatricality that I hadn't known he was capable of, raising his eyebrow as he lowered his voice to a gravelly rasp. Eventually the family died off or something, because it became an orphanage of sorts, taking in troubled children that were having a difficult time at home or at other orphanages that couldn't or wouldn't tolerate their behavior.

"Are you saying this was a baby prison?" By this time we were actually walking with him away from the finished campsite, and I regretted the question as soon as I asked it. I liked Colby, and I didn't want him to think I was making fun of his weird attempt at a scary story. But he just nodded and grinned at me.

"Kinda yeah. Not babies, but some of the children were very violent or deranged. That lasted a few years, but it seems like a lot of the children got worse living at the orphanage, not better, and eventually the place fell into such ill-repute that business dried up and the house was shuttered for good. Since that time, no one has lived there, but there are several accounts of people hiking or camping nearby and having…incidents." Again, the raised eyebrow as he looked around at us like an old vaudeville villain. It was kind of cute in a dopey way.

Bonnie tittered at him. "What kinds of incidents, Colby-poo?" That was one of her cloying nicknames for him when she was feeling especially whorish. Like usual, he blushed when she said it, looking away before continuing. I wanted to punch her.

"Well, hearing voices when no one is there for one thing. And more than one account of seeing lights or faces at the windows of the old house. That kind of stuff."

Susan, not wanting to be left out, grabbed his arm dramatically as she looked up at him with doe eyes. "This sounds scary. You going to protect us?"

Colby gave an awkward laugh and nodded. "Yeah, sure." He looked up at me and smiled. "I'm sure we'll all get through it okay."

****

The house was both impressive and impressively creepy. Large swaths of moss lay draped across most of the roof, but even with several of the windows broken and its weathered skin of yellowed paint and warped, rotting wood, you could see what a beautiful house it had once been. Four stories tall, with thin columns going up to a large balcony on the second floor, it looked far too stately and regal to be stuck in the middle of these dark woods being slowly consumed by decay.

Yet at the same time, it somehow seemed to fit its locale perfectly. The front of the house reminded me of a face—an ancient, moldering face that stared at us with cold contempt as we shuffled across what had likely once been a well-manicured front lawn. I suppressed a shiver as I unconsciously dropped my gaze.

Looking back at Alan and Janet, I saw they had similar expressions of both awe and apprehension. I leaned toward them and tried to sound nonchalant. "This place up to snuff, spookinesswise? It seems to be pretty creepy to me, but I'm no expert."

Janet looked at me and beamed. "Yeah, this place is badass!" Alan nodded his agreement before going back to fumbling with his phone as he tried to take a picture. Colby noticed him and frowned.

"Come on, man. Leave off with the phone, will you? We're here to experience it, not look at our phone screens the entire time."

Looking sheepish, Alan nodded and stuffed his phone back into his pocket. I almost said something then, as I didn't like Colby bossing Alan around like he was some kid, especially when in truth Alan was probably five years older than any of the rest of us. But then Colby was excitedly telling us to come on, that he had a key for this place too, and I went along, pushing my irritation and doubts aside.

He unlocked the front door without any problem, but it took him and Alan shoving it hard to create a large enough opening for us to squeeze through. The afternoon light had already been fading, and once we were inside, I realized we had left the sun behind. We all pulled out our phones then, using flashlight apps to light our way as we moved down a trash-strewn front hall that led to a large room that had possibly once been a small ballroom or massive parlor. Now it was a black ruin—a tangy, putrid smell filled my nose as I sent a wash of electric light over moldy walls and dangerous-looking floors.

"I don't know about this, Colby." I didn't want to be a party pooper, but I was already having images of someone falling through the floor or getting sick from breathing in all this rot. I could see that Alan and Janet were feeling the same way, and even Susan was starting to look uncomfortable. I noticed Bonnie scowling at me, but I ignored her as I went on. "I'm just worried this place might not be structurally sound, you know? I don't want someone getting hurt."

He nodded and smiled. "I know it looks rough. But listen. I've been here once before and it really is safer than it looks. Just go where I go, and if anyone get too worried, we'll stop and leave. Fair?"

I wanted to say that I had *already* said I was too worried and wanted to go, but I let it go. I was probably being overly cautious, and as long as we were careful it should be fine. And it was, at least at first. The house was very creepy, and we heard the odd sound or two, but there was nothing too remarkable.

After walking around inside for a few minutes, we split up into smaller groups to explore a bit. Surprising no one, Bonnie and Susan had gone with Colby, while I had gone with Alan and Janet. I didn't like splitting up, but I was trying to not worry and get into the spirit of our adventure.

We spent some time wandering around the main floor, as I had no interest in trying the stairs or the flooring on the upper levels. The house truly was massive, with numerous halls weaving between different rooms large and small. Alan, Janet and I finally started working our way back toward the front of the house when I turned a corner and ran into Susan, the odd bubblegum-scented perfume she always wore assaulting my nostrils as we bumped into each other. She let out a yelp and then smiled nervously at me.

"Shit! I got turned around and separated from Colby and Bonnie. Glad to see a friendly face again in this place!"

I smiled and then winced slightly. "Poor Colby. Bonnie has probably attacked him by now." Susan surprised me by letting out a short laugh and nodding.

"Yeah…I think he's cute and all, but not really my type. I just like joking around a bit. But Bonnie…yeah, she may hurt that boy." We both laughed again, trying to stifle it as Alan and Janet came around the corner.

We walked on for a bit when I thought I heard Bonnie's voice. Thinking about what we'd just said, I decided I might as well try to intervene…if Colby wanted any intervening. I dropped back and went in the direction of her voice, making a point to call out to them well before I walked up on something I shouldn't see.

I got no response, and as I walked to where I thought she had been, I saw no sign of either of them. I was in what had once been a large kitchen, white tile walls painted with blue roosters and hens forming a weirdly quaint procession around the perimeter of the room. There was an old-fashioned kitchen hearth containing a large cast-iron pot along one wall, and as I watched, I thought I saw shadowed movement in the ashes underneath the pot. My first thought was *rat*, but whatever it was, I wanted no part of it. I headed back the way I came, regretting ever leaving the group in the first place.

That's when I rounded another corner and saw Bonnie and Colby. At first I thought they were embracing, but then I realized he was behind her and she didn't seem to realize he was even there. His light was off and I could only make out his outline from the reflected illumination of her phone's light hitting the rotting wall in front of them. It struck me as odd so I stopped and watched for a moment. Colby lifted his hand and placed it on the back of her head while uttering a single word.

"Selah."

Bonnie jumped and let out a little scream as she turned around. I couldn't see much of their faces in the phone's meager glow, but I could hear the fear in her voice as she spoke, although she tried to hide it and turn it into a joke once she saw who had touched her. "You scared me, you asshole! You're going to have to make that up to…"

"Hey, you guys ready to go?" I don't know why I blurted it out, but I didn't want to be in the house any longer and for whatever reason I didn't feel right leaving Bonnie alone with him any more. I expected a glare from Bonnie as I shined my light on them, but instead she looked relieved. For Colby's part, he just gave me a thin smile and nodded.

"Yeah, I think we're done here."

****

We were all fairly quiet on the way back to the campsite, though I noticed that neither Bonnie or Susan seemed interested in sticking close to Colby this time. I didn't know what to make of what I had seen, and as we settled into cooking hotdogs and joking around, things began to feel more normal again. By the time we were taking turns telling scary stories, I had almost decided I'd just made a mistake thinking anything was going on beyond a guy trying to scare a girl he liked.

But when it was getting close to my turn to tell a story, I got up to go to the bathroom. I was racking my brain for something that could even vaguely compete with Janet's story about her mother's dead twin sister or Alan's tale of "waterbabies" that drag people into a nearby lake. I found what I hoped was a non-poisonous bush and squatted down, my gaze going back to the campfire and my odd collection of friends laughing and talking there. Their shadows were flung giant against the tents and surrounding trees, dancing and shifting in the ever-changing flicker of the firelight. That's when I noticed it.

Bonnie had two shadows.

One was like the others—vague and ill-defined, but still an amplified and distorted version of her silhouette. The second…the second was something very different. It was much darker and almost seemed to have a substance to it. It moved, but in a way that was discordant and wrong, out of sync with the fire or the other shadows. And its shape. Its shape was more defined than the others and much more horrible because of that added definition. I didn't know what it was, but it didn't resemble anything human.

I pulled up my pants and strode back to the camp. My heart was thudding, and the last thing I wanted was to be near either Colby or Bonnie, but he had the only car and I wasn't staying out there any longer. I told them that I was sick. Badly sick and I needed to go home.

Alan and Janet made disappointed noises, and Bonnie and Susan gave no real argument or comment at all other than Susan asking if I needed anything, but my focus was primarily on Colby. He just looked at me, his expression seeming sad or disappointed except for his eyes. His eyes were hard and distant as though he was considering something, doing some kind of dark arithmetic behind that gaze. After a few heartbeats, he just nodded with a small smile.

"Sure. There's always next time."

The ride back to his house was the longest three hours of my life. I was exhausted, but there was no chance I was falling asleep in the car with either of them. And while I didn't know what was going on, I was past doubting myself or putting myself in any more danger than was necessary to get home and away from them.

So I sat in the back with my hand on the door handle in case I needed to make a hasty exit, fast-moving asphalt or no. I talked very little, and when we reached Colby's house, I was out of the car before it made a complete stop. Someone yelled that I was leaving my sleeping bag behind, but I didn't turn around. Fuck it. They could keep it.

When I got home, I locked my door and checked all the windows. It was after sunrise before I finally fell into a fitful sleep, and even then I was plagued with dreams of being trapped in that house with shadows chasing me through the dark. In the first few days after that, I kept expecting to see Colby or Bonnie or both. Coming around to check on me or deal with me or…something. But there had been no sign of anyone.

I have stayed in my apartment most of the time since then, but this afternoon I finally had to go out to get groceries. I was nervous the entire time, but I never saw anyone I knew, and I made it back home uneventfully. Yet when I walked into my apartment, I froze.

Bubblegum. I smelled bubblegum.

I dropped my bags and stepped back into the hallway. After several seconds of silence, I reached in enough to turn on all the lights I could get from the switches next to the door. Nothing seemed out of place, and there was no sign of anyone. My heart thudding, I picked up one of my grocery bags containing several weighty cans and began to explore my apartment with the makeshift weapon. There was nothing there. Well, except for the singular smell of that bubblegum perfume in several spots throughout.

I locked the door back and went to sit down at my laptop to write this all out when something made me stop and go to the window. I had gotten in the habit of looking outside frequently in the last few days, always wary of some sign of Colby or Bonnie. But there had never been anything out there. Until now.

Across the street on the far sidewalk, I saw Susan and Alan standing together holding hands. Holding hands and staring up at me. That was five hours ago, and they're still out there.

They haven't tried to come in or communicate with me, but they also haven't moved from their spot in all that time. They just stand and stare, waiting. Waiting for me to give up and come out so they can get me for…something. And while I don't understand enough to know exactly what they want to do with me, I have a strong suspicion.

I think they want to take me camping again.

The Trick

When I was twelve years old, I went trick-or-treating by myself. A month earlier I would have said I was going with my best friend Jimmy Miner, but that was before his mother got sick and they moved away the week before Halloween. In my parents' eyes, that left me open to taking my eight year-old sister with me trick-or-treating, which served the dual purposes of freeing themselves from taking her and giving me some company.

While I protested a little bit when they initially made the suggestion, in truth I didn't mind carrying her along. I was lonely, and I loved my sister Mary a lot. Loved being her big brother and how she looked up to me, wanting to do what I did and go where I went. Sometimes it was a pain, sure, but as Halloween drew near, I was looking forward to spending it with her.

Then she came down with a bad cold and I wound up back on my own. I almost didn't go at all, but I didn't want my family thinking I was that down in the dumps, and I *did* want to score some candy beyond the handful of "healthy treats" my mother was letting us eat.

So on Halloween I went out, made my rounds, and came back with a large sack more than halfway full of the good stuff. My father was watching a horror movie in the living room when I got home, and I announced my return briefly before heading upstairs to my room with the idea of squirreling away my loot. When I passed Mary's closed door, I heard my mother in there reading her a story. Poor kid. I could tell she was really sick when I was heading out, but she was also sad about missing out on Halloween with me. Easing my door closed, I promised myself I'd save her some of the best candy as I got ready to go through my trick-or-treat loot.

Normally I would have just stuck some of it away in a drawer and then headed back down to eat from the rest while we watched t.v., never really reaching the bottom of the bag until at least a day or two had passed. But I really did want to save Mary some good stuff, and to do that, I needed to see what I was working with. After a moment of indecision, I dumped it all out onto my floor.

It was a nice neighborhood, so there was always a lot of good candy in my bag, almost as though the neighbors were competing with each other to see who could give the local children diabetes first. But that year, I noticed that there were several weird squares of white paper or something mixed in with the brightly colored bits of waxed paper, plastic and foil. Frowning, I picked one up and turned it over.

It was a picture from an old instant camera. My dad had shown me one before—a Polaroid. I remember thinking it was like magic that the square of film would fill in as you shook it, almost as though being drawn in by some invisible hand. But this one was still blank, and shaking it did nothing. I looked back down at the floor and counted eight more potential pictures down there.

I was curious to look at the rest, but at first I just stood there trying to figure out how they would have gotten into my bag in the first place. I knew the bag was empty when I left home, and I watched everyone that put candy into my bag while I was out. I think I would have noticed someone slipping a stack of nine instant camera pictures in with a candy bar or a handful of gum.

Unable to think of an explanation for the undeveloped picture in my hand, I set to looking at the rest. I think I half-expected them all to be blank, maybe with the idea that someone had just accidently stuck some unshot film in my bag while trying to give me candy. The idea sounds dumb now, but the growing worm of worry in my stomach was demanding some kind of explanation. As I bent down and turned over the next photo, I felt that worm burrow deeper into my core.

It was a photo of me. Taken just that night as I was leaving the house in my pirate costume, fake parrot on my shoulder and big Halloween bag in my hand. Judging from the angle, it was taken from somewhere near the bushes beside our garage.

At the time, I didn't think about the practical realities of a picture like that. For instance, how was the picture was so clear and not grainy when it was already getting dark, yet clearly no flash had been used? And as I went to the next picture, how had I not seen whoever was taking these photos?

Because the second developed picture was again of me, but a closer up shot. Based on the distance and angle, I'd have guessed the photographer was no more than five or ten feet in front of me. Again, the picture was almost unnaturally clear, this one at a slight upward angle, as though taken by someone smaller than my five foot height. Judging by the background, in the picture I had just left from getting candy at Penny Johnson's house.

My hands were trembling as I went through the remaining seven pictures. Photos Four through Six were blank. Seven showed me from behind as I was cutting through a side yard to get to the street behind ours. Eight was also blank, while Nine showed me returning home just a few minutes ago.

My mind reeled. That was impossible. How could *anyone* have given me these photos if they were still taking them when I was walking into the house? The bag hadn't left my hands all night long, and yet I was looking at photos of events that were only ten minutes old.

This led me to recheck the ones that were blank. I felt my mouth go dry as I saw the start of an image beginning to ghost its way onto what I thought was number Eight. Swallowing, I grabbed the photo and gave it a shake. It was another of picture of me, this time looking with sympathy at Mary's room as I headed to my own to divvy up the candy.

It had been inside. Maybe it still was.

The thought pushed itself up from the black, burning in my mind like a coal as I began frantically looking around my room. I was truly afraid now, and I wasn't sure what to do. I was on the verge of yelling for my mother when I saw another picture starting to fade in. I gave it a shake and then dropped it as I recognized a close-up shot of my bedroom door.

Turning away from the pile on the floor, I ran to the door and quietly thumbed the button lock. Now I was worried about calling out to anyone out of fear they might get attacked by whatever was outside my door. And back then, kids my age didn't have cellphones, and I didn't have a land line in my room. My mind raced through several bad plans before I settled on the least terrible of them. I would climb out my window, go down and around to the living room where I could tell my father, and he could help me get Mary and our mother out of the house safely.

That's when I heard the voice.

"Candy?" It was a low, soft voice, with a rasping strangeness and hesitancy that reminded me of when animals make noises that sound like they're speaking human words. And then again, slightly louder and insistent, *"Candyyyy?"* This was followed by a loud thump as something hit the door, causing me to let out a yell in spite of myself.

Its demand made no sense, but none of this did. Working largely off of fear and instinct, I plunged into the pile and began raking the candy back into the bag. I hesitated when it came to the photos, deciding at the last second to leave them out since the voice had only asked for candy.

I went back to the door and called out. "I've got your candy. All the candy I have. Please take it and go." Sitting the bag of candy on the floor, I gently unlocked the door before opening it just far enough to shove the bag through with my old baseball bat. Slamming the door shut, I relocked it. I sat down and braced my feet against the door in case it decided it was unsatisfied with my offering, but everything was quiet.

Looking over at the photos, I saw another one, Four, was filling in. The photo's view was like the photographer was going back down the hall. *Thank God*, I thought, wondering how long it would take for it to leave the house so I could go tell my parents what had happened. Then I heard it again.

"Candy?"

The voice was more distant, and it only took me a moment to realize why. When I looked over at the pictures, Five confirmed my fears. It was outside of Mary's door now. Mary who was in bed sick and had no candy to give.

I'll always regret the decision I made next. I was scared of opening the door, but I also worried that if I didn't get my father involved right away, I might be making a dangerous situation that much worse. So I went to my window and climbed out onto the roof. Taking a deep breath, I jumped into the bushes below, and while I felt a flare of pain in my left ankle, I kept moving and was back inside the house within seconds.

My father was still in the living room, but he was asleep in his chair now. I went to him, my eyes fixed on the nearby stairs as I shook him and yelled. He didn't wake up. I shook him harder and his head lolled forward. I had a terrifying moment when I was sure he was dead, but when I leaned close I could hear him softly snoring. Panicking, I stepped back and kicked him as hard as I could in the leg, sending a fresh bolt of pain through my own hurt ankle in the process. Still nothing.

My frustration at being unable to wake him and my worry over Mary and my mother was turning to anger by this point, and since I had left my bat upstairs, I grabbed the fireplace poker and headed for the stairs. Every moment I climbed the steps I expected to be attacked, but no attack ever came. When I reached the top, I could see that Mary's door was standing wide open.

I ran into the room, ready to try to fight off whatever might be in there with them, but all I found was my mother, lying on the edge of the bed and fast asleep. I searched the room and the closet, but there was no sign of anyone else, including Mary.

I started shaking my mother, and after a few moments she came awake. I was hysterical by this point, but I was able to convey enough that she woke up the rest of the way and began screaming Mary's name and searching for her. Within seconds, my father was groggily climbing the stairs to find out what was going on.

I kept helping to look for Mary too, but when the house had been searched and the police were on their way, I thought and returned to my room to collect the photos for the police. That's when I saw that Number Five had filled in as well.

The picture was of Mary, clearly crying and terrified. It was hard to make out much of her surroundings, but I could see dirt walls with roots threaded through them above her and to her sides. One of her bare feet was in the frame, and next to it I noticed what looked like a scattered collection of small bones and candy wrappers half-buried in the dark, subterranean earth.

They never found my sister, though the case is technically still open even after nearly twenty years. That's mainly because every year, on Halloween, I find a new instant photo of Mary. Sometimes it's in my mailbox. Sometimes it's in my shoe. Once I found it in the middle of a loaf of bread I had just bought that same morning. But every photo shows my baby sister as she's grown up in some dark hell. Pictures of her running, fighting, huddling in the dark. Doing inscrutable tasks or looking bleakly into the camera, her eyes so different now than when she was a young girl. Though she's four years younger than I am, she looks much older than me now, and while I always turn the pictures into the police after showing them to my parents, we've never been any closer to knowing where she actually is.

As you might imagine, Halloween is a hard time for me. In some ways I look forward to the brief, if terrible, glimpse I get of my sister every year. It lets me know she's alive, though I don't know if that's really a blessing. But it also fills me with dread at what new terrible thing I'll have to see and know when I look at the latest photograph.

Today is Halloween, and as expected, I got a photograph. Except this one was different. I recognized the location. It was my daughter's school. The picture looked like it was taken from out in the hallway, looking in to where my little girl sat in her third-grade classroom. In a panic, I immediately called the school, but they said she was perfectly fine. Not willing to take a chance, I picked her up right away and had my wife meet us at a hotel two towns over for the night.

My wife understands some of it, enough to be properly scared, but she thinks it's just some psycho who kidnapped my sister as a child and is weirdly fixated on me. And there's no real point in me trying to explain that its more than that. But I did point out the other thing I noticed about the photo before turning it over to police this afternoon. You see, the picture of our little girl was actually taken through the window of the classroom's door, and in the glass of that window you could see a faint reflection of the one taking the picture.

It was Mary.

I've always loved my sister, and for most of my life I've felt guilt and sadness over her being taken. I've prayed every night for her to return home. But now we're holed up in a locked hotel room with a loaded gun on the table and three huge bags of candy stacked against the outside of the door.

I still love Mary, but I no longer want her to come home. Better for her to stay in whatever world she's been raised in and leave my new family in ours. I hope the candy will be enough, and if it's not, I hope the gun can stop her.

Just stay away, baby sister. Just stay away.

I found a serial killer's cell phone.

Part One

Text Log (11/4/18) Beginning 10:42pm

BRNR3: Hello? Did someone find my phone?

You: Yeah, I did. I work maintenance at the hospital and it was in the discard pile for old lost and found.

You: I wasn't trying to steal it or nothing, they just get rid of unclaimed lost stuff after a month. The tag said this was left there back in late September. If you want it back though, that's cool.

BRNR3: What hospital was this?

You: River North Hospital. The tag said it was left by a John Doe…guess that's you…in the ER. So is that you?

BRNR3: It is. I didn't have money for the doctor, so I decided to leave without giving my name.

You: Damn, man. That sucks. Nice phone tho. I thought I'd hit the jackpot tonight. Just charged it and turned it on when you sent the text. You must have been looking for it, huh?

BRNR3: Yeah, I got an alert when it powered on. When can I get it back?

You: Well, I can bring it back into the hospital tomorrow afternoon. Tell them to hold it for you until you can come by to pick it up.

BRNR3: Well

BRNR3: That might work.

BRNR3: Or I could just come get it from you tonight. I'm not that far from you right now, as a matter of fact.

You: Lol. Good joke man. Points for being creepy. But nah, I'll just leave it at lost and found tomorrow. Have a good night.

BRNR3: I'm not joking.

BRNR3: You live on Abercorn Street, right? I can see the GPS location for my phone too. And I'm familiar with that area. You live in the big apartment building I bet.

You: Look, man. I'm not trying to be weird or nothing. But I don't know you. And I'd rather just drop it by work and let you get it officially if that's cool.

BRNR3: It would be, but I'm flying out in the morning. Going to be gone for two weeks and I need that phone. Been using a burner for over a month and I have too much stuff on there that I need while I'm gone. That's why I've been watching so close for it to come back on.

BRNR3: Please. I'm not some nut. But I really need to get my phone tonight.

BRNR3: Please. I'll pay you a finder's fee.

You: Nah, no need for that. Look, I live in Belvedere Apts. You text when you get here and I'll run it down to you. Will that work?

BRNR3: Yeah! Awesome! Thanks so much. I'll text you in about 15 minutes.

BRNR3: Thanks again!

Text Log (11/4/18) Beginning 11:08pm

BRNR3: Okay, I'm about to be outside.

You: Cool. Omw down.

You: Where are you?

You: I'm standing right outside the front door of the building. Gray sweater.

You: Hello? It's cold and I'm about to head back in. You here or not?

You: Ok. Fuck this. Sorry, dude. Idk if you got lost or what, but you'll just have to pick it up at the hospital. Later.

Text Log (11/5/18) Beginning 1:18am

BRNR3: Sorry I didn't come get the phone. It's just that

BRNR3: I got to thinking. Did you look through my phone?

BRNR3: Did you?

You: Wtf? No. I didn't look at your fucking phone. I'm trying to sleep. Fuck off and get it back from the hospital.

BRNR3: Are you sure? Are you sure you didn't look at my phone?

You: Look at what, you freak?

BRNR3: I think you did. I think you saw all the pictures. The videos. Everything.

You: Get your phone at the hospital. You text me again and I WILL look through your phone and call the cops for harassment.

BRNR3: No. You call the cops and you die.

You: Who the fuck is this? Is this Jamie? Jamie, is this some kind of fucking prank? Not cool. I'm too tired for this shit.

BRNR3: This isn't Jamie.

You: Then who is it?

BRNR3: A friend. For now.

You: Don't text me again.

Text Log (11/5/18) Beginning 2:42am

You: Okay. I'm sorry. I'm sorry I took your phone. I will drop it wherever you want. I don't know who you are, and I don't want to know. I haven't called anybody. I just want you to get your phone back and leave me alone.

BRNR3: So you did look at the phone.

You: Yeah. I really hadn't before. But I did now. Just a little. Was that all real? Please tell me it was fake. I won't be mad.

BRNR3: It was real. Though if it makes you feel better, nothing is traceable back to a particular known crime, so you're not withholding evidence by not calling the cops.

You: I swear I didn't. I won't. I just want out of this. Let me get you your phone back or destroy it or whatever you want. Just let me be rid of it and I'll forget you even exist. I swear.

BRNR3: I believe you. Mostly. The problem is, mostly believing you still means you have to die.

You: What? I don't know anything, I don't!

BRNR3: But you do. And so if you're going to avoid dying, you have to make me fully believe you.

You: Ok. What do you want me to do?

BRNR3: Well, for me to fully believe you, I need you to be invested in this. Invested in what I do. What's on that phone. Be a party to it. So that telling on me is also telling on yourself. Understand?

You: I can't do that. I can't hurt someone.

BRNR3: I think you'd be surprised what you can do when you're given a little push. But I don't expect much from you. You're new to all that, and I'm not unreasonable. So we'll start with something simple.

BRNR3: You need to pick.

You: Pick what?

BRNR3: You need to pick the next person I…meet. The next person I treat like you've seen on that phone.

You: I can't do that. I won't do that.

BRNR3: I think you can and will. If I'm wrong, I'll accept my mistake. And I'll console myself by coming to see you instead.

You: I'll call the cops instead.

BRNR3: Go ahead. There's nothing on that phone that can be traced back to me. They won't find me now any more than anyone has before.

BRNR3: But I'll find you. I always find the things I really need. And if you betray my confidences like that…well, I will NEED to meet you.

You: Okay, okay. I was just bluffing. No cops. But I can't tell you to hurt someone.

BRNR3: I didn't say you had to tell me what to do. I'll decide what happens to them. But I do need you to give me a name. Share enough responsibility that I know you won't tell on us.

You: Fuck. I don't know.

BRNR3: You've got until sunrise. Think carefully. I'll expect an answer by 7am. TTFN.

Text Log (11/5/18) Beginning 7:01am

BRNR3: Cock-a-doodle-do. Time's up.

You: Jim Purvis.

BRNR3: Oh? Who's he?

You: Why does it matter?

BRNR3: Who's he?

You: He was a piece of shit drunk that used to date my mother. Beat her too.

You: When I was 15 I tried to stop him. He broke my arm and then broke his hand on my head. Guess which one of us Mom stayed with at the hospital.

BRNR3: Interesting. Is he still alive?

You: Last I heard he was working upstate for a logging company.

BRNR3: Physical description?

You: Idk. Old, fat white guy?

BRNR3: Won't your mother be sad at your choice?

You: My mother died when I was 20.

BRNR3: Did he do it?

You: No. The piece of shit left her for some bar skank he met. I think Mom died of a broken heart.

BRNR3: :)

BRNR3: I like your choice. You get to live today. Keep the phone on you and charged up. I'll be in touch.

Part Two

Text Log (11/6/18) Beginning 12:13pm

BRNR3: Video Received. thislilpiggy.mp4

BRNR3: Watch it.

You: Fuck

You: That was him. You did it.

BRNR3: We did it.

You: Is he dead?

BRNR3: Lol. What do you think?

You: Is he?

BRNR3: Of course.

You: Ok. So this is done? We're done?

BRNR3: No.

BRNR3: You'll know when we're done.

You: Please let me just give you the phone back. You have dirt on me now, okay? I will say right here, I ASKED YOU TO KILL JIM PURVIS. YOU ONLY DID IT BECAUSE OF ME.

You: Okay? Isn't that good enough?

BRNR3: The more you talk about not going to the cops, the more I think you will. You're eroding that trust you just built.

You: I'm sorry.

You: Fuck. I'm just scared. I just want this to be over.

BRNR3: You're not scared. You don't know how to be really scared yet.

BRNR3: I am really trying to work with you on this. Give you a chance to earn my trust. But your whining is boring. If I get too bored, I'm going to give up and come see you. Understand?

You: Yes. Got it. What do you need me to do so you can fully trust me?

BRNR3: The next thing I need you to do is hurt someone. I'm not saying kill anybody. And though it should go without saying, don't get caught. Don't make the mistake of thinking you'll be safe if you get arrested.

You: How bad do I have to hurt them? Like punch them or something?

BRNR3: I didn't say it had to be physical, though it can be. Do what you think will satisfy me. You'll either be right or wrong.

BRNR3: But whatever it is, record it with the camera on my phone. Send me the video as soon as it's done.

You: Not trying to whine, but I don't know if I can do this.

BRNR3: That's up to you. Time to see if you value someone else's discomfort more than your own life.

BRNR3: You have until 6pm tonight to send me the video.

BRNR3: Happy hunting. ;)

Text Log (11/6/18) Beginning 5:45pm

You: Video upload failed.

You: Video upload failed.

You: Video uploaded. done.mp4

You: There. I did it.

Text Log (11/6/18) Beginning 6:21pm

You: Did you get it? Was that okay?

BRNR3: I got it. I've been thinking about it. Weighing it.

You: You said it didn't have to be physical.

BRNR3: I remember what I said.

You: Look, maybe the video doesn't do a good job of explaining it. That car belongs to a homeless girl that lives near me.

BRNR3: A homeless person with a car?

You: Well, she lives out of her car. Been doing it at least six months. She swaps out between a few different parking spots so she gets less hassle. So busting out her windows like that, especially as cold as its getting, is going to hurt her a lot. And I did like you said. She wasn't around, and no one saw me.

BRNR3: Hmm.

BRNR3: I think that a person's actions tell you a great deal about what they believe. What they value. You agree?

You: Yeah, I guess so.

BRNR3: What you did was mean-spirited, I suppose. It will cause this woman some degree of discomfort.

BRNR3: Assuming that your little story is even true. You could have just vandalized some random car and then made up the part about a poor homeless girl to make it more compelling.

You: No, I swear! You can even see all her clothes and the sleeping bag in the video! I made sure.

BRNR3: Either way, the real question is

BRNR3: Does this act represent how much you value your life? This petty act of breaking windows? This act of an unruly child?

You: You said that it didn't have to be physical.

BRNR3: Or do you want more time to prove how much you value living? Another chance to show me that I can fully trust you? Or are you just wasting my time?

You: No.

You: No you can trust me I swear you can and Ill do better

You: Please let me have another chance. Ill do better

You: Please

You: Hello? Please

Text Log (11/6/18) Beginning 8:49pm

You: Video uploaded. molly.mp4

You: Did you get it? I'll do more. Just want to make sure you got it.

You: The little girl is named Molly. She's the daughter of a woman I used to date. They've had the same dog for years. Chester. They love that fucking dog.

You: Loved. That's why she's screaming like that when she found him in the yard.

You: I think I understand now. I think you want to see how it hurt her more than you want to see me hurting the dog. If I'm wrong, tell me. I recorded the other too.

You: That was really hard for me. I really care for that girl and her mother. I've never hurt an animal before. But I want to give you what you want. I want you to trust me.

You: Please let me know if this is okay.

Text Log (11/6/18) Beginning 9:11pm

BRNR3: That's better.

BRNR3: I noticed you shot the video where I could see it was a little girl but not what she or her house looked like. ;)

BRNR3: Her name isn't Molly either, is it?

You: No, it is. But yeah, I don't want you knowing who or where they are for obvious reasons.

BRNR3: Is that why you didn't carry my phone with you like I told you? Is that why you recorded the footage on your own phone instead and then transferred it to mine before you sent it?

BRNR3: I give you some credit for thinking about me tracking my phone, but you still disobeyed my instructions.

BRNR3: If you don't trust me, how can I trust you?

You: I'm sorry. It won't happen again. I was just trying to keep anyone else from getting involved.

BRNR3: I wonder if ol' Chester thinks he's not involved. Or "Molly".

BRNR3: How did you kill him?

You: I fed him poisoned food. Then I cut his throat after he was dead. To make sure she would scream for the video.

BRNR3: Was Chester an outside dog?

You: Yeah.

You: Well, he stayed in the backyard during the day. At night they would always let him in when they got home for a few hours. Sometimes he slept inside too.

BRNR3: How did you know when they'd find him?

You: Molly goes to her mother's store after school. They don't get home until after 8 most weeknights. It was tight, but I was done by the time Molly came out to get Chester tonight.

BRNR3: How long has it been since you saw "Molly" and Chester?

You: Idk. A year maybe.

BRNR3: What would you have done if Chester hadn't been there?

You: What do you mean?

BRNR3: Well, you went there to make a second video. With poison and a knife. What if Chester had died or ran off since you had last been around? What would you have done then?

You: Idk. I'd have figured something else out.

BRNR3: I see.

BRNR3: Good enough for tonight. Sweet dreams.

Text Log (11/7/18) Beginning 6:38am

BRNR3: Video Received. sleepytime.mp4

BRNR3: You're cute when you're asleep.

You: You were in my apt?

You: This was from last night. Why? I'm doing what you asked.

You: Why?

BRNR3: Because I need you to trust me. Before this you might have thought that I wasn't sure who you were or where you lived. Or that I couldn't get to you. That something other than my word was keeping me from meeting you.

BRNR3: Now you know better, don't you?

BRNR3: Now we're getting closer to knowing where each other stands in this.

You: Are you still in here?

BRNR3: No. I'm absolutely not watching you from your bedroom closet.

BRNR3: J/k.

You: Leaving the phone at the hospital wasn't an accident was it.

BRNR3: ;)

You: Look, I'll do what you want, but I just want your word that there is a way for me to get out of this. Other than you killing me, I mean.

BRNR3: There is. You don't have to die to finish this. You have my word.

You: Thank you.

You: Do you need me to do something else today?

BRNR3: Initiative. I like that. Today I only need two simple things from you.

BRNR3: First, I need you to pick another person for me. This time it needs to be someone you don't know.

BRNR3: Meet someone today. Get their name and take a pic of them. Send me both and also where you met them.

BRNR3: I'll take care of the rest.

You: Ok. What's the second thing?

BRNR3: Go into the app drawer on my phone. I want you to open up an app and familiarize yourself with it for later use.

You: Ok. What app?

BRNR3: It's called "Polterzeitgeist! Find that ghost!". Can't miss it.

You: Okay. You just want me to look at it?

BRNR3: For the time being, yes. And get me your next pick by 3pm. TTFN.

Part Three

Text Log (11/7/18) Beginning 10:23am

You: Image uploaded. 1A23110718.jpg

You: His name is Harry Parks. I met him at a coffee shop near the hospital. I've seen him before but never talked to him. I just made small talk in line and then took the picture after making contact. He shouldn't know I took the pic or suspect anything.

BRNR3: Very good. I like you being careful. I'll be in touch soon.

Text Log (11/7/18) Beginning 2:18pm

BRNR3: Are you at work?

You: You know that I am.

BRNR3: :) I know that my phone is at the hospital. Are you at work?

You: Yes, I am.

BRNR3: Go to a secluded place and open the Polterzeitgeist app.

You: Ok. Just a min.

Chat Log from "Polterzeitgeist! Find that ghost!" app (11/7/18) Beginning 2:23pm

Revenant: Hello there.

You: Is this you? BRNR3?

Revenant: Of course.

Revenant: I liked your pick. You failed to mention in your "detailed report" of how you met him that he was an armed out-of-uniform police officer. I'm assuming you knew he had a gun and that he was law enforcement?

You: Yes. I didn't lie to you. I had never talked to him before. But I had seen him in uniform at the coffee shop a couple of times, and he did have a gun in a back holster today. It was under a jacket, but I saw it when we were in line.

You: But I figured it wouldn't be any problem for you anyway.

Revenant: :P

Revenant: I appreciate your confidence in me. It's well-placed.

Revenant: Video Received eating.mp4

You: Oh god.

Revenant: Yes.

Revenant: Now it's your turn again. Listen carefully, because while I appreciate your attempt at being clever, I am not in the mood to repeat myself or listen to you whine. Are we clear?

You: Yes.

Revenant: Good.

Revenant: This app has many functions, but one of them is to serve as a guide. It contains a map that will show you where you need to go. When we finish talking, go to the map and you will find a yellow star on it. You need to reach that star no later than 4:45pm. Do not leave work to reach the star earlier than necessary, but keep watch on the map regularly. Make sure you can reach it on time. Get stuck in traffic or lose your way, and you will have failed.

Revenant: And what happens if you fail will make what the cop went through look like a paradise.

You: I won't fail. I promise.

Revenant: Good. I have faith in you.

Revenant: When you are within 15 meters of the person the star represents and the time is 4:43 or later, you will receive further instructions from the app on how to complete your task.

Revenant: It should go without saying that you should avoid being conspicuous, be aware of any security or surveillance, and generally avoid getting caught. If you get caught, that counts as failure too.

You: Ok. I'll do it.

Revenant: After you hit "Accept" on the task it gives you, the app will start recording video. Leave the app open until the task is completed. When you are finished, hit "Send" and wait for me to contact you. Understand?

You: Yes. I won't mess it up.

Revenant: We'll see.

Chat Log from "Polterzeitgeist! Find that ghost!" app (11/7/18) Beginning 5:15pm

Revenant: Good job.

You: My hands are shaking. Fuck. You made me do that.

Revenant: No, you chose to do that. You decided you valued yourself more than a stranger.

You: Who was she?

Revenant: Her name was Alison Murphy.

You: Why her?

Revenant: She used to have a fairly boring job as a law clerk that one day led to her having some excitement. Seeing a small part of how this all works.

Revenant: She was invited to participate, but declined. Instead, she decided to just talk to others about things she didn't understand. Her talking about it wasn't the problem. Her lack of participation, however…well, you know how I feel about people that don't want to participate.

You: Did you know where she'd be? That she'd be alone at the top of that parking garage like that?

Revenant: I knew she'd most likely be at one of six places at that particular time. She had established several relevant patterns of behavior in the past few weeks. One of those patterns was parking her car occasionally at the top of that particular garage, which she did this morning at 9:44am. Another was returning to her car between 4:40 and 4:55pm when it was parked at that location. All of this, combined with the app tracking, made the place you found her the most likely place she would be.

You: But that's still just an educated guess. What if she did something different? Came back early or late? What if at 4:45 she was in the middle of a grocery store full of people?

Revenant: Then you would have had to "figure something else out". Just like you would have had to find other places to stick your poison and knife if poor old Chester wasn't there to kill.

You: Okay. But what if she had just left her car this morning, got on a bus and went to another state? Went somewhere I couldn't reach in time?

Revenant: Lol! Oh no. Did you think this was all about you? That you're the only one I'm connecting with? You did, didn't you? (͡° ͜ʖ ͡°)

Revenant: Wherever she went, whatever she did, Alison Murphy was going to die today. Luckily for you, she was close to your hospital. Even better for you, she was pushed from the sixth story of a sparsely populated parking garage that has no cameras.

You: So there are others like me?

Revenant: There are others, but each of you is special and unique. :)

Text Log (7/4/18) Beginning 1:01am

BRNR6: So you found the phone I added to the box? Can I assume you've gone through the rest of my "Private Valuables" then?

You: Yes. I did. I didn't know the combination to open the lock on the book. And I don't know how to open the small metal box. But yeah, I looked at the rest. You're insane.

BRNR6: Sanity is a relative concept. You think that Independence Day is a good movie, for example, yet I don't judge.

You: Okay.

You: What do you want from me?

BRNR6: Do you appreciate the fact that I can find you now?

You: Yes. I just want this to be over.

BRNR6: Well, you're about to take the first step towards that.

BRNR6: Look in the box. You see the little clay pumpkin?

You: Yes.

BRNR6: Great. Now pull up the app drawer on the phone you're using. I want you to familiarize yourself with the app called "Polterzeitgeist! Find that ghost!"

You: Why?

BRNR6: Because tomorrow it's going to show you where you need to take that little pumpkin and what to do when you get there.

Chat Log from "Polterzeitgeist! Find that ghost!" app (7/7/18) Beginning 12:19pm

You: I can't keep doing this. Whatever sick game this is, I can't do it. I can't keep hurting people, helping you hurt people.

Revenant: I think you can. I think you will. You've done so well so far.

Revenant: But I do think it's time for you to open the book and read it. It will help you understand. The combination is 10925.

Revenant: I'll expect a thorough book report tomorrow morning. ;)

Chat Log from "Polterzeitgeist! Find that ghost!" app (7/8/18) Beginning 9:35am

Revenant: Do you understand now?

You: I don't know.

You: Maybe.

Revenant: Are you ready to continue?

You: Do I have a choice?

Revenant: You always have a choice.

You: I'm ready.

Revenant: Good. Find the little cornhusk ghost in the box.

Chat Log from "Polterzeitgeist! Find that ghost!" app (7/12/18) Beginning 8:42pm

You: I'm inside. Everything is prepared.

Revenant: Good.

Chat Log from "Polterzeitgeist! Find that ghost!" app (7/12/18) Beginning 9:25pm

You: Sam Morris has been claimed. The work is done.

Revenant: The work is far from done. But you have taken another step down the Dark Path I've shown you. I'm proud of you.

You: I think I enjoyed it this time.

Revenant: I know. That's good.

You: What is happening to me?

Revenant: You are finding your true self.

You: Can I look in the metal box yet?

Revenant: In due time, my love. All in due time.

Part Four

Text Log (11/8/18) Beginning 11:14am

BRNR3: Good morning.

You: Is it time for me to pick another person for you?

BRNR3: No, we're past that I think. Open up the app.

You: Another gold star? Another for me?

BRNR3: Yes.

You: This is over four hours away.

BRNR3: Which is why you need to start getting ready. You'll need to leave within the hour.

You: Why this person?

BRNR3: I have my reasons. Just because I have shared things with you doesn't mean you're entitled to know everything.

You: Sorry. I was just curious.

You: I'm nervous.

You: Can you tell me the time and location? I like to know so I can plan.

BRNR3: Not yet. You need to be adaptable. But I will tell you to expect more of a challenge than pushing a frightened girl off a parking deck.

BRNR3: Now get going. When you get within 2 miles of the star, you'll receive the specifics of your task.

You: Ok.

You: Thank you.

Chat Log from "Polterzeitgeist! Find that ghost!" app (11/8/18) Beginning 4:23pm

You: Okay, I made it here and got the instructions. So I have to kill this guy between 5 and 5:15? But I'm at a shopping mall. If the star is right, he's in there somewhere. Can't I wait until there are less people around?

Revenant: No.

You: Does it have to be this Alex Turney guy anyway? How about if I just pick out someone else?

Revenant: You're wasting time. If I were you, I'd spend more time looking things over and formulating a plan rather than whining like a petulant child.

You: Ok. I'm going.

You: Wish me luck.

Revenant: ;)

Chat Log from "Polterzeitgeist! Find that ghost!" app (11/8/18) Beginning 6:01pm

You: What the FUCK was that?

Revenant: What was what?

You: You set me up.

Revenant: What do you mean?

You: I mean you fucking set me up. He knew I was coming. There's no way he didn't know I was coming.

Revenant: Why do you say that?

You: Because

You: Look, I went into the mall, okay? I used the star as long as I could, but it took me into a department store and there were a lot of people around. The star wasn't accurate enough to be useful at that point. I had his picture from the app, but it still took awhile to find him without being obvious.

You: Then I turned a corner and saw him looking at shoes like ten feet away. I didn't catch him looking at me, but he suddenly sat down the shoe he was holding and starting moving fast toward the back of the store. I saw he was heading to the bathroom, so I figured this was my best shot. I followed him.

You: I saw the door to the men's bathroom closing as I got near. I took out the gun I had brought. I hadn't been sure how I was going to muffle the shot, but then I saw he was wearing a thick coat. I figured I'd make him take it off, wrap the gun in the coat, and shoot him in the mouth. Try to make it look like a weird suicide if I could, or at least buy enough time to get away.

BRNR3: What were you going to do about the security cameras? Or anyone who saw you and remembered?

You: I wore a hat and tried to blend in. Never looked up at any cameras and never touched anything after entering the mall until I touched the door handle going into the bathroom. I'd planned to wipe it down on my way out, but things didn't go according to plan.

You: When I went into that bathroom, he jumped me. From above. That fucker was holding himself up above the door somehow. Just waiting.

BRNR3: Interesting.

You: No. Fuck that. He almost killed me. He pinned me down and took the knife away. I think he broke my wrist. He's a big fucker, but he was way faster than me.

You: I've never seen anyone so fast.

BRNR3: So why aren't you dead?

You: He said he didn't want to end it yet. Then he told me "Run. Hard and fast. Don't worry. I'll find you again soon enough."

BRNR3: That sounds like him. Always so dramatic.

You: So you did set me up.

BRNR3: No, not really. I didn't tell him that you or anyone else was coming for him. But he is further along the path you are starting down. He's not easily taken.

You: So you're pitting all your little pets against one another, is that it?

BRNR3: Pets. Your petty indignation and complaints are tiresome. You are being given a gift and yet all you ever do is complain.

You: Look, I'm sorry. I'm just hurt and scared. I thought I could trust you.

BRNR3: You can.

You: Then what do I do? This maniac you had me go after will hunt me down, I can feel it. So what's next?

BRNR3: It sounds to me like you should run.

BRNR3: Hard and fast.

Text Log (11/10/18) Beginning 2:41pm

You: Video upload failed

You: Video upload failed

You: Video upload failed

You: Shit. My service sucks here. I'll have to send the movie later. Can you get this?

BRNR12: Yes.

You: Cool. Sorry about the delay.

You: It was everything you said it would be. I wish I could show it to you.

BRNR12: Tell me.

You: The guy...Simon. He knew Alex was coming for him just like you said. I followed him from the mall, he went to some cheap motel for a couple of hours, but I guess he got too antsy, because he left there before midnight and spent yesterday moving from place to place.

You: First an all-night diner. Then a grocery store. Then a library. Then he went to the airport and bought a ticket for a domestic flight. I thought he was going to actually fly off, but he just spent the next several hours sleeping at one of the gates in those uncomfortable chairs.

BRNR12: Poor baby.

You: Lol. Yeah.

You: Security finally started hassling him today though, asking about what flight he was waiting for and stuff. So he wound up going to a little restaurant down the road from the motel he'd stayed at for half a minute. This was just over an hour ago, and it was kind of a shitty place, but it was still busy that close to lunch.

You: I went in a few minutes after Simon did. Got a booth against the far wall where I could keep an eye on him. It was funny. He kept looking around like somebody was goosing him. Super skittish, right?

BRNR12: Right.

You: Then his head came up. I had a bird dog once. That's what it reminded me of. But I'll be damned if Simon didn't look up right as Alex came in. It was like you said it can be. When you're following the Path, you can sense other travelers.

BRNR12: Pilgrims.

You: Shit, yeah. Pilgrims. Well Simon was sure as shit feeling something, though it might have just been piss in his pants. :P

BRNR12: Continue.

You: Sorry, yeah. So Alex comes in. Dressed normal, but not trying to hide. As he heads up the aisle toward where Simon is sitting, Simon loses his shit. Gets up from his table, starts screaming for someone to help him. That this guy (Alex) was crazy and trying to kill him. Had been stalking him.

You: Now all while he's doing this, Simon's looking around. He's waiting for a reaction. He expects the waitress to start freaking out and calling the cops. He thinks that old couple with the kid is going to huddle down or run for the door. But then he realizes none of that is happening.

You: They're all just watching. Watching and smiling. I realized I was smiling too, and I don't mind telling you it freaked my shit out a bit. But it was really good too. It felt right. Like truth. Capital T truth.

BRNR12: Yes, that's the way it is sometimes.

You: Well, Simon has realized by this point that he's alone. No help coming and only ten feet from the monster that's after him. I'll give him credit. When he got up from the table, he'd taken a steak knife with him. You said he'd had a gun, but he either didn't bring it in or he panicked and forgot about it. But he still tried. When Alex came for him, he didn't try to get away until he was already screaming and instinct had kicked in.

You: I stayed until the end. After Alex was done, he and two of the others took Simon away. The other people…I don't really understand. It was like nothing had happened. I watched that old couple with the little boy finish eating lunch with drops of blood on the side of their glasses. Were they all plants by you or Alex? All in on the joke?

BRNR12: What do you think?

You: I don't see how. That would be like 20 ppl. But what else could it be? Mass hypnosis or something? I don't know which idea spooks me more.

You: Anyhow, I recorded all of it, but like I said, I'll have to wait and send it in a bit.

BRNR12: That's fine. Just make sure you do.

You: Sure. But do you mind if I ask a question?

BRNR12: Go ahead.

You: Who was Simon anyway? Just some dude?

BRNR12: lol. Yes. Just some dude who found my phone. And he tried walking the Dark Path for a moment, but like most, he failed. So he wound up as meat for Alex.

You: The Path is a razor that bleeds you. Until you finish it or it finishes you.

BRNR12: So they say.

Chat Log from "Polterzeitgeist! Find that ghost!" app (11/10/18) Beginning 5:15pm

Revenant: I haven't heard from you since you dealt with Simon. Alex, are you all right?

You: I am. I've just been thinking.

Revenant: About?

You: About him. There at the end, he knew he was going to die. But he still fought. And for a second, I though I could see the glow around him. Like he really was a Pilgrim like me. Like us.

Revenant: For a second I think he was. But that's the point. The journey we're taking, the path is narrow with room for only a few. Only one of you could progress any further, and he had little chance against you.

You: I guess.

You: I don't dream any more. Did I tell you that? For all the changes, I think that bothers me the most.

Revenant: I didn't either when I was where you are. You'll have new dreams soon enough.

Revenant: It's time I told you how to use the box.

You: I know it's mentioned in the book, but I don't understand what it really is. What's inside.

Revenant: It's called a box of shadows. And if your heart is right, it will show you the place that the Dark Path is leading us.

You: The Realm? The Kingdom of Dust?

Revenant: Yes, my love.

You: Are you sure I'm ready?

Revenant: I am. I wouldn't risk it if I wasn't.

You: When can I see you again?

Revenant: Look up. I'm already here.

I thought my neighbor was dressing up like a scarecrow.

Growing up, I lived only about thirty minutes from my grandparents' farm, so it was a regular thing that we would go and visit them on the weekends and holidays. I remember playing with the handful of ducks and goats that they had, running around in the small grove of trees behind the house, and exploring all the intriguing differences between the farm and my mundane city life. Back then, the idea of their farm was more akin to a magical land I was lucky enough to visit regularly—vast and lush and full of animals that seemed exotic and exciting.

But the counterpoint to this sense of childish wonder and joy were my young fears about the large field that lay between my grandparents farm and the house next door. Most years it was planted in corn and sunflowers, their rows of tall stalks and reaching leaves resembling an invading army of monsters waiting impatiently at the border of my grandparents' land.

And presiding over that terrible horde was the scarecrow—an old shirt and overalls stuffed with hay and topped with a torn potato sack head and a worn straw hat. My father told me it was to keep birds away, that he wasn't a real man and couldn't hurt anybody, but I would always check to make sure the scarecrow hadn't moved from its high perch among the crops when we were coming or going from my grandparents' house. Even as a teenager, when I thought I was well-past being scared of corn and stuffed shirts, I would find myself glancing out into that field to make sure the scarecrow wasn't off its post and marauding between the rows.

It was an engrained habit that I found myself repeating two months ago when I pulled up to the farm again for the first time in three years. My grandfather died when I was twenty-one, and my grandmother had followed him just a week before my arrival back at the farm. She had managed to outlive my grandfather and both my parents, but she'd had to leave the farm for nursing home care during the last years of her life, and I hadn't returned to the house since she had left it. Still, it was in good repair—she had someone to look after the place and they had done a good job overall.

That's when I realized I was unconsciously checking for the scarecrow.

There was none, but there were no crops either. The old man who had owned it for decades had died the same year as grandfather, and whoever owned it now, they kept to themselves and didn't seem too keen on farming. Weeds and grass grew tall as my chest throughout the twenty acre strip, and in the middle of it, the old wooden post that had held the scarecrow was bare and faded with age. Shaking my head, I got out and started checking the house more thoroughly for problems.

If all of this had happened a year earlier, I would have said I was going to do minimal repairs and then immediately sell the place for the best price I could get. I had sentimental attachment to the farm, but my career and my life were over five hours away and didn't involve raising ducks or planting a garden. I was only a few years out of school, but I had a good, high-paying job at an architecture firm, and I had no intention of going anywhere.

But things changed. In the past six months the firm had been dissolved due to an embezzlement scandal between the partners and I had been forced to live off my meager savings and a handful of short-term contract jobs. With my ever-looming student debt and no real prospects, I decided that I would give up my apartment and come stay at the farm for the next few months. The contract work I could do from pretty much anywhere as long as I had internet, and it would give me some financial relief while I figured out where I was going to land.

I had been prepared to find the house in terrible condition—even well-cared for empty houses have a remarkable ability to fall apart, as though the lack of people inside cause them to age prematurely. But aside from some bad plumbing and a hot water heater on its last legs, it wasn't in bad shape at all. Which was more than I could say for the house next door.

Much like the weedy field, the house had developed into a ramshackle eyesore. Over the next few days I would find my eye drawn to it, a voice whispering in the back of my head that the new neighbor was probably going to take about 30 grand off my asking price when I got ready to sell the place. Still, there was nothing to be done about it, and for the time being I was enjoying being back at a place filled with so many good memories. I even got in the habit of taking walks every morning and sitting on their wide front porch as evening would come on, taking in the beautiful scenery and the blissful silence.

But still my eyes would wander back to my neighbor's house on occasion, a constant irritant in the corner of my eye. I never saw the owner, and as far as I could tell, his old red pick-up truck never moved from its spot in the front yard. Nothing ever changed at all, until I saw a new scarecrow in the field between us.

It was larger than the one from my childhood, and even at a distance I could tell it was better constructed and defined. It had a weight and substance to the way its body hung on the post, and its hands were fully formed and covered with dark gloves as opposed to the tied-off sleeves and jutting hay straw of its predecessor. And several things occurred to me about the scarecrow as I studied it from the porch.

First, I didn't understand what the point was. There was no sign of the field itself being tended or cleaned up in any way, much less anything being planted. Second, it seemed odd that it looked so well-made when there was such an obvious lack of attention to everything else over there. Third, it being better made and more substantial somehow made it more off-putting than the old version had been, perhaps because it more closely resembled an actual man.

Finally, whatever the reasons, even at thirty-two, I thought it was creepy as fuck.

****

Over the next few days, I was busy with several new contract projects, and that combined with finicky internet and working on the plumbing had me preoccupied most of the time. But I still thought about that new scarecrow frequently, and every time I went outside I found myself checking to see if it was still in his spot. I kind of hated the little surge of relief I would feel when I saw that he was, and over the next several days I came to realize I had started to think of the scarecrow in terms of "he" rather than "it". I was irritated with myself for being spooked by an inanimate object, but that didn't stop me from peeking over there, just in case.

I pushed down the initial flush of panic I felt, telling myself the owner had either taken him (damnit, *it*) down or it had fallen down on its own. I was in the middle of finishing up a draft for a client, but I forced myself to sit down in one of the porch chairs and hang out for a few minutes. I knew it was only to prove to myself that I wasn't scared, but I didn't care. If I was going to be out here by myself for the next few months, I had to get over being unnerved by every little thing.

So I sat, looking around and trying to empty my mind, but really just waiting for the next time my roving gaze made its way back over to that field and the empty post. When I first saw movement in the grass near the post, I froze, my mouth going dry as I suggested to myself that it might be a trick of the fading twilight. When it happened a second time, my rational mind declared that it was either a critter or the man had decided to put the scarecrow back on its perch.

When I watched the scarecrow climb back up on its wooden post and settle there, all thought fled from me. I was rooted there by fear and some low-level instinct to stay still. To not be seen. I knew it was no trick of the light. I had watched that thing climb back up on the post under its own power. It was alive somehow.

That's when it turned its head and looked at me.

Even across the distance I could feel its gaze hot on my face, and after a moment of boiling horror I bolted inside. When I looked out through a window, I saw it had already turned back to contemplate the field and my logic started to reassert itself from behind the safety of window panes and locked doors.

Clearly it was a costume. There was a person wearing a scarecrow costume for whatever bizarre reason, and I had seen them getting back up on the post. There was probably a little platform lower on the post that they stood on, and they were playing a practical joke on me. Or making a movie. Or just being weird. It didn't really matter, because it being a person was the only thing that made sense.

Besides, they were on their own property, I reasoned, and whatever odd or silly shit they wanted to get up to over there…well, that was their business. The main things were that it wasn't a monster and they were over *there*, not over *here*. I repeated these points to myself throughout that night and the next couple of days, and while the continued presence of the scarecrow (the person dressed as a scarecrow, I would correct myself) was creepy and weird, he hadn't moved again that I had seen. It still preoccupied my thoughts, and I realized I had abandoned going for my morning walks or hanging out on the porch in the evening, but I tried not to dwell on it more than I could help.

So by the third night after the scarecrow looked at me, I had resigned myself to watching t.v. and eating a microwave lasagna while studiously *not* looking out the windows. Until I did, and saw the scarecrow at the window looking in at me.

Its face was partially obscured by a dark, wide-brimmed hat, but what I could see looked to be made of a swarthy, oiled leather. There was a leering slash of a smile stitched up with some kind of thick, red thread, and above that twin silver buttons shaped like long, sickle moons stared in at me, dancing in the reflected light and motion from the television. The rest of the thing's face was riddled with black marks of some kind, reminiscent of Norse runes but different. As I watched, the sack skin bulged slightly in spots as its smile turned up at the ends.

I took this all in during the brief two-second window of shock and surprise before I lost my shit.

Then I was yelling, peddling out of my chair and away from the window like the house was on fire. I grabbed up my phone and locked myself in the bedroom I'd been using, moving to pull the curtain on the room's windows as I called 911. Over half an hour later, a sleepy-looking deputy pulled up and took my statement before going over to talk to my neighbor. When he came back, he looked less sleepy, but I could tell by his expression that he didn't have good news.

"Look, I talked to your neighbor. He's a weird fella, no doubt about that one, but he says he doesn't know anything about it. He told me he put up a scarecrow a few days ago, but it hasn't moved from the spot since." We were standing on the front porch now, and he gestured to a shadowy shape above the field. "And as you can see, it's up there now."

I gritted my teeth. "It took you over half an hour to get out here. He had plenty of time to put the scarecrow back up there after taking off the outfit."

I realized my mistake as his gaze hardened. "Listen, bud. We have four deputies to cover nearly six hundred square miles, and you live far out. You'll have to forgive us if you have to wait a few minutes." He puffed out a breath, and when he spoke next, his voice was softer. "Look, I knew your grandparents. They were good people. I'm sure you are too. But country life is a bit different. Try not to spook so easily, okay? It could be you fell asleep and had a dream, or maybe the guy next door was playing a prank. Call us again if you need us, of course, but sometimes you just have to let things go or handle them yourself." With that he patted me on the shoulder and headed back to his patrol car.

I wanted to feel angry or offended at being brushed off, but I knew he was probably right. I either needed to ignore it or try dealing with it myself. When I woke up the next morning and still felt scared and angry, I decided I was better off just going to talk to the neighbor. I'd be nice about it, but maybe if I let him know I took it serious, it wouldn't happen again.

It didn't work out that way.

****

The neighbor's house was in even worse shape up close, and I felt my stomach roll slightly as I started getting various whiffs of decay as I made my way up to his front door. I saw the source of at least some of them. There were two dead birds and a dead possum littered across his yard in various stages of decomposition. Swallowing down my rising gorge, I focused on the door and knocked.

The man who came to the door was likely only a few years older than me, but he had the worn-out, prematurely aged look of a junkie. He was short and balding, with sallow skin that hung loose on a dirty frame that was barely covered by a soiled wifebeater and a discolored pair of underwear. A fresh bouquet of stale sweat and beer had struck me when he first opened the door, and when he spoke, the smell of decay grew stronger as well.

"What do you want?" His voice was low and gravelly, with an accent I couldn't place. His red-rimmed eyes were full of contempt as he waited for me to respond, and I could tell by the way he was holding the door he was on the verge of shutting it back in my face.

I swallowed again and began. "Um, well. I just wanted to let you know that I wasn't trying to hassle you last night by calling the deputy. I really did have someone at my window wearing a mask that looked like your scarecrow."

He let out a dry, cawing laugh. "Wasn't a mask. Was the scarecrow, I reckon."

I frowned. "Well, yeah. I guess. I mean I saw some guy in the full costume climb up on that post the other day. Are ya'll making a movie, or…"

He was shaking his head, his lips pulled back in an ugly smile as he continued to chuckle. "You're not gettin' it, mate. It's not a costume. It's the scarecrow." I wanted to immediately discount him as crazy, but the thing was he didn't *seem* crazy. Hostile and condescending, yes, but not crazy.

I found myself taking a couple of steps back from him. "That's impossible."

He shrugged. "Maybe so, but it's the truth. That thing there comes from the Rot, and there's a whole lot of impossible that can come from such as that."

I blinked. What the fuck was he talking about? Maybe he was crazy after all, or into some odd religion or something. "The rot? I don't know what you're talking about."

He laughed again and waggled a yellow finger at me. "Of course you don't, sheep. But maybe you'll find out."

I felt a new surge of anger. "Is that some kind of threat? Look, if you or your fucking scarecrow come back on my property your ass is going to have a problem."

His laughter cut off as his eyes grew dangerous. "You need to mind yourself talking to me, boy. And I have no interest in you. As for the scarecrow..." He paused and looked out into the field, and for a moment I saw fear pass across his face. "I can't control that thing. Thought I could, but it's too strong." He looked back at me, his expression of hard arrogance returning. "So you best be watching out yourself, 'cause it seems it's taken a liking to you."

****

I got little accomplished the rest of the day, and when I went to bed that night, I felt sure I would never get to sleep. I hadn't fired a gun since my early twenties, but I had my grandfather's shotgun loaded and in the bed next to me as I stared up at the ceiling. I found myself jumping at every creak and groan of the old house, and every few seconds I was glancing out the window, despite the fact it looked out into the backyard and not toward the field. The last thing I remember was patting the stock of the shotgun for the twentieth time to make sure it was still close by, and then I was waking up.

The scarecrow was standing over me.

It was nearly a full moon that night, and while the room was still dark, I could see well enough to watch as it leaned down toward me. Letting out a yell, I tried to scramble away off the other side of the bed, but it was too fast. One hard, gloved hand pressed down on my chest with enough pressure to both hurt and pin me to the spot while the other hand pulled back the sheets and began pressing on my stomach.

The pain from my chest was overtaken by a thudding ache that spread across my abdomen as its fingers probed. And while my mind was lost in a tumult of blind animal struggle and fear at the time, later it occurred to me that it was almost as if he was looking for something or examining me. Then, just as swiftly as it had begun, it was over. The scarecrow jerked his hand away from my stomach as though it had fallen on a hot stove, and with a last warning push on my chest to stay down, it moved quickly from the room. A moment later I heard the front door slam open and the creak of the porch as the thing left.

I stayed deathly still for several moments, and when I finally did move, it was only to rub my chest and stomach. I wanted to call for help, but I knew there was no help to be had and I feared going outside to my car in the dark. So I crawled off the bed and over to the door to lock it, and once that was done, I pulled the forgotten shotgun free from its tangle of sheets and held it tightly as I sat in a corner of the room and waited for sunrise.

Light was still returning to the world when I heard the first sirens. First closer by, then farther away, then closer by again. I was curious, but I was also still petrified. Whatever was going on out there, I planned to wait until things were quiet and then bolt for my car and never come back. So when someone began to knock at the bedroom door, I let out a scream. Three seconds later, the same deputy from before was busting in the door, eyes wide and gun raised.

His gaze found me in the corner and he raised his other hand. "Put the gun down." I dropped it immediately and he lowered his own slightly as he looked around the room. "Are you all right? Are you alone in here?"

I nodded, unembarrassed tears springing to my eyes. "Yeah. I am. Unless that thing came back."

His eyes went to mine and I could tell something had changed. When he didn't respond, I went on. "What happened? I heard sirens and I didn't call anybody this time."

He sighed as he stowed his gun back on his belt. "Bad things. Worst I've seen I think. The guy next door? His house burned down. Fire crew has it mostly out now, but from what they've seen he's dead. Not from the fire but from his guts being ripped out." I started to respond, but he wasn't finished. "We were getting the call about the fire when another call came in. A couple of miles further down the road, a young woman and her nine-year old son were murdered. Father found them when he came home from the late shift. They were hollowed out too."

The deputy's eyes had lowered to the floor as he had been talking, but now they lifted past me to stare out the window at the back yard and the grove of trees beyond. "I don't know what happened, but I think I believe you a lot more now than I did the other night. I doubt you had anything to do with any of the rest, but you'll still have to be examined and questioned, of course." He looked back in my direction. "My advice is to leave off trying to convince anybody that there's a living scarecrow prowling the woods." Meeting my eyes meaningfully, he went on. "In fact, my report is going to say that I woke you up during a welfare check and you were surprised that anything had happened. How does that sound to you?"

I nodded, my throat painfully dry and tight. "Yeah...But why help me?"

He shrugged. "Because I meant what I said the other night. I figure you're a good kid in a bad place, and I've lived long enough to know there's enough bad already in the world without me making more. Or maybe because I should have done more sooner, and I saw some things tonight that made me realize that. Either way, go ahead and get dressed. We'll try to get you done quickly."

I wanted to ask what else he had seen, but looking at his haunted expression, I thought better of it. So wiping at my eyes, I just nodded and started thinking of what I would say.

****

I haven't returned to my grandparents' farm since that day, and I don't plan on that changing in the future. A week after the murders, the deputy called to tell me that the sheriff's office had concluded their initial investigation and I was no longer considered a person of interest. And although they had no suspect yet, they would continue to investigate until they did. I could hear in his voice how he expected that to go.

And while I'm not going back there myself, someday I'll put the farm on the market for a very cheap price and hope someone snaps it up, severing my last ties with that place and those memories forever. But for now my mind is on other things.

Because tomorrow I'm going into surgery for a partial colectomy—the removal of part of my colon. I started having stomach pains and bleeding last month, and when I got it checked, the doctors figured out I have stage two colon cancer. Treatable, and with a good likelihood I'll recover, even if I'll always live in the shadow of the cancer coming back down the line.

But a month ago, when I was sitting in the doctor's office as he gave me the news, his face full of practiced concern and his words no doubt a canned recitation of standard disclaimers and assurances, I barely heard any of it. All I could think about was the scarecrow jerking its hand back as it explored my abdomen. Almost as if it had discovered something unsuitable about the guts coiled inside.

The doctor jumped slightly when I let out a snort of relieved laughter at the thought. Not only had the colon cancer possibly saved my life, but it made me doubt the scarecrow would ever try to find me again. I was damaged goods, I guess.

And cancer sucked, but at least I could understand it. Try and fight it. And compared to facing that rotten thing? A horror that was still roaming the dark somewhere with its silver moon eyes and blood-red smile?

I have to say, I like my odds.

The Ghosthound

My nephew Grayson was always a smart kid. A good kid. My sister was raising him by herself, and while she had to work a lot to make ends meet, he never complained or acted up because of it. Instead, he would fill his time with books and games of his own creation. And while I didn't get to see them as often as I would have liked, it never ceased to amaze me how much they loved each other and how happy they were.

I was part of that love too. We were the only family each other had, and while distance and work kept me from visiting them more than every few months, it was something I always looked forward to. In between, we would keep in touch through texts and funny videos. Then I got him the "Ghosthound"—a stuffed brown hound dog to go with his recently developed interest in ghost hunting.

But the Ghosthound wasn't just a simple stuffed toy. Supposedly it contained temperature sensors and an electromagnetic field (or EMF) meter. According to what Grayson had told me and what I found out researching the toy, "ghost hunters" use changes in EMF and temperature as two big indicators that a ghost is possibly around. When you turn on the Ghosthound and it picks up a significant change in the nearby EMF, its chest will glow a pulsating green. If the temperature drops suddenly, the left front paw will glow blue. If the temperature spikes upward, the right paw will glow red. And all of these lights are accompanied by an audio cue—the toy dog will howl to let you know that a ghost may be near.

Cute stuff, but I was still unsure how much use Grayson would get out of it. Fortunately, his initial excitement over the toy didn't fade. He started making ghost hunting videos and sending them to me, using the Ghosthound to help scout around their house, his school, and at the local park. It was great seeing him so happy, and the videos really were cool. He was genuinely funny, and he would always adopt this overly dramatic narration as he and the Ghosthound patrolled for lingering spirits.

But then late last year, him and my sister Amber were both murdered during a home invasion. No witnesses, no known motive other than possibly theft or just a desire to hurt someone. The investigation is still technically open, but I know the likelihood of them ever catching who did it at this point is slim to none.

I was actually planning on visiting them soon when it happened. I moved up my flight to plan their funerals and attend to all the other details that have to be dealt with when a life ends. Most of their possessions I gave to charity, though I kept all the photos I found, as well as a battered old trumpet case containing the instrument Amber had used since junior high. From Grayson's room I took a couple of trophies, a collection of drawings he had done over the years, and the Ghosthound.

For the longest time I kept everything squirreled away where I wouldn't see it. The loss of them was still too fresh, and I needed time before reminders of them would bring me at least as much joy as they did pain. Still, last week I was starting to consider bringing some of their stuff out when I came home to find the Ghosthound sitting in my guest bedroom.

It was on a small stack of boxes next to the closet I kept both the boxes and the toy in, and my first thought was that someone had broken into the house. I searched the whole place, checking all the doors and windows, looking everywhere for any other sign of disturbance.

But then I remembered. A few days earlier I had been pulling out stuff from that closet in my search for an old receipt. I had been busy and distracted at the time, and I couldn't remember if I had put the boxes back. I didn't specifically recall sitting out the toy dog, but I couldn't say I didn't, and I hadn't been back into the room since. It seemed like the only reasonable explanation.

I contemplated putting the Ghosthound back up again, but instead I took it with me to the living room and sat him on the coffee table. Later that night, I was watching television when I suddenly heard a loud and mournful howl. I jumped, my eyes scanning the room for the noise's source until I saw the pulsating green glow of the toy dog's chest.

Licking my lips nervously, I reached for the dog. It had stopped howling now, but the green light continued to flash as I turned the toy over to look at the power switch. It was switched on, but I knew I hadn't done it. It also seemed odd that the batteries would still be working if it had been left on since Grayson had last used it. The green glow died when I flipped the switch off, and I found myself surprised by the sadness that came over me as the light went away. So after a moment's deliberation, I turned the Ghosthound back on and put it back on the table. It sat quiet the rest of the night.

Over the next few days I found myself waiting for the dog to do something again, but nothing happened. I don't really believe in ghosts, but I don't *not* believe in them either, and I'd be lying if I said I didn't grow more disappointed every day. By the third night I decided to change out the batteries, promising myself that if nothing happened that night, I would move the Ghosthound to a less-conspicuous place and get it off my mind.

That evening I tried to watch television, but my eyes kept going to the dog. When nothing had happened by midnight, I went to bed with a heavy heart, and after staring into the dark for nearly an hour, I finally found my way into troubled sleep.

I was awoken by the Ghosthound's howl.

Jumping out of bed, I ran into the living room, but was unable to find the toy dog, even after flipping on the light. I was looking under the table when I heard the howl again. It was coming from the kitchen.

I went slower into the kitchen, my sleepy excitement being slowly penetrated by concern and fear as I entered the room and saw the Ghosthound. It was sitting on the counter next to the oven. And I knew there was no way I had put it there.

The next twenty minutes were spent patrolling the house with a butcher knife. But like before, I could see no signs of any intrusion other than the Ghosthound itself. I considered calling the police, but what was the point? They were unlikely to find anything beyond what I could tell them, which wasn't much. So instead, I picked up the Ghosthound and went back to the living room.

Sitting down with it still in my hands, I tried to think of possible explanations for what was going on. Possible explanations aside from the toy dog being haunted, which I wasn't prepared to believe.

It could be a cruel prank of some kind. Or it was possible it was all in my head. I didn't think I was going crazy, but then crazy people rarely do. Maybe I really had taken it into the kitchen with me and left it. I was very tired when I went to bed, after all. Or I could have gotten up and moved it in my sleep.

Or the toy dog could be haunted.

I looked back down into the blank-eyed stare of the Ghosthound. "Is anyone there?"

Immediately the dog let out a howl and the right foot lit up red. I almost threw the thing in the floor then, but instead I forced myself to grip it tightly as I steadied myself.

"Does red mean yes?"

Red foot again. *Yes*.

I felt my chest tighten, though I couldn't say if it was more out of excitement or fear. Still, I needed to keep going while it was responding.

"Are you a ghost?"

Red foot. *Yes*.

"Are you Amber?"

The left foot lit up blue. *No*.

"Are you Grayson?"

Red foot followed by blue foot. *Yes and no*. I couldn't help but be happy at that, though the double answer worried me.

"Are you haunting the Ghosthound?"

Blue foot. *No.*

"Are you haunting me?"

Red foot. *Yes.*

I swallowed, my mouth feeling like I had eaten a pound of sand. "Do you mean me any harm?"

The Ghosthound sat silent for several moments, to the point that I thought it wasn't going to answer at all. Then the chest began to glow green again, the light pulsing like a heartbeat. After a few seconds it stopped, and the dog remained silent the rest of the night.

The next morning I called my friend Parker. We had been college roommates, with me studying history while he worked on his engineering degree. He was a very successful and busy electrical engineer now, but he still loved building and taking apart gadgets in his spare time.

I knew I wouldn't have any idea what I was looking at if I opened the Ghosthound up, and I was afraid of breaking the toy if something important or miraculous really was going on. More importantly, I knew I could trust Parker—both to be honest with me and to not judge me for asking for his help.

We met that afternoon, and after some brief chit-chat, he led me to his hobby workshop. Gently taking the Ghosthound from me, he looked it over carefully before turning it upside down. He used a small razor to cut along the edge where the plastic battery casing met the plush fabric of the toy, taking all the care and precision of a surgeon. I still sucked in an involuntary breath at the cutting, but he looked up at me with a comforting smile.

"I'm going to be careful. I know this is important. Believe me, it'll work just the same when I'm done."

I nodded, not trusting myself to speak. Parker went back to work, slowly delving into the internal parts of the toy. He took notes and pictures as he went, and it was half an hour before he was done with his examination. Still silent, he carefully hot-glued the incision he had made closed, leaving no real trace the toy dog had been cut at all.

Sitting back, he puffed out a breath and looked up at me. I had been perched on a stool in the corner of the room while he worked, and I couldn't help but feel like I was in the waiting room of a hospital, hoping for good news.

"Ok, so this morning I did some research after you called, both on the toy and common components used in this kind of thing. So right off, I can tell you I found a digital thermometer and an EMF meter in there, along with sensors running from them to the backs of the plastic eyes. It's actually kind of a neat way to do it." He gave me a sheepish look. "Sorry. I'm a nerd, I know."

"Anyway, I saw the LED lights in the front feet and chest. The voice box and small speaker that generates the howl. All of that stuff is connected like I'd expect and makes sense." He was frowning slightly now, and I could tell he was trying to hide the concern in his voice.

"But?"

He shrugged. "Look, I'm not a toymaker. And people manufacture things in weird and various ways. But it seems like there's extra stuff in there."

I felt my hands tighten on my knees. "What do you mean, 'extra stuff'? What's in there?"

He shrugged again, his brow furrowing as he tried to pick his words carefully. "I'm not sure. The extra components are covered by pretty solid casings, and without knowing what I'm dealing with, I wasn't going to risk cracking one open and breaking the toy. I can tell you that based on everything I've read about this particular model, all of its features are covered by what I can identify. So you're left with mystery parts that are connected to the rest." He saw my expression and raised a hand. "It's probably nothing. Like I said, weird and various ways. But I got a couple of serial numbers off the casings, and with luck I'll be able to track down what these things are. Probably something stupid I'm overlooking."

Picking up the Ghosthound, he looked at where he had repaired the cut. "I can always go back in if we find something needs double-checking, but I kind of figured you would want to take him home with you." He didn't meet my eyes, but when I quietly nodded he stood up and handed the toy back to me. "Try not to worry about it. We'll figure it out."

****

It was already dark when I got home, and after eating some leftovers I settled onto the living room couch. The Ghosthound was back at its spot on the table, and this time I didn't even bother turning on the t.v. Instead, I wanted to try something.

"Are you there?"

Red foot. *Yes.* Okay, now for the test.

"Blueberry."

No response.

"Blueberry. Blueberry. Blueberry."

Again, the Ghosthound was silent.

I had been thinking about this since leaving Parker's house. Maybe the "extra stuff" was some kind of microphone set-up. What if, when the toy heard someone talking, it would flash lights and howl in response? If that was the case, then me saying a random word repeatedly should get the same reaction as the questions I had asked it. Unless it somehow was able to tell when it was being asked a question based on intonation. That seemed unlikely, but still…

"Blueberry, blueberry?" I made sure I went up on the last word like I was asking something. But still no response.

Suddenly it hit me. Maybe it really was a smart toy. The extra stuff might be connecting it to the internet and it was able to answer complex stuff by using cloud technology or something. Why they wouldn't market that as a feature and charge more for the toy was beyond me, but maybe this was some prototype that got shipped out by accident.

I got up and disconnected my modem and router, killing any wifi in the house. The fact that the toy wouldn't have my wifi password hadn't escaped me, but I was growing desperate. Desperate to know the truth before I gave myself permission to actually believe that Grayson or Amber might be watching over me and communicating through the Ghosthound.

There was a tendril of dread coiling around my heart as I sat back down in front of the little dog. Feeling a grim certainty that I had finally killed its ability to mimic messages from beyond the grave, I asked another question.

"Is there an afterlife?"

Red paw. *Yes.*

I felt my eyes welling up with tears. "Can you see me?"

Red paw. *Yes.*

I was about to ask my next question when my phone buzzed. Letting out a small scream, I fumbled it out of my pocket and accepted the call. It was Parker.

"Hey, man. You almost gave me a heart attack."

He let out a short, nervous laugh. "Sorry, sorry. Look, everything cool over there?"

I glanced at the Ghosthound as I wiped my eyes. "Yeah, it's good. Been trying to figure this thing out. Why? Is something wrong?"

He paused. "I don't know. Probably not. But I finally figured out what two of the mystery components are. They're used for RF. Radio frequency antenna and stuff. Kind of like a remote controlled car or something, just a lot more expensive and weirder."

I felt my skin prickle slightly. "Weirder how?"

"Well, you don't normally put RF stuff in that kind of casing, especially the antenna. Kind of defeats the purpose, you know? It degrades the reception. Now this stuff is fairly high-end, so its designed to pick up signals even through the casing. But the whole point of the case it to make it hard to tell what it is. Typically you'd see something like this on a spy gadget or even a short-range bomb trigger."

"What the hell? Why would that kind of stuff be in a toy? What would it be used for?"

I could hear the worry in his voice. "I'm not sure. The most likely answer is that it would be a way to trigger the lights and the howl it makes. Someone could have a remote and make it do what they wanted. But that isn't the thing that has me spooked. It's the range it would have with that kind of design."

"What do you mean?"

"I'm not trying to freak you out, but unless I'm wrong, I'd estimate the remote control would have to be no more than fifteen or twenty feet from the toy to work. It hasn't gone off again tonight has..." His voice was suddenly gone, and when I looked at my phone I saw I had no signal at all any more. Panicked, I was about to stand up to leave the house when the Ghosthound's chest started flashing green again, this time without the usual accompanying howl.

I froze, unsure of what to do next. That's when I saw motion reflected in the television screen. There was someone standing in the doorway of the kitchen. They were large and dressed in dark clothing except for a silver mask that covered their face. In one hand, they held something small, possibly the remote. In the other, they held a long, gleaming hunting knife. It reminded me of the one they had found the night Amber and Grayson were murdered.

"Are you going to kill me?"

My eyes were fixed on the reflection, but out of the corner of my eye I saw the right foot silently light up red.

Behind me, the killer began to howl.

Made in the
USA
Monee, IL